PRAISE FOR
CAFÉ M...

"Fun and intriguing, *Live and Let Chai* is filled to the brim with Southern charm."

—Kirsten Weiss, author of A Pie Town
Mystery series, for *Live and Let Chai*

"Bree Baker's seaside town of Charm has everything readers could want: an intrepid and lovable heroine who owns an adorable iced tea cafe, a swoon-worthy hero—and murder. Fast-paced, smartly plotted, and full of surprises, it's as refreshing as a day at the beach!"

—Kylie Logan, bestselling author of
French Fried, for *Live and Let Chai*

"A sun-filled cozy-cum-romance best enjoyed by beach readers."

—*Kirkus Reviews* for *No Good Tea Goes Unpunished*

"This is a food- and tea-filled story, but Baker never loses sight of moving the mystery plot forward and providing ample opportunities for fans to catch up with the engaging series cast."

—*Booklist* for *Tide and Punishment*

"A swarm of bee-centric suspects, a bit of sweet romance, and a surprise sting add up to a honey of a tale."

—*Kirkus Reviews* for *A Call for Kelp*

ALSO BY BREE BAKER

SEASIDE CAFÉ MYSTERIES

Live and Let Chai

No Good Tea Goes Unpunished

Tide and Punishment

A Call for Kelp

Closely Harbored Secrets

PARTNERS *in* LIME

SEASIDE CAFÉ MYSTERIES, BOOK 6

BREE BAKER

Poisoned Pen

PRESS

Published by Poisoned Pen Press, an imprint of Sourcebooks
P.O. Box 4410, Naperville, Illinois 60567-4410
(630) 961-3900
sourcebooks.com

Library of Congress Cataloging-in-Publication Data

Names: Baker, Bree, author.
Title: Partners in lime / Bree Baker.
Description: Naperville, Illinois : Poisoned Pen Press, [2021] | Series:
    Seaside café mysteries ; book 6
Identifiers: LCCN 2021003878 (print) | LCCN
2021003879 (ebook) | (paperback) | (epub)
Subjects: GSAFD: Mystery fiction.
Classification: LCC PS3602.A5847 P37 2021 (print) | LCC PS3602.A5847
    (ebook) | DDC 813/.6--dc23
LC record available at https://lccn.loc.gov/2021003878
LC ebook record available at https://lccn.loc.gov/2021003879

Printed and bound in the United States of America.
LSC 10 9 8 7 6 5 4 3 2

CHAPTER

ONE

I smiled at the sound of seashell wind chimes jangling over my front door. "Welcome to Sun, Sand, and Tea!" I called, waving to the café's newcomers from my position behind the cash register. It was nearly seven o'clock, closing time, and the final rush of folks were arriving to pick up to-go orders and after-dinner sweets.

I handed my current customer her change, then lifted my eyes to welcome the next in line.

My seaside iced tea shop was a favorite of locals at any hour, but I'd noticed a definite pattern in the two years since I'd opened. Folks liked to have lunch on the decks of my historic Victorian home, and in the dining room overlooking the sea. I'd done my best to play up the fantastic location and majestic views by showcasing the abundance of windows and carrying the beachy color scheme inside. The efforts were a hit, and the place stayed busy through the afternoon most days. But after five, the bulk of my regulars purchased snacks and drinks to-go, then peppered the beach and boardwalk outside, enjoying my culinary handiwork along with the balmy ocean breeze.

"Hey, Mrs. Waters," I said, recognizing the general store owner's wife and my former babysitter's mom. "I've got your cookies right here." I plucked her bag from a lineup of ready orders, then passed the treats her way. "One dozen Colonial Cutouts and a bag of Her Majesty's Munch Mix." I scanned the receipt, then lifted a finger. "And…" I turned briefly to retrieve a chilled container of my best selling brew from the refrigerator. "One quart of Grandma's Old-Fashioned Sweet Tea."

"Bless you," she said, extending a stack of cash in my direction, eyes glued to the bag of goodies before her. "I'm addicted to these cookies. Please tell me they aren't going away after opening night."

I grinned. I'd started to learn a thing or two about sales since opening my shop, and one of those was that people loved themed and limited-time items. Especially when those items had adorable names. My cutouts and munch mix were two more in a long line of examples. Both were named in honor of *The Lost Colony*, a historical outdoor drama preparing for its eighty-fourth season. The Roanoke Historical Society organized the massive annual production, which required more than one hundred people to fill roles from actors to stage crew. The show's popularity made both recipes impossible to keep on the shelves.

"Mr. Waters and I have season tickets, you know," she said, looking immediately younger and wistful. "He took me to opening night on our first date, and we've been together ever since. Haven't missed one in forty-three years."

"I love that," I said, passing her change and receipt. "I'm taking some refreshments to the cast and crew after I close."

She beamed. "Lovely. Oh, how lucky they are. I'd better not keep you."

The Lost Colony was a big deal for locals of Charm and all the other little towns sprinkled along the barrier islands of North Carolina, known to many as the Outer Banks. The play depicted the story of the lost colony at Roanoke, where more than one hundred English men, women, and children landed in the sixteenth century, established an English settlement, then vanished without a trace soon after. The settlers' disappearance was a four-hundred-and-fifty-year-old mystery that still baffled today. Some folks considered the show the heart of the islands. I didn't disagree. Who could resist a good mystery?

My ancestors arrived in Charm about one hundred years after the Roanoke settlers, but thankfully they didn't vanish. Instead, Swan women had settled in and stayed. We were woven into the fabric of the town now, rumors, legends, and ghost stories included. I'd hated the whispers about my family as a kid, but I'd grown quite proud of my heritage as an adult, quirky bits and all.

My great-aunt Fran stepped into view as Mrs. Waters took her leave. "Everly, thank goodness. I thought I might miss you. I'm running late, and I believe my head has literally fallen off sometime during the course of my day," Aunt Fran announced, hoisting her giant handbag onto the counter.

"Anything I can do to help?" I asked.

She pushed a long, salt-and-pepper braid off her narrow shoulder and sighed. "The whole town is up in arms over my proposed agenda for the rest of the year. Half think I've gone mad, and the number of events I've slated is way too high. The other half can't understand why we aren't doing more. It's absurdity."

"I'm sorry," I said, pushing my bottom lip forward in sympathy and resting my hand briefly on hers.

Aunt Fran had been elected mayor last fall and was still adjusting to the job.

The previous mayor, and most of the town council, had worked diligently for decades to discourage tourism in Charm. They feared too many visitors would bring chaos to our perfectly manicured and well-mannered streets. Aunt Fran thought outsiders should come and enjoy the place we were all so proud of. Maybe spend a little money and increase local commerce. So far, finding a balance her constituents could live with had been a struggle.

"Tell me you had time to make my rum cakes," she said, offering me her credit card with desperation in her large brown eyes. The dark sleeves of her painfully old-fashioned blouse clung to her thin arms and wrists as if it had been made for her. More likely, it had been made for an ancestor long before Aunt Fran was born.

My logoed T-shirt, on the other hand, had been made in bulk by machines in a town I'd likely never visit, and fit me like a burlap sack. Aunt Fran and I were cut from the same genetic cloth, but most of the similarities ended there.

We did, however, look a bit alike, save for the sixty or seventy pounds and forty years separating us. My dark-brown hair was shorter but nearly the same color as hers, minus the gray, and usually kept in a ponytail fighting for freedom. Our olive skin and brown eyes were a near-perfect match. It was our personalities that were another story.

Aunt Fran liked to take stands and make change. Her sister, my great-aunt Clara, and I preferred to keep the peace and still a rocking boat whenever we could. I wasn't sure who I'd inherited my curiosity from, but as far as personality traits went, my severe inquisitiveness was as unruly as my hair.

I stacked her bakery boxes into a handled bag then returned her credit card with a receipt. "I added extra rum, just the way you like."

"Thank you," she said, clearly meaning it down to her bones.

"Who gets the special order tonight?" I asked, resting a hip on the counter. Aunt Fran's schedule had been nearly nonstop since taking office. She was perpetually on the move and exhausted, but seemed happier despite it.

"Crooked Oaks Retirement Community," she said, returning her handbag to her shoulder. "I promised the residents more action in Charm while I was campaigning, and there are a few ladies over there who're holding me to it. The rum cakes are a peace offering while I figure out how to make them happy without pushing Charm traditionalists over the edge with more community-wide events."

"When in doubt, spike the dessert," I said, lifting the massive bag in her direction. "Do you need any help out?"

"No. I think I've got it." She stuffed her wallet back into her purse, and her gaze caught on the flyer I'd taped to a mini chalkboard on my counter.

After months of diligence and hard work, I'd finally finished restoring my home's former ballroom, and I planned to introduce the town to the space through a series of cooking classes. The first was tomorrow night.

"Any chance there's room for three more?" she asked, sweeping her gaze from the flyer to me.

"Sure," I said. "Who do you have in mind?"

"Corkers," she said. "I'll tell the ringleader when I get there. You're a lifesaver."

"Corkers?" I repeated, laughing as I marked a line through the flyer, indicating the class was now full.

"Crooked Oaks Retirement Community," Fran clarified. "It's a mouthful, so they abbreviated and nicknamed."

I snorted, then rounded the counter to give her a hug and walk her out.

I flipped the closed sign as my nemesis appeared.

Mary Grace Chatsworth-

Vanders, my childhood nemesis, strode into the foyer with a faux grin. "You weren't closing up before I got my order, were you?"

I matched her smile, then led the way back to my register, having mentally blocked the fact she'd placed an order at all. She only came by to gloat and/or deliver annoying news. It was usually a toss-up.

I snagged her bag from behind the counter and set it between us, eager to see her on her way. Mary Grace had once told our entire middle school that my mother didn't actually die when I was very young, but had instead run off with the circus to avoid raising me.

I wasn't over it. And she made it unfathomably easy to keep the animosity flowing.

She slid a little white business card in my direction while I rang up her bill. "You should hang onto this, for when you need to downsize," she said. "I imagine you'll be selling the café and your home once it all goes under."

Mary Grace and her giant marionette of a husband had turned to selling real estate after losing the mayoral election to Aunt Fran. She blamed me for it, at least partially, and like me, she wasn't over the offense.

I dragged her business card across my countertop with a fingertip, then tipped it into my trash bin. "I'm doing just fine, thank you," I said, refusing to take her bait. "Here you are." I set the bag with her order between us. "That'll be twenty-seven-twelve."

She paid with cash and an annoying cat-that-ate-the-canary smile. "Thanks. Here's your tip. Eloise Maisley bought the Deeter estate on Bay View and opened a teahouse. Considering her atmosphere is exquisite and delightful, and you have sand on your floors, I expect you'll need me soon." She pocketed her change, lifted the bag of food, then set another business card on the counter and laughed all the way out the door.

My phone buzzed with a text, and I glanced briefly at the familiar Manhattan number. Ryan, an investigative reporter who drove me batty but adored my best friend, Amelia, would have to wait. I was still trying to unclench my teeth.

I hurried to the door and locked it behind Mary Grace, then marched back across my foyer to the café, wondering if she'd been pulling my leg about the Deeter estate. I'd been incredibly busy lately and wholly distracted, but had I some-how missed the opening of a second tea shop in Charm?

I took a long hard look at my café while Buddy Holly sang merrily on my radio.

Sun, Sand, and Tea stretched through the entire south side of my first floor. Walls had been strategically knocked out by the former owner, to merge the kitchen and formal dining area into one large space for entertaining. I'd known it was the perfect setup for my café the moment I'd stepped foot inside.

Seating was a hodgepodge of different but coordinating pieces. Twenty seats in total, five at the counter and fifteen scattered across the wide-planked, whitewashed floor. Padded wicker numbers circled low tables at the center, while taller bistro sets stood along the perimeter. I'd used the color palette of my breathtaking views as inspiration for the decor. Pale blue for perfect cloudless skies and vast, endless water. Gray and tan for driftwood and sand. Pops of yellow, orange, or red on throw pillows and accent rugs to reflect the other things visible from my windows, like sunsets, kites, and Frisbees.

And Mary Grace was right, there was sand on the floor.

I moped my way upstairs to my private living quarters to change before my handsome ride arrived, because the night could surely only get better.

CHAPTER

TWO

I grabbed my phone, keys, and purse when the doorbell rang, then ran to meet my date. The silhouette was easily recognizable, as were the electric vibes zigzagging through the door between us.

I dropped the long strap of my purse over my head, securing it crossbody as I stepped onto the porch, towing my childhood wagon, and inanimate employee, behind me.

"I'm all packed up and ready to go," I announced, greeting my unofficial boyfriend, Detective Grady Hays. I hadn't seen him in more than a week, and I desperately needed my fix.

He smiled as he took me in. "Hi."

"Hi," I returned, more breathlessly than intended, and heat scorched across my cheeks.

"You look fantastic."

I forced myself not to look away. I'd crammed my size-fourteen behind into jeans I'd slowly outgrown during the winter, then paired them with a more forgiving A-line tank top and cardigan. I'd slid my feet into leather booties. The look was casual in the extreme but a definite step up from the cutoffs, T-shirt, and flip-flops I'd worn all day at work.

"Back at ya," I said, admiring his equally comfy ensemble.

He'd traded his Charm PD windbreaker for a worn-out denim jacket and covered the ever-present detective shield on his belt with an untucked heather gray T-shirt and unbuttoned flannel. His jeans were nearly worn through at the knees and hung low on his hips.

I tried not to stare, but failed.

"I guess I'd better move the goods," he said, closing in on Wagon.

The previously red Radio Flyer had been repurposed and given a fresh paint job when I'd opened my shop. She was my first method of transport for distributing samples and spreading the word that I'd opened a shop. Now, Wagon was one in a fleet of three matching helpers that assisted in delivering orders all around Charm, weather permitting. I'd also acquired a thrift-store bicycle with basket and a fixer-up golf cart I called Blue. Wagon mostly worked around the house these days, helping me move big orders from my café to the porch in just one trip. The convenience was priceless.

I watched in sincere appreciation as Grady lifted the jugs of tea, then carried them to his truck. I grabbed a pile of boxes and followed on his heels. "Thanks for giving me a ride tonight," I said, stacking the snacks and sweets into the back seat of his extended cab truck before stuffing both hands into my pockets. I wasn't gifted with an incredible amount of self-control, and in Grady's presence, watching my tongue and my hands at the same time had always been a challenge. "I've missed you."

"Back at ya," he said, tossing my words back to me with a grin. His gray eyes twinkled as he took a confident step forward and slid his palms against the curves of my waist, curling long fingers against my back. "How else were you going to get to Manteo? Your golf cart isn't exactly highway worthy, and I couldn't let you hitchhike."

I decided to overlook his use of the word *let* and smiled up at him instead. "It's handy to know a guy with wheels."

Grady's smile grew as he nodded. His head tilted and dipped slowly closer to mine.

"It's especially nice when the guy's a perfect kisser," I whispered, bracing myself for the fireworks that shot through me with every press of his mouth to mine.

"You know anyone like that?" he asked, our lips brushing as he spoke.

"Uhm." My mind went fuzzy, and my hands sprung free of my pockets, burying themselves deep into the hair at the back of his head as I rose onto my toes. The world seemed to lose gravity, as it always did when we were this close, and the heady scent of him curled my toes inside my booties. "I don't know what you asked, but please kiss me again before I explode from anticipation."

Grady chuckled, then easily obeyed.

My bones turned to jelly, per the usual.

He broke the kiss far too soon, also per the usual, then set his forehead against mine. "We have to go or we'll be late."

I groaned in disappointment, and he laughed once more, this time lacing his fingers with mine as he led me to the passenger door and helped me inside.

I powered my window down and stuck out my hand, the

night air rushing through my fingers as we turned onto the highway connecting island towns. "How was DC?" I asked, eager to hear everything I'd missed while he'd been away.

"Not bad," he said. "Different than I remembered it. The city seemed busier and more intrusive than I'd thought before I moved here. Olivia, however, was thrilled to be home."

Olivia was Grady's former mother-in-law and a U.S. senator, who'd tried her hand at island life but decided it wasn't for her. Grady had cheerfully helped her move back to where she'd come from, which had kept him away for a week. I couldn't say I'd miss her, but I was disappointed for Grady's son, Denver. He'd already lost his mother to cancer at an unjustly young age. It seemed doubly unfair for him to see his grandma go so soon after she'd moved to Charm to be near him.

I'd vowed to myself, long before Grady and I had started dating, that if we ever became an item and anything later went wrong, I would continue to be a part of Denver's life until he or Grady ordered me out. Denver wasn't my child, but I cared far more about his feelings than my own, and any need I might have to nurse my pride following a breakup would take a far back seat to the assurance of his happiness and well-being.

Planning for a breakup was admittedly not the most emotionally healthy thing to do, but Grady and I had an unconventional and complicated relationship. From the way we'd met, when he'd accused me of poisoning an old man, to the complexities of our families and our pasts. It was abundantly fair to say the odds were not in our favor. Grady had already had an epic love, and her loss had nearly killed him. Giving his heart to another person like that would take something, or someone, miraculous. And if he did, my family's alleged love curse might still do him in.

Grady swore he didn't believe in curses, and I knew logically the idea was bananas, but I cared too deeply not to at least consider it might be true.

Grady glanced my way, one eyebrow cocked. "What are you thinking about?"

"I was thinking you're devastatingly handsome, and your truck smells nice," I answered quickly, inhaling deep and slow to prove my words. It was all true.

"Anything else?" he asked, a goofy smile tugging at his lips.

I straightened, recalling the thing that was officially under my skin. "Did you know there's a new tea shop in town?"

"Sure," Grady said. "I drive past it on my way to the station every day. It seems a little uptight and pretentious. This is a beach town. Folks live here to get away from all that noise."

I crossed my arms. "You say that now, but what happens when I'm homeless?"

"What?" He snorted softly as the amphitheater appeared. "You really should've tried out for this play," he teased.

"I'm not being dramatic."

"No," he agreed. "Never."

I narrowed my eyes as he shifted into park. "Mary Grace came into the shop to taunt me. She makes me nuts, and she was so satisfied with herself when she saw my expression. She knew she'd dropped a bomb. She even gave me her business card for when I need to sell my home."

He smiled. "Sounds like she's a little dramatic too."

"She is the absolute worst."

A round of cheering and applause pulled our attention to the darkening world outside. Actors from the various island towns gathered on the stage, carrying scripts and dressed in period clothing. We'd arrived just in time for Matt Darning's performance as a sixteenth century longbowman.

Grady groaned, then climbed down from the cab and circled around to meet me.

Matt was a paramedic and friend. He'd only been a member of Charm's community for a handful of years, but he was already beloved for his compassion and kind nature. He'd helped me more than once after I'd taken a spill or tumble. Or when someone had tried to kill me. He'd also beaten Grady to the punch, asking me on an official date last fall. The date, like Matt, was perfect, barring an unforeseen hiccup. And the fact he wasn't Grady.

I climbed out, then helped pile my teas and treats back into Wagon after Grady set her on the pavement.

He took my hand in his as I pulled the food and drink toward waiting tables.

The Waterside Theatre was huge in comparison to any typical indoor venue, three times larger than the average Broadway stage, and set against a backdrop of the sea. Surrounded by ancient trees and a handful of related buildings, the sunken stage faced a crescent of abundant seating.

On stage, Matt wore loose-fitting trousers and nothing else. A spotlight followed him as he struck a pose, then pulled the string of his longbow, engaging the muscles of his bare chest, arms, and back. The gently lunging posture drew the eyes of every female on stage. "As a skilled longbowman I can fire six aimed shots a minute," he recited, not needing the help of a script. "With the wind at my back, I can pierce targets two hundred yards away." He released the string and a second spotlight trailed the projectile through the air, to a target illuminated in the distance, nearly a football field's length away. The arrow lodged in its straw-stuffed core.

Applause erupted, and I released Grady's hand so I could stuff my fingers into my mouth and whistle.

We paused at a row of empty tables, erected in the grass, then began to unpack Wagon.

"I can't get over how good he's gotten with that longbow," I said. "It's huge. I don't even know how he can carry it without falling over it, let alone actually use it to hit anything."

Grady sucked his teeth, utterly unimpressed. "I don't understand why his costume didn't come with a shirt."

"I'm pretty sure that's the wardrobe department's fault," I said, nodding to a cluster of maidens vying for Matt's attention on stage.

Grady rolled his eyes.

Aunt Clara hustled in our direction, loaded down with paper plates, disposable silverware, and napkins. "There you are! Right on time!" she called, beaming ear to ear. "This is lovely! Oh, it all smells so good and looks delicious!" She slowed to hug me, then Grady, before turning to the spread.

Ham and cheese pinwheels, homemade chips, dill spears, an array of Colonial Cutouts, and two dispensers of old-fashioned sweet tea. The actors and stage crew were sure to love it all.

Aunt Clara set her tableware at the beginning of the

yummy lineup then clapped her hands silently. "It's perfect. Thank you so much for doing this."

"Of course," I said. "Anything for you." I leaned in to kiss her cheek as a wave of hungry thespians arrived for the food.

The low droning sound of an argument between two men pricked my ears, turning me away from the tables. Two shadowy figures moved in unison along the side of the stage, passing briefly under an unattended spotlight before going dark once more. I recognized Matt easily, the longbow in one hand, the other hand waving wildly. The second man was new to me, as was Matt's deep, pointed tone.

The steady roar of the ocean drowned the words, making it impossible to guess the problem.

"Who's that with Matt?" I asked anyone within earshot, my eyes fixed on the partially concealed pair.

A round of mumbled uncertainties followed.

Whoever he was, I wasn't the only one who didn't know him, and that was incredibly peculiar in the presence of a cross section from so many local towns.

The second figure was as tall and broad as Matt, his voice equally heated. His hair puffed and lifted in tufts on the breeze, reaching out in every direction, but that was all I could discern at such a distance.

"What are you doing?" Grady asked.

I turned to find myself several steps away from him, then looked back to Matt on the other side of the vast amphitheater seating. "Nothing," I said, though my inflection made it sound more like a question.

I hadn't realized I was drifting away.

Grady frowned slightly, unimpressed with my fib.

Curiosity scratched at the nape of my neck, urging me to get to the bottom of Matt and the stranger's rift. "Maybe I should take them some cookies and tea?" I suggested, straining to make out their words, now flying faster and more fervently.

"They don't need snacks," Grady said. "They need some privacy."

I sighed, knowing he was right, and reminding myself that some things simply weren't my business. When that didn't work, I found consolation in the fact I'd probably get the scoop later from our town's gossip blog, or tomorrow at Sun, Sand, and Tea.

A sudden smile bloomed as I recalled something I kept in my bag. Something I could use to get more information. I fished out a pair of binoculars, and Grady groaned.

"I knew that gift would come back to bite me in the—"

"Hey," I said, raising the viewers to my eyes. "Language." I smiled as I focused the zoom.

My binoculars had been a gift from Grady after a set of birders who'd stopped by my café for lunch last fall piqued my interest in their hobby. I'd spent a lot of time since then looking for various species of birds and checking them off a list in my book on the subject. Grady loved seeing me busy myself safely, and I liked tracking the most elusive migrant species.

"There," I said, bringing Matt and the other man into view. "It looks like he's arguing with one of the surfers from those Back to the Beach billboards that have been popping up all over the islands."

Back to the Beach was a week-long annual event that

took places in a different beach town every summer. The Outer Banks was a popular spot for the event because our string of islands made it possible to spread the individual events out geographically, peppering them through multiple nearby small towns. A barbecue cook-off in Duck, followed by a kite competition in Kitty Hawk, a sand sculpture event in Corolla, and a surf competition in Manteo, for example. Tourists loved to rent a beach house, then visit a different island town and event each day all week long. It was like a vacation within a vacation. And thanks to Aunt Fran's diligence, she'd convinced the scheduling committee at Back to the Beach to bring the events back to our islands this summer. Something that hadn't been done in decades. Best of all, she'd offered Charm as host-town for one of the daily competitions. Though a committee would ultimately determine which town held which event, I was hoping for a dessert festival. And maybe a judgeship.

Suddenly the men stilled and silence rang against the ocean's waves.

The stranger's arm shot out, and Matt's head jerked back before I had time to process what was happening. Matt stumbled, nearly falling from the force as his feet collided with the massive longbow.

"Well, hell," Grady moaned, starting off in a jog toward the men.

I hurried after him a heartbeat later. Both men turned in our direction before parting ways.

Grady stayed his course, determined to speak with the puncher, while I chased Matt toward the beach.

"Wait!" I called, heart sprinting from exertion and

the eight pounds I'd collected during the winter. I'd been trying to lose at least twenty-five for the last two years, but it seemed my slow progress had begun moving backwards, and all those extra dress sizes were currently sitting on my lungs. "Stop," I panted, fingers grazing Matt's shoulder as I cut him off on his path.

"Don't!" he snapped, stopping to glare at me with an expression of anger and distrust I'd never seen on him before. "Leave it alone, Everly. This has nothing to do with you."

"You're bleeding," I rasped between heaving breaths. The smear of blood from his nose stretched across one cheek. "Let me help you."

"I don't need your help," he growled, stepping around me. "I should've dealt with this a long time ago. So, please, just stay out of it."

I stopped cold as he walked away, embarrassed at his hurtful tone and harsh dismissal.

The line from the refreshments table had relocated to the grassy knoll nearby, watching with rapt attention as they noshed on my goods.

My eyes stung with unexpected emotion.

Matt had never been anything but kind to me. To anyone, as far as I knew. But he'd scolded me and blown me off in front of an audience. Stupidly, I felt my bottom lip quiver.

"Everly," Grady called, turning me on my toes as Matt shrank in the distance.

I nearly sprinted into Grady's arms.

"I wasn't able to catch up with that guy," he said. "You learn anything from Matt?"

"No." I wrapped Grady in a hug and pressed my cheek to

his chest, regrouping and licking my wounded feelings. "He didn't want to talk to me."

"I'm sorry." Grady rubbed his palms against my back. "You okay?"

I shrugged, then stepped away. "Yeah. He just caught me off guard. I've just never seen him so angry."

"We all have an ugly side," Grady said. "I can't say I'd have been much nicer after getting punched in the nose."

I laughed at the thought.

Before Grady lost his wife and moved to Charm to focus on single-parenthood, he'd spent time in the military, then become a rising star at the U.S. Marshal's office.

"I'd like to see someone try to get the best of you," I teased.

His gray eyes flashed with mischief as he pulled me back toward the table and poured me a glass of iced tea. "Me too."

I took one last look in the direction Matt had gone. He might've wanted rid of me tonight, but I had a feeling Grady would take me home and stay a while. And I couldn't wrap this night up fast enough.

CHAPTER
THREE

Grady dropped me off about an hour later and promised to be back after a quick trip home at his son's request. A nap after swim practice had thrown off Denver's internal clock, and he wasn't falling asleep again very easily. His au pair, and my morning shop keep, Denise, had called to request backup from Grady, and he had easily agreed.

I hurried inside to change clothes and collect my marbles after a long, flirtatious ride home. Thanks to Grady's demanding job, single-parenthood, and my nightly hours of baking in preparations for the next day, we didn't get to see one another as often as we wanted. As a result, our dates often happened in impromptu spurts. We stole a day together here and there, if our days off and the stars aligned, but I rarely had a day off, and Grady was the island's only detective, which kept him busy. We joked that it would be impossible to tire of one another this way, and the truth in that was incredibly frustrating.

I locked up behind me as he drove away, then used the key again on an interior staircase off the main foyer, which provided passage to my second-floor living quarters. The stairs were beautiful, worn into gentle dips from nearly two-hundred years of use and stained a faded red, with delicate carvings along the edges. I'd hung dramatic black and white photographs of the town, beach, and sea in deep red frames over creamy, cashmere-colored paint. A little personalization for the private stretch made it truly feel like my own.

Upstairs, I raked excited fingers through my unruly mass of brown curls, then let them fall around my shoulders. I traded my too-tight jeans for a butter-soft pair of navy yoga pants and paired them with a white V-neck T-shirt I'd bought from a boutique in town.

Back in the living area, I opened the sliding glass doors to my deck and let in the spring ocean breeze.

Moonlight crept across my living room carpet, stretching toward the kitchen beyond, where I set the small table with glasses for iced tea and a pedestal for one of my family's lemon cakes, Grady's favorite. He loved the recipe so much that I'd stopped making it for anyone else, and I always kept one on hand just for him.

My phone buzzed with a text at the same moment Maggie, the cat who kind of lived with me, appeared. I checked my phone as I crouched to stroke her fluffy white fur.

Ryan again.

I sent a quick response this time, letting him know I was busy and that I'd call him tomorrow. I still had to check my lip gloss and mascara before Grady's return.

Maggie arched and brushed against me as I rubbed behind her ears. She blessed me with her presence several times a week, then vanished as quickly as she appeared. She, like Lou, a friendly seagull, had come with the house. My great-aunts believed both creatures were reincarnated souls. Maggie, the former mistress of a wealthy businessman who'd commissioned the house to keep her, and Lou, the businessman. Their love affair had been illicit and ultimately deadly, so I tried not to imagine my aunts being right about this one.

I filled Maggie's glass bowls, one with food and the other with water, then I gave her space to enjoy.

I'd nearly finished touching up my face when the doorbell rang downstairs.

I checked my watch as I ran. Grady hadn't had enough time to get home and back. Had he? And he would've needed at least a few minutes to tuck Denver in, even if he'd already fallen asleep before his dad's arrival.

The silhouette waiting on my porch was familiar, but decidedly not Grady.

"Hello, Matt," I said tightly, offering a warning smile as I opened the door then crossed my arms. My expression fell as I took in his overwrought and disheveled appearance. His nose was red and swollen where he'd been hit. His lost puppy expression said he needed a friend, not a scolding, even if he deserved it. "Come here," I said, pulling him into a hug.

He immediately squeezed me back.

"I'm sorry I was such a jerk earlier," he whispered into my hair. "I had no right to speak to you like that, and I wasn't thinking, or I never would've behaved that way. I was embarrassed and angry, and I just wanted to get away from all the onlookers." He stepped back, appearing impossibly more humbled. "Please forgive me. You've been nothing but wonderful from the day we met, and I don't want to lose that."

I pursed my lips and shrugged. "I'm not ready to write you off yet," I said. "I know you weren't yourself. I've never seen you so angry before."

"I don't normally get mad," he said. "Not like that." Matt pushed his fingers into the front pockets of his jeans. "It's stupid that I let him get to me."

"Maybe," I said, "but he shouldn't have hit you." I raised one hand limply toward the darkening evidence on his face. "You're allowed to be ticked. Do you want to come inside? Have some tea? Talk?"

Matt shook his head. "I should go." He glanced over his shoulder, then turned back with a frown. "I'm sure you're busy."

"Not at the moment," I said breezily. "Grady's coming back in a bit, but until then, there's no reason we can't talk." I motioned to the set of rocking chairs I'd recently added to my home's wraparound porch.

He nodded, then took a seat.

I followed suit. "So, what happened tonight?" I asked, shamelessly thrilled to get the inside scoop I wanted. "Before you got socked."

He puffed his cheeks out in a sigh. "Kai Larsen happened," he said, slowly beginning to rock. "You know how you and Mary Grace have that thing between you?"

"A near lifelong animosity that still makes me want to push a cupcake in her face every time I see her?" I asked. "Even though I am far too close to thirty to have such ridiculously childish fantasies and should be ashamed?"

Matt laughed, then winced, gently touching a finger to his reddened nose and cheek. "I guess. But change the cupcake thing for something less adorable."

"So that guy was your childhood nemesis?" I asked, wondering again if I was right about him being on the new rash of island billboards.

"Thankfully, no," Matt said. "I didn't meet him until I was eighteen, and we haven't spoken in several years. We were teammates when I surfed. He's here doing promo for next month's Back to the Beach event. There's going to be a Spring Classic surfing competition near Rodanthe as part of the festivities. He's the reigning champ."

I watched Matt as we rocked, trying to imagine why Kai had hit him, especially when they hadn't spoken in so long.

"Kai still surfs professionally?" I asked.

Matt nodded solemnly. "He's a bit of a celebrity on the circuit. Has all the best sponsors and everything else he's ever wanted." Matt's tone soured and his expression turned grim.

I was sure there was more to the simple statement, but I didn't ask. Not when there was so much more to know. "So, he sought you out at play practice to argue with you?"

"No. He came to brag," Matt said, rolling tired eyes in my direction. "I think he knows that I could've been where he is now if I hadn't walked away so soon after turning pro, and he hates it. Seeking me out and punching me in the nose is his way of making a statement."

"That he's a jerk and a bully?" I asked.

"That he's tough, I guess," Matt corrected. "Some folks said he only became the star he is because I left, and it bothered him. Then, he was hurt at the pier while filming some promotional footage this morning, and I got the call. He didn't want my help when I got there. Made a big scene. I think seeing me come to his rescue brought up those old emotions."

I considered that a moment. "I can see Mary Grace punching me in that situation," I said, not completely sure it wasn't true.

Matt smiled. "The competition between me and Kai was fierce. The crowds loved it. I didn't. I just wanted to surf. Kai wanted to win. He needed to win. He sabotaged anyone and everyone who got in his way. He'd mess with their boards, their wax, their girl. If none of that worked, he'd apologize and invite them out for one too many drinks the night before a big competition to hinder their performances. Whatever worked."

"Gross."

"Yeah," Matt agreed.

"You didn't fall for his stunts, I take it?" I asked, certain I already knew the answer.

"No. I've always believed in good health, good choices, and good karma. I don't drink. I took good care of myself and my equipment during training and competitions." He ground his teeth, eyes glazing with unspoken memories as he looked into the distance. "It wasn't an attack on me that drove me away from surfing." He leaned forward, elbows on thighs, and he kneaded his hands. "A new kid, Jamal Sanders, was a fast-rising crowd favorite. He was good looking, good spirited, and only twenty. Kai took him out the night before a big competition, where I assume he bought him alcohol, because the next day, Jamal was a mess. He looked sick but wouldn't talk about it. He couldn't keep his eyes open, then he fell asleep in the baking sun while Kai made a big joke about it. I urged Jamal to stay in the shade and stay hydrated, but he just wasn't himself."

"Hungover?" I asked, wondering how awful that must've felt on a day he needed to compete. A day he had to spend in the sun with all those spectators and competitors watching.

"I think. I don't know because he never said. If Kai confessed or was accused of contributing to the delinquency of a minor, he'd have lost everything that day, and I suppose Jamal thought that keeping the secret was better than being a rat or maybe that he'd be in trouble somehow too if he told."

"What happened?" I leaned forward, matching Matt's posture and turning my head to look at his tightened jaw.

"Jamal wiped out, epically. He went under and didn't come up. I saw it and left my position in the lineup to help lifeguards search for Jamal. He'd been caught in a riptide and was too weak to swim free. He was the first person I ever saved using CPR. He was unresponsive when EMTs arrived, but they brought him around and said he would've died if I hadn't kept him going until they got there. It was the day I realized I didn't need recognition for doing something I loved. I can surf anytime. For fun. What I really wanted was to make a difference in people's lives. Maybe even make a difference in the world."

I leaned across the arms of our rockers and wrapped him in a side hug as pride swelled in me. "You're a good man. You know that? You've made a big difference in my world. And you didn't even punch him back tonight."

Matt straightened when I released him from the hug. "I

wanted to," he said. "But I've been done arguing with Kai for years. I couldn't let him reduce me to his level with all those people watching. All the actors and stage crew. You." He slid his eyes in my direction.

"You knew I was there? Before I went after you?"

"I always know when you're near," he said. "It's weird, but it's true. I can't explain it."

I smiled. "Well, I'm glad you didn't hit him. You did the right thing. One more reason everyone loves you. We can count on you to be the good guy we know you are. Even when a really bad guy provokes you."

Matt rubbed his palms against his thighs and sighed. "I should probably apologize to everyone from the play. They shouldn't have had to see any of that." He patted his coat pockets. "I can't call them all, but maybe you can help me write a decent email to send to the group?"

"Sure."

He shifted hip to hip, searching his jeans' pockets when the phone didn't turn up in his coat. "My phone's gone," he said, confusion lining his brow. "Wait." He deflated. "I left it in on the stage with my costume's jacket, which still doesn't fit right. It's hanging on the prop tree beside the stage." He stretched onto his feet, then offered me his hand. "Feel like a moonlight drive?"

"I can't," I said.

"Right. Grady." Matt shook his head and smiled. "I forgot."

"It's no problem," I said, fishing my vibrating phone from my pocket. "I would go if I didn't already have plans."

The message was from Grady.

Duty calls. Rain check?

I frowned at the offensive text, then lifted my eyes to Matt.

"Something wrong?"

"Nope." I smiled, slipping the phone back into my pocket. "My plans just cleared up. Is that moonlight ride still available?"

～

"Thanks for the talk," Matt said, as we raced down the highway in the night. "I didn't know I needed it, but I guess I did. I feel a lot better now that someone in Charm knows who Kai really is. Telling anyone else would've felt like gossip." Matt flashed me a smile that warmed me to my toes. "I'm glad we met. The conditions were unfortunate, you always being nearly killed and everything," he teased. "But I'm glad we did."

"Me too," I agreed. "And your secret's safe with me."

Signs and billboards flew by outside the window. They'd all been changed to reflect upcoming island events. And now that I was paying attention, I'd recognize the floppy-haired Kai Larsen anywhere. He stood, arms crossed, wearing board shorts and mirrored sunglasses, before a similarly outfitted man and a woman with a blue bikini and longboard. Each wore rash guards with the Surf Daddy Lessons and Gear logo emblazoned across the fronts.

"That's him?" I asked, pointing as the next sign came near.

"Yep."

I studied Kai's cocky stance and what I could see of his expression beneath the glasses.

I still hadn't gotten a good look at his eyes, and I wondered what I'd see there if I met him. "Is it weird to see him on billboards?"

"He's on everything." Matt sighed.

I patted his arm, hating that Kai's presence on the islands had already escalated into a physical attack. "Do you know the others?"

"Not personally," Matt said. "But I keep up with the sport. Locke is Kai's number two. He's younger, but learning fast. He might be number one before Kai's ready to concede. Ava's the newest member of the team. She's one of the best female surfers in the sport. A huge fan favorite."

I was sure the bikini didn't hurt. "Did you know Surf Daddy is a local brand?" I asked. "It was founded last year by James Goodwin and his family."

"In Rodanthe, right?" Matt asked.

"Yes." I smiled. Rodanthe was a small village on Hatteras Island, south of Manteo, where the amphitheater was located. The village had been made semi-famous following the release of a Nicholas Sparks book-turned-movie, *Nights in Rodanthe*, and fans still went out of their way to photograph the house featured in the film.

"The Goodwins are the absolute nicest people you'll ever meet," I said. I pictured the laid-back couple and their towheaded children at street fairs and farmers' markets. They always had warm smiles and kind words. I'd imagined, more than once, that I might have a similar life one day. A toddler on my hip. A preschooler on my husband's shoulders. All of us enjoying the town and people we loved.

The slim chance I might be cursed and kill a man with my love kept the fantasy brief and me from getting carried away.

"How long will Kai be here?" I asked, hoping it wouldn't be long.

"I don't know. He usually takes his money and whatever else he wants, then goes. He'll likely head home as soon as the promotion work is finished. I hear the beach house he bought in Malibu is really something to behold." Matt shot me a droll look, then hit his turn signal as signs for the amphitheater came into view.

"Malibu," I repeated. "How much money do professional surfers make?" I'd assumed competitors lived like cowboys on the rodeo circuit. Chasing glory they'd never quite get their hands around. Earning enough money each time to buy into the next competition but never quite enough to make a living.

"A lot." Matt eased onto the smaller road, casting a cautious look my way as he spoke. "Sponsors give the top surfers hundreds of thousands, even millions, of dollars every year. They're brand influencers. Everyone wants to wear what the winner wears, ride the boards they ride. Good brand ambassadors are everything."

"Wow." I watched him when he turned away, expression flat, gaze distant. "You walked away from a lot when you left surfing."

"I did," he agreed. "But I got to keep my sanity, and my integrity. That was priceless."

My heart swelled impossibly further with complete respect for him. "You never regret leaving?" I asked, not sure I could've been so content in his shoes. Saving small-town residents from certain doom in exchange for an average income seemed a pale comparison to life in Malibu.

"Sometimes," he said, a sheepish grin on his handsome face. "I didn't hate the money."

"So you are human after all," I teased.

The flash of emergency lights stalled our conversation, and we both sat a little taller, leaning forward as we made the final turn into guest parking.

An ambulance blocked our view of the crowd, but it was clear by the number of uniformed people something bad had happened. Spotlights had been erected on the beach beyond the stage. An officer unspooled yellow crime scene tape between a set of trees.

Matt shifted into park, concern marring his brow. "I should go see if I can help."

I hopped out, then met him at the front of his vehicle, and we moved together toward the carouseling lights.

"That's Grady's truck," I said, lifting a finger. "What's he doing down here?" Manteo was definitely not Grady's jurisdiction, unless he'd been given on loan by Charm PD, and I couldn't imagine why that would happen.

"Maybe the injured party is from Charm?" Matt suggested. "Someone who might've called our police department, not thinking about being in the next town?"

My feet turned to stone as another vehicle I recognized came into view. I grabbed the sleeve of Matt's shirt as he passed. "Look."

Beyond the ambulance, in the shadow of the amphitheater's stage, was the coroner's van.

CHAPTER

FOUR

Matt immediately picked up his pace.

I curled my fingers around his elbow as I hurried along at his side, taking in every detail I could manage, and terrified the victim was someone I knew or loved. It was a selfish thought, of course, because every life mattered, and whoever the coroner had come for, someone's heart would be broken.

"I guess you know why Grady canceled on you," Matt said. "Something really did come up."

I'd never doubted Grady, but the situation begged another question. "I wonder why he didn't tell me what happened."

Normally he'd say something about the case that interrupted our plans. *I have to settle a domestic squabble.* Or, *There's an accident on Sunnybrook Lane.*

Had he been intentionally vague this time? And if so, what was the point?

"Oh, I don't know," Matt said, a teasing note in his tone. "Maybe because anytime someone dies, you get involved somehow. And you usually need a medic afterward."

"I don't get involved when everyone dies," I said. "Only when the cause of death is murder and I'm worried about the accused. Or when I am the accused." I rolled my eyes, recalling the absurdity of Grady once thinking I was a killer.

"I think you're safe this time," Matt said, finally reaching the crime scene line. He ducked underneath, then held the tape up for me to follow. "Grady took you back to Charm, then I showed up. You've got a solid alibi."

I squatted under the flimsy plastic barrier, then straightened at his side.

A swath of floppy hair came into view where the coroner crouched, and I felt the wind rush from my lungs.

A lean, muscular man lay prone on the sand, his slack face turned our way. His logoed Surf Daddy shirt was marred by a broad circle of crimson blood spreading out from the center. An arrow like the ones shot by Matt and his longbow was sunk deep into his back.

"I have an alibi," I whispered. "But what about you?"

Matt bolted forward.

I tried and failed to hold him back. Though I slowed him a bit by yanking his arm. "Matt," I whispered. "No. Stop!" I leaped in front of him seconds before we reached the body. Then, I pushed him back a few feet, drawing the attention of everyone nearby. "You can't help him now," I said, appealing to his medical training. "But you can help yourself by not talking."

"What?" He turned wide, frightened eyes on me.

I watched as understanding slowly sank in.

Matt covered his mouth with one hand. "No."

"Yeah," I said softly, visually tracking a uniformed officer who was headed our way. "Don't say anything more than you have to until you have a lawyer present. We don't know what happened, but that arrow might as well be pointing directly at you."

"Hey!" the officer called. "What are you two doing here? This is a crime scene."

"Sorry," I said, backing slowly up and towing Matt with me. "We were just looking for something left behind at play practice."

"Not so fast," the officer said, taking long purposeful strides forward, faster than we could reasonably retreat. "What are your names?"

"Uhm," I stalled. "This is Bob, and I'm Mary Grace Chat—"

"Do not," a low growling voice interrupted my lie.

I hung my head as I turned to find Grady looming behind me.

"Surely you weren't about to lie to an officer of the law."

I shook my head slowly. "Never."

"I've got this," he said, speaking over my head, presumably to the officer who'd confronted us.

I raised my eyes to peek, and Grady frowned.

"What are you doing here?" he asked. His keen gaze slid to my fingers, curled tightly around Matt's arm.

I released him immediately. "Matt forgot his phone and you canceled on me, so I came with him to find it," I said. "Why didn't you tell me there was a murder?"

"Why do you think?"

Matt chuckled, and Grady's eyes flicked to him. "Where did you go when you stormed off earlier?"

"Nowhere," Matt said, his attention returning to Kai's body on repeat. "I drove around, trying to cool off."

"Did you?" Grady asked, shifting his weight and seeming to pull his broad shoulders back by a fraction. "Cool off?"

"Yeah. Of course. I realized fighting with Kai was useless. Our beef is ancient history, and his punch was about him, not me. Then I went to Everly's house to apologize for the way I spoke to her when she tried to comfort me before."

Grady worked his jaw, apparently unimpressed with all of it. "I suppose you got a look at the murder weapon."

"I did." Matt folded his arms, then rubbed his face roughly with one hand.

My limbs were stiff and noncompliant from the shock of Kai's death and being busted by Grady inside the yellow crime tape.

"The arrow looks like one of the props from the play," Matt said.

"It's from the play," Grady said. "But it's not a prop. It's a very real arrow. Made especially for your longbow. I can't think of anyone this side of the fifteenth century, other than you, who could hit the broad side of a barn with that thing. Can you?"

"No," Matt said, flatly.

"Any idea how the arrow wound up in Kai Larsen's back?"

Matt's expression tightened, a mix of pain and betrayal crashing over his features. "Of course not."

"No?" Grady pressed, eyes hard and seeking.

"I'm not a killer," Matt said. "You know that. I save lives. I don't take them."

"Not even when someone pushes you to your limit?

Shows up at play practice uninvited, then punches you in the face?"

"Not even then."

Grady's steely eyes narrowed. "Did you kill Kai Larsen?"

Matt gaped, clearly knocked off-balance by the directness and horror of the question. Then he sealed his lips and slid his eyes to me.

I gave a small, reassuring nod. The less he said now, the better.

Grady turned his intimidating cop face on me. "Is there something you need to tell me, Everly?"

I blew out a breath. "Yeah. For starters, I'm positive someone other than Matt can operate a longbow, because the proof is right there." I lifted a finger in the victim's direction. "And Matt can't be a suspect because he was with me tonight."

"Not all night," Grady said, an unnecessary chill in his tone. "You left play practice with me."

"Any word on time of death?" I asked, cocking my head to the side and hurrying to ask the questions that counted before Grady escorted me from the premises.

"Not yet."

"Who found him? Nearly everyone was gone when you took me home. Maybe we should start with a list of who was still here."

Matt angled to look at me. "You think someone from *The Lost Colony* could've done this?"

I shrugged. "It seems more likely than thinking someone just happened to be out here and ran across his body." I motioned along the scene in both directions. The amphitheater was essentially secluded. Tucked into the trees of the

Fort Raleigh National Historic Site. No neighbors. And at this hour, there shouldn't have been any guests.

Grady shifted his weight, debating perhaps, how much he wanted to say.

I guessed he was torn between not wanting to tell me anything and wanting to engage Matt in a way that would bring about a confession.

"Maybe you're overthinking this," I pressed. "Maybe the real killer is already here. His or her encounter with Kai escalated, and he or she tried their hand with the bow."

"Unlikely," Grady said finally, tossing a pointed look into the distance. "His manager, Ted Osier, found him."

I followed his gaze to a uniformed officer speaking with a gray-haired man outside one of the buildings on site. The man wore a remorseful expression, with a yellow polo shirt and khaki pants.

Matt barely spared the guy a glance. His attention was fixed on the coroner and crime scene officials circling and prodding Kai.

"What do you think his manager was doing out here at this hour?" I asked Matt, pulling him back to the conversation.

Matt rubbed a hand against his jaw, then dragged his fingers through his hair. "He tracks him."

"What?" I yipped, shocked and appalled. "Like *tracks him*, tracks him?"

Grady nodded. "That's what he told us."

"Why?" I asked, unable to fathom why neither man before me thought tracking another adult was beyond batty, not to mention illegal—or at least a breach of privacy.

"Kai's a handful," Matt said, looking as if he might like to collapse. "He liked to go out and be seen, hit the clubs, crash house parties, stay out till dawn. He loved the attention, and he had a reputation for being extremely unreliable, among other equally unfortunate things."

"So he tracks him?" I said, still unable to process. Hearing it out loud again only made the words sound more ridiculous. "That's stalking."

"Not if it's in the contract," Matt said.

I waved my hands wordlessly, at a total loss for such nonsense. "Okay, but how do we know he tracked him here because he was concerned? Maybe he followed him here because it's a dark, quiet place to commit murder without witnesses."

Grady locked eyes with the man at my side. "Because Matt is the one who asked Kai to meet him here."

Matt's eyes shot wide. "No I didn't." Sincere confusion quickly replaced the shock on his brow. "My phone is here. We came back for it." He motioned from me to himself. "Kai showed up here on his own."

"After you called him," Grady said.

"No," Matt repeated. "I haven't called him in years. I don't even know his number anymore."

Grady whistled, and a young officer turned in our direction. Grady waved a hand in the air, beckoning the younger man.

"Detective?" he asked, quickly jogging our way. "Anything I can do for you?"

"Do you have the victim's cell phone?" Grady asked.

"Yes, sir." The officer fished an evidence bag from the duffel draped over his shoulder, then passed it to Grady before stepping back.

Grady snapped on a pair of blue plastic gloves, then

removed the phone from the bag and entered a code. He scrolled and tapped before turning the device to face us. "Is this your phone number?"

The text on the screen appeared to have come from Matt's cell phone. As promised, the message requested Kai meet Matt at the amphitheater.

"That proves I didn't do this," Matt said, confidently. "I told you I don't have my phone. I left it here, which is why we came back."

Grady's eyes seemed to narrow further at Matt's use of the word *we*. "Where is it now?"

Matt turned in the direction of the stage and began to move. "On the stage, I think." He called the words over his shoulder as he rushed to find out if he was right.

I turned to Grady the moment Matt was out of earshot. "Why are you treating him as if you think he actually could've done this?"

"I'm just following the evidence," he said. "Why don't you know that's how I work?"

Matt bypassed his costume jacket, hanging with his quiver on a tree limb, then lifted his phone from the edge of the stage. The light from the screen illuminated his stunned face. "It says I sent that text."

Grady moved past me to his side. "Uh huh." He took the phone in his gloved hands, then beckoned the younger officer back again. "Let's get this checked for prints."

The younger man returned, nodded, then dropped Matt's cell phone into an evidence bag.

Grady swung his attention back to Matt when the officer walked away. "When did you arrive at Everly's home?"

"I'm not sure."

The men looked at me. "I didn't check the time."

In my periphery, I saw Kai's manager shaking someone's hand. I turned to watch as he said goodbye to the officers and headed back toward the parking lot.

I gaped after him. I wasn't a detective, but it seemed to me that releasing the man who'd found the body, and was probably the killer, was a terrible idea. I watched as he made his way through the night, trying to discern his secrets from his stride.

Grady cocked his head. "It takes twenty-minutes to get to Everly's place from here," he said, still working out the time it would've taken Matt to kill Kai, then come to my house and pretend he wasn't a cold-blooded murderer. "Twenty to get back," he continued. "The message was sent shortly after Kai punched you, and everyone saw you leave. Around the same time the cast and crew were having refreshments and clearing out of here. You had plenty of time to return, shoot your bow at an unsuspecting Mr. Larsen, then arrive at Everly's."

I cringed because Grady was right. Based on the time-stamp of the text, Matt could've been the killer. I just couldn't see how anyone would believe it.

"Someone must've known I left the phone," Matt said, trying to work the available pieces into some sort of sense. "They knew it was here, then they helped themselves to it," he said.

I wrinkled my nose. "Don't you keep a password on your phone?"

"Sure. It's nine-one-one," he said, a self-deprecating smile lifting his lips.

"Cute," I said. "Have you ever accidentally made the call, thinking it was the lock screen?"

He frowned. "No."

I nodded, kicking away the question, and pretty sure I would make the mistake eventually with a password like that. "I draw a star on my home screen," I said, daring a look in Grady's direction.

Grady had carried a star as a marshal, and he'd mended the headrest in my golf cart with a star-shaped patch after someone stabbed it with a knife. A star was kind of our thing now.

I caught his eye, briefly, anticipating the butterflies of a secret silently exchanged, but Grady simply looked away. Whether because he didn't understand how much the star now meant to me, or because he'd missed the fact I was trying to communicate that with him, I wasn't sure. Either way, it was kind of a bummer.

Matt paced in a small circle, beginning to lose his cool. "No one has ever bothered anything of mine since I moved to Charm. I don't even lock my truck at night. Because everyone in town knows it's *my* truck."

"Who is in town that would want to kill Kai?" I asked. "Who even knows he's here besides Matt and the manager?" I turned to Grady. "The man who found the body." I formed air quotes around the word *found*, then tented my brows, waiting for him to get my drift.

Before he responded, something else came to mind, and I fixed my eyes on Grady. "How'd you get into Kai's phone?"

"Fingerprint recognition," Grady said grimly.

I shivered at the thought of using a dead man's hand to gain access to his phone. "Ew."

Matt gave a withering sigh, then dropped into a squat before rolling back onto his bottom in the grass, the way I suspected he'd wanted to for a while. He dug his fingers into his hair and released a ragged breath. "I can't believe this is happening."

I took a seat beside him.

"This is a lot to process," Matt whispered.

Grady stepped into our personal space, forcing us to tip back our heads to see his face. "Murders usually are."

"Someone killed Kai Larsen, and they're framing me for it," Matt said.

I looped my arm with Matt's and offered a supportive squeeze. "It's going to be okay. Grady knows you aren't a killer, and he's really good at what he does. We'll figure this out. Promise."

Matt nodded, and I beamed up at Grady, thankful for the opportunity to show support for him and brag about his skills to the latest wrongly-accused.

Grady glared back, jaw tight and eyes fixed on my arm linked to Matt's.

I released my friend before I unintentionally provoked the detective any further, but it didn't feel great that he'd missed a second silent signal I'd tried sending. I moved my attention back to the man at my side and put on my tightest thinking cap, because the sooner we proved Matt's innocence, the sooner Grady could find the real killer.

CHAPTER
FIVE

I woke early the next morning, after tossing and turning through the night. Grady had grudgingly allowed Matt to drive me home while he stayed at the crime scene, and he hadn't called or texted afterward. Matt had barely spoken on the ride back to Charm, and I'd cleaned my café to within an inch of its life trying to burn off my nervous energy.

I poured my second mug of coffee as the sun began to rise, then went onto the deck to talk things over with Lou.

He appeared a moment after I took my seat.

We watched in companionable silence as the day blazed to life over the Atlantic, then he turned one beady eye on me.

"You've probably heard by now that there was a murder in Manteo last night," I said.

He didn't respond, so I filled in the details as I knew them.

"Crazy, right?" I asked. "Who would want to frame Matt? Everyone loves him, and no one here even knew Kai."

Lou puffed his feathers until his face became unrecognizable and his stumpy orange legs disappeared.

"See," I said. "It's frustrating. You get it. Something foul is definitely afoot." I finished my coffee, then said my goodbyes to Lou, promising him shrimp leftovers at lunch. "Be careful out there," I added, sliding the glass door closed behind me.

I'd barely made it down my steps to the foyer when the doorbell rang.

Denise waved and peeked around the lacy curtain on my front door. "I'm early," she called through the glass when she saw me.

I welcomed her with a hug. "This must mean Grady told you what happened last night."

She closed the door behind, then turned to me with wild blue eyes. Her long, blond hair hung in thick beachy waves down her back. She'd tucked her logoed work shirt into faded and distressed blue jeans, then slid bare feet into sneakers. Denise was younger than me by a few years, taller by a few inches, and thinner by fifty pounds. She looked a little like a Barbie doll come to life, except more physically proportional, and with the ability to flip a grown man on his back inside a second. I'd seen that last part for myself.

"Are you kidding?" she asked, exasperated. "Grady came in late, then barely spoke with me over breakfast. I had to get the scoop from the *Town Charmer* this morning."

"Matt didn't do it," I said.

"Of course not," she agreed, leading the way across my foyer to Sun, Sand, and Tea. She dropped her purse beneath the counter, then tied an apron around her narrow waist. "But it doesn't look good."

"I know." I took a seat at the counter and rested my

elbows on top. "I searched the internet for everything I could find related to Kai Larsen's surfing career last night. He's known for his good looks, bad boy charm, and frequent outbursts. Apparently his fans love the chaos and unpredictability that's always surrounding him. They're the ones buying up all the brands and products he uses to support him. So Kai's sponsors were essentially supporting, if not enabling, his behaviors."

Denise bobbed her head. "All publicity is good publicity. But I bet he's made an enemy or two along the way. Bad boys usually have at least one known nemesis."

"I couldn't find one," I admitted, "but I know he or she is out there somewhere." And whoever they are, they know how to shoot a longbow. "Oh!" The most interesting piece of my research popped into mind. "I also learned that Kai was married to a total diva named Tara, and she came with him to the islands for the promotional stuff he had going on this week. They were an attention-seeking, overly dramatic match made in heaven. She threw fits frequently for the paparazzi's benefit, and they ate it up. She lists her career as budding actress on all her social media sites."

Denise grimaced. She righted two glass jars from the rack behind the counter, then filled both with ice and flooded the cubes with bubbling basil raspberry tea from the dispenser containing the weekly special. "She does not sound like my cup of tea," she said, passing one of the jars to me.

"Agreed." I wrapped my fingertips around the offering and smiled. "Thanks."

"Of course," she said. "Find anything else that's interesting?"

"There were a lot of articles about Matt in his surf days," I offered, casting a sideways look in her direction. "Pictures too."

Denise whipped her phone out and began to tap the screen. When her eyes lit up and her mouth popped open, I knew she'd found what she was looking for. "Holy eight-pack, Batman! I knew he was trim under that EMT uniform, but I had no idea he was packing this much heat."

"Surfing definitely requires stamina," I said, remembering the strong, lean body I'd had before leaving Charm for culinary school. "Maybe I should get back on a board. Walking hasn't been making the impact on my waistline that I'd wanted." That was the understatement of the century. I didn't mind walking, and I enjoyed being outside, but it was hard to keep up the pace and not stop to chat when I knew everyone I came upon. Or when I saw sales in store windows and ice cream in people's hands. Basically, my power walks always fizzled into leisurely strolls with plentiful conversations and delicious snacks.

"You surf?" Denise asked, her expression offensively shocked.

"I grew up on an island," I said. I was pretty sure sand and salt water made up half my DNA. "I'm not any good, but that never really mattered." My gaze drifted to the view outside my café windows, where sunlight glistened on cresting waves. I'd been hard to get out of the water for at least my first decade of life. After that, I came out for good reasons, mostly food and boys. The pull to get back into the ocean hadn't been as strong since I'd moved home a couple years ago, but maybe that was because I literally lived on the beach now.

"You doing okay?" Denise asked.

"Yeah," I lied, my distracted mind racing back to Matt and wondering why anyone would want to frame him for a murder. I sipped my tea and let the familiar flavors soothe me. "I'm all right."

"Just all right?" she challenged. "Because there's nothing you like more than to investigate a good mystery. Except maybe the opportunity to stick up for someone. And from where I'm standing, Kai Larsen's death gives you a grand opportunity to do both."

"True," I said. "But you should've seen Grady last night when I asked a few questions and tried to comfort Matt."

Denise barked a laugh. "I can imagine. Have you seen Matt lately? And let's not forget he's the same guy who beat Grady to asking you out on an official date last fall."

"But," I countered, "I've been seeing Grady exclusively for months, and things have been great. He can't go all angry-faced on me for being myself."

She tented her pale brows. "The two of you have gotten along so well because you haven't been stepping all over his toes trying to look into one of his murder investigations."

"Because no one has been murdered."

Denise set a finger on her nose.

I rolled my eyes and hopped off the bar stool. "Well, I can't fight fate," I said. "I've got people to see and questions to ask. Let me know if you hear anything good while I'm gone."

"You didn't even try to fight the impulse," she called to my back as I strode away.

"I'm a lover, not a fighter," I returned, already heading down the porch steps.

I hustled up my short drive to the mailbox, then hit my stride on the historic boardwalk a few feet beyond. Brisk spring air nipped my cheeks, even as the brilliant southern sun worked to warm them. I smiled at the thought. Beach life was the best life.

My muscles loosened slowly as I moved, basking in the perfect April day. I tipped my chin and inhaled the heady scent of home that hung thick in the air. The signature salty fragrance that clung to my skin and hair long after I'd gone inside. The humidity and seagrass, wet sand and sunblock. I pulled it all deep into my lungs and smiled.

My fitness bracelet buzzed against my wrist, thrilled that I'd taken more than a dozen steps in a row for a change. I had a love-hate relationship with the little rubber tyrant. I'd threatened to throw it into the ocean more times than I could recall, but each time I remembered I'd left home in a size six and returned in a size twelve, now a fourteen, I'd decide to let the bully do its job.

The boardwalk curved up ahead and cut a path through the marsh, leading me away from the beach, the families flying kites and the multitude of colorful tents staked into the sand. I caught a glimpse of brightly colored shops a moment later.

I parted ways with the historic wooden planks and stepped onto a fallen tree. In three short strides, I was over the marsh and onto solid ground beside Ocean Drive.

The restaurants in town were open for breakfast, filling the sidewalks with a hearty mix of freshly fed shoppers by ten o'clock. The faint aromas of waffles and lattes brought a smile to my face.

I stared at a large Back to the Beach promotional banner while I waited for a car to pass. Apparently Charm was hosting the cook-off and sandcastle competition next month, in addition to the opening of a historic estate and gardens in July. The estate had recently been returned to the town's historical society, after Grady's mother-in-law, Senator Denver, vacated it. I could only imagine the number of feathers Aunt Fran had ruffled by packing the town's summer calendar like that.

I dashed across the street a moment later and onto the sidewalk outside Blessed Bee, my aunts' holistic honey shop. Theirs was just one in a row of pastel-colored houses, long ago converted into a delightful selection of cafés, shops, and second-floor apartments. Blessed Bee boasted a bright-yellow clapboard exterior and was bookended by two matching homes. The blue shop on the left was an ice cream parlor, and the pink one on the right was Charming Reads, my best friend Amelia's bookstore. Each of the shops had a small Back to the Beach poster in the window, featuring the Spring Classic surf competition and Surf Daddy logo.

I waved to Aunt Clara as I approached.

My aunts, like the centuries of Swan women before them, were beekeepers. They used honey from their personal hives, plus dried flowers and herbs from their extensive gardens, to make uniquely fabulous, holistic potions like lip gloss, facial soap, and mouthwatering condiments. My near-paralyzing fear of bees meant the tradition would end with my aunts.

All the Blessed Bee products were figuratively, but not literally, magical, though plenty of islanders whispered about the possible woo-woo in our Swan family juju.

I didn't mind the speculation my aunts were something more—or something different. What I minded were the alleged curses that hung over my head and heart like a guillotine. Thankfully, there were only two, and everything was fine as long as I didn't believe, fall in love, or try to leave the island.

"Everly!" Aunt Clara called, a bright smile on her pretty face. She set a stack of products on a table erected outside Blessed Bee's door, then came at me with open arms. "Good morning! How are you?" She wrapped me in a hug and squeezed.

Her cream-colored ankle-length gown hung from her thin frame like bed sheets on a mannequin. Long silver and blond hair stretched down her back, and cornflower blue eyes searched me for my secrets.

"I'm good. How are you?"

"Excellent! I'm setting up a nice sidewalk sale. No sense sitting inside all day when I can enjoy the beautiful weather before it gets too hot to breathe." She stepped back and looked me over, then her smile fell. "You're upset about that man who died after play practice."

"Grady and the Manteo police think Matt killed him."

"Pishposh." Aunt Clara turned back to her boxes and began unpacking the contents onto a bright-yellow tablecloth. Handstitched bees flew a loopy pattern along the hem in every direction, and the store's logo was embroidered front and center. "Grady will figure it out," she assured. "He always does."

"Maybe," I said. "Assuming he stops looking at Matt long enough to find the real killer."

I scanned the clusters of people chatting on the sidewalk and waiting in lines to enter busy cafés. Did one of them know something that would be useful? Would they tell me if they did?

"As long as you don't get involved, it doesn't matter to me how long it takes," Aunt Clara continued. "Grady will do the right thing, and if he doesn't already know Matt's innocent, he will," she said. "They're both such good boys."

I pursed my lips, unable to disagree. Though neither of the brawny men in question would qualify as a "boy" to me. "Can I help you?"

"Absolutely. Grab my bag of lip balms and face scrubs from the front seat?" Aunt Clara raised one hand and pressed the button on her car key, unlocking the electric blue Prius several parking spaces away.

"On it," I said, hurrying in the car's direction. Aunt Clara had begun to drive more in the last year, visiting other towns' historical societies and getting involved in new things after Aunt Fran was sworn in as Charm's mayor. They'd been inseparable before, but being mayor had taken Aunt Fran away for long hours and forced Aunt Clara to find out who she was without her sister.

Aunt Clara hated the amount of damage she was doing to the ozone with her mom's hand-me-down Bel Air, so she'd sold the car to Aunt Fran, then bought a more eco-friendly Prius to put her mind at ease. Aunt Fran rarely drove anything other than a bicycle, but she knew what it cost Aunt Clara to say goodbye to their mother's car, and she couldn't let her do it. Not completely. So, Aunt Fran now had two cars sitting in one of the homestead's outbuildings. The Bel

Air and an old VW Bug I hadn't seen since I was in elementary school.

I, on the other hand, got around town on my feet, or in Blue, my fixer-upper golf cart, as needed.

I grabbed the handwoven bag of freshly made goods from her passenger seat, then locked up on my way back to Aunt Clara and set the bag on her table. "Any chance you saw or heard anything about the murder or the victim's fight with Matt after I left last night?"

"No, but I saw the way you were looking at your detective, and that's a dangerous road you two are traveling. You know that, and surely he does too." She tipped her chin low and rolled her eyes up to me in warning as she worked on her table's display.

"Grady doesn't believe in our curse," I said.

"And you?" she asked.

I pressed my lips together. I didn't believe, because it would be ridiculous to think a two-hundred-year-old curse killed men for being loved. How would a curse even know how I felt when I barely knew?

Still, deep inside, I feared there was a chance things existed outside my understanding, and I had to decide if the possibility of a curse was a risk I was willing to take. Would I risk the life of a man who meant so much to me? What about the possibility of making his son an orphan?

"Mm-hmm," Clara said, apparently satisfied with whatever look was on my face.

"Just because you believe in something, doesn't make it true," I said.

"And just because you deny something, doesn't make it false."

It was a conversation we'd had far too many times, and I decided to change the subject. "Where's Aunt Fran?" I asked. "I thought I might see her here this morning."

Aunt Clara straightened, then shook her head. "Last night's murder caused a public relations nightmare. Especially since the victim was directly related to the Back to the Beach event, and so many Charmers were against getting our town involved."

I cringed as I imagined poor Aunt Fran walking a proverbial tightrope.

"She's having brunch at the teahouse if you need her," Aunt Clara added, checking her watch for the time. "You can catch her there in an hour."

"Treason!" I huffed.

Aunt Clara smiled.

"I can't believe she approved a teahouse in Charm without telling me. And now she's having lunch there!"

"Well, she's busy, and Subtle Teas isn't officially open. I'm sure she'll report back once she has something to share."

"Subtle Teas?" I asked, crossing my arms in frustration and biting out the words. "Well, that's a ridiculously adorable name."

"Isn't it?" Aunt Clara agreed. "I'm sure the place is lovely too, but just remember Eloise's business has nothing to do with you. It's stuffy and froufrou and hoity-toity. Not at all like your wonderful little escape."

"How do you know?" I asked, my stomach knotting unreasonably in betrayal. "Have you been there too?"

"Oh, no," she said. "I'd love to go, but I hear there's a waiting list."

I guffawed. "Are you kidding?"

"Don't give it another thought," Aunt Clara said, setting her final line of goods on the table. "Subtle Teas has nothing to do with your wonderful café."

"We both specialize in tea," I argued, trying not to wonder when my aunt had come to first-name terms with an interloper.

"Proper teahouses are stuffy and fussy and require women to wear dresses and hats," Aunt Clara said. "You'd hate it, and so would your clientele."

I glared at her cream dress with lacy sleeves, then dragged my eyes over her matching floppy hat. She and Aunt Fran always dressed exactly as she'd described. Aunt Clara in cream and Aunt Fran in black.

A sleek red convertible slid into the spot beside Aunt Clara's Prius, pulling my attention away.

Amelia climbed out. "Good morning!" she called, looking magnificent in her black and white vintage dress and Mary Janes. Large, white-framed sunglasses covered her pale blue eyes, and she'd swept her silky blond hair into a tidy chignon.

I hugged Aunt Clara, then took a step in Amelia's direction. "I'm going to pop over to the bookstore for a minute before I head home. Are you still coming to my cooking class tonight?"

"I wouldn't miss it!" Aunt Clara said, dropping a kiss on my cheek.

I darted along the sidewalk, sidestepping window shoppers and groups heading in every direction. "Hey," I called, slipping inside as Amelia flipped on the lights.

"Hi!" she chirped. "Is Clara having a sidewalk sale?"

"Yeah. Completely impromptu," I said. "She told me she wants to enjoy the spring day, but I think she gets lonely inside when Fran isn't with her. At least outside, she can talk to everyone who walks by."

"Fun! Help me carry this table?" Amelia asked, dragging a collapsible unit in my direction. "I think I'll join her. It really is beautiful, and I adore Clara."

I grabbed one end, and we toted the table through her door, then set it up on the sidewalk.

We waved at Aunt Clara, and she smiled brightly but didn't respond. A trio of women had her attention, chatting animatedly across the table from her.

The women paused to stare at me, then lowered their voices before continuing.

I made a mental note to ask my aunt about them later.

"So, how are you holding up?" Amelia asked, smoothing a white linen cloth over her table. "You were pretty upset when you texted last night. Did you manage to get any sleep?"

"Not much," I admitted. "Thanks for reading my zillion rapid-fire panic texts, by the way. I was too upset to talk, but I had to get it all out of my head."

She smiled sweetly. "That's what friends are for. I would've gladly listened to you ugly cry in person if that was what you needed."

I smiled back. "I know. You're really appreciated. I don't tell you that enough."

"It's fine. You always show it. That's what matters." She headed back inside with me on her heels.

I followed her around the shop as she selected books, then went to arrange the tomes outside. "I was online reading everything I could find on Kai Larsen and professional surfing in general," I told her.

"How'd that go?" she asked, putting the finishing touches on a multibook display.

"It was interesting to learn about Matt's and Kai's pasts, but I'd rather have answers about the present."

Amelia nodded as she admired her work. "Spend any time online this morning?"

"Not really," I said. "Why?"

"Did you read the *Town Charmer*?"

I swallowed a groan as I pulled my cell phone from one pocket and navigated to the town's gossip blog without any further questions. No one seemed to have any idea who ran the wildly popular site, but the information found there was both current and brutally honest, much to the dismay of anyone who'd ever drawn the blogger's attention. Like me, for example. Multiple times. Folks said they tuned in every day for the weather and tide schedule, but the sheer volume of comments and responses to every poll and story told the whole truth. Locals might've logged in for the weather, but they stayed for the scoop.

A set of images centered the screen. Me with Grady walking on the beach. Me with Matt riding in his truck. Me with Matt and Grady at the crime scene, arranged in an actual triangle, both men scowling. "This is completely out of context." I looked back to the ladies whispering with Aunt Clara and suddenly understood the looks they'd given me.

"They probably saw the blog and are curious," Amelia said, following my gaze to the lookie-loos. She lifted a hand and waved.

"You know them?" I asked, not matching any of the faces with names in my memory bank, though all three women looked vaguely familiar, thanks to life in a small town.

Amelia smiled. "Sure. They all come to my book club for the over-sixty crowd. They're Corkers."

I turned my attention back to her slowly. Did everyone know about the Corkers, except for me? "Promise me that we will call ourselves something completely ridiculous too when we're old?"

Amelia nodded. "Try to stop us."

I scanned the blog's headline and grimaced.

CHARM'S FAVORITE LOVE TRIANGLE: BACK IN ACTION? OR NEVER LOST ITS SHAPE?

"Are they trying to say I've been dating both men for six months?" I asked, hoping I wasn't reading it right.

Amelia wrinkled her button nose. "Maybe not so much dating them both, as you just never stopped seeing Matt on the side."

"That's the same thing!"

She raised her shoulders to her ears. "I'm trying to put a nice spin on it. Can you blame me?"

I rubbed my temple. "A man was murdered, and some anonymous blogger is more interested in my love life."

"In fairness, it's not just the blogger," she said. "Everyone is interested in your love life. Myself included." She pointed to my phone. "Look at the comments."

"Two-hundred-seventy-one comments?" I gasped.

"That's nuts!" Who were these people, and why didn't they have better things to do?

Upon quick inspection, I determined there were only about fifty or so actual commenters. The rest of the comments were conversations made by the same few dozen people.

I put the phone back in my pocket. I'd deal with the gossip later.

"Just when you and Grady stopped making the daily news, you had to go and get a late night visit from Matt," she teased.

"If I ever find that blogger," I started, then stopped when the women, including Aunt Clara, turned to look my way. "I'm going to thank him or her for doing such a bang-up job." I improvised, inching closer to Amelia and lowering my voice. I checked to see who else might be listening before I continued. "Any chance you saw Kai Larsen around here?" I asked. "He followed Matt to play practice, so I'm guessing he started by asking around Charm for Matt's location."

Amelia's rosebud mouth turned down. "Yes. I saw Kai at the ice cream shop when I went to grab milkshakes for me and Dad. He hit on the waitress, who was barely twenty, then on me, when he was on his way out. It's easy to believe the rumors of him as a womanizer. He seemed thrilled to hit on every female in sight."

"You read about him too?" I asked.

"Of course." She grinned. "I didn't see any way to stop you from looking into this since it's Matt's reputation and future at risk. So I figured I should at least try to be informed."

I cupped both hands over my heart. "Thank you."

"Someone has to keep you out of trouble," she said. "And I love Grady, but he's cut it pretty close the last few times your life was in danger."

"You aren't going to try to stop me?" I grinned.

"Would it work if I did?"

"Nope." I rocked onto my toes then back down, a zing of adrenaline rushing through my veins. "Thank you."

"Sure."

"Hey," I said, thinking of something else I'd been meaning to ask her. "Any idea why Ryan is texting me?"

She shook her head slowly, a small set of creases forming between her brows. "He said he had business on the island soon, but he was pretty vague about it. I hope he's going to swing by for a visit while he's here."

"I guess I'll let you know after I talk to him then," I said.

"Wouldn't it be great if he relocated to Charm?"

I nodded, not sure I felt as warmly about the notion as she did, but not willing to disagree. The word *relocate* brought something else to mind, namely the tea maker who'd recently relocated to my town. I checked the time on my watch. "I'd better get going. I want to run over to Bay View and take a look at this new tea place everyone's talking about."

"Right." She nodded conspiratorially. "Subtle Teas. That's good market research."

I smiled back. *Something like that*, I thought. But mostly, I wanted a look at the woman who'd had the audacity to roll into my town and set up shop as my competition.

Because I was wholly freaked out about it.

CHAPTER
SIX

I hurried through town, smiling and nodding to locals and anyone taking a good long look at me as I hustled past. I tried not to wonder how many of them had read the morning blog or what they thought of the content. Did anyone in Charm truly believe I'd secretly dated Matt behind Grady's back? That the town's only detective hadn't known I was sneaking around on him? I wasn't sure who that scenario painted more poorly, me or him, but I didn't like either.

I crossed the street with a group of pedestrians at the corner of Middletown and Bay View, then headed toward the teahouse. The group turned toward Northrop Manor, the historic property being opened as a museum next month. The grand estate was seated on the sound, and had a rich island history. Grady's mother-in-law had lived there nearly a year after buying it out from under the Charm Historical Society. Now that she was gone, the history buffs were in possession as originally planned, and there would be a major celebration very soon.

Foot traffic was lighter in my direction, and the former

Deeter property came into view rather quickly. The small, two-story home was covered in cedar shake that had been weathered gray with age, salt, and the searing southern sun. I felt an instant kinship upon approach.

The door had been painted red. The window trim and porch, sage green. Flowers had been planted in mass along the walkway, then set in large planters up each side of the steps, where a large checkered mat was topped with a smaller, oval one, lined in scarlet and sage. The word *Welcome* was scripted across its center.

Beds of brown mulch ringed the home, and baskets brimming with still more blooms swung from hooks in the porch ceiling. The aesthetic was ridiculously inviting.

Chills swept down my spine, and I froze briefly when my steps stuttered in response. I swung my gaze wide, convinced someone was watching me, but unable to find anyone looking my way. I scanned the area in wide passes, turning slowly as the sensation increased, certain I was right. I imagined the women I'd seen speaking with Aunt Clara peeking around the bushes, or whoever ran the *Town Charmer* taking photos of me from across the street with a telephoto lens. No one was near, however, and those in the distance weren't paying any attention to me.

I hurried up the walk to the front porch, suddenly eager to get this adventure over with and return home where I wouldn't be alone.

A paper sign in the window announced the shop's hours in stiff black font and instructed interested parties to call during those hours or check the website for information on how to make a reservation.

I cupped my hands at my temples, then pressed my nose to the beveled glass window beside the sign, peering into the shadows.

Mismatched tables, chairs, and centerpieces were sprinkled over a white tiled floor. Paintings in elaborate, gilded frames lined the walls, and a life-size cardboard cutout of the Queen of England leaned against a set of stairs in the corner. The words *Gift Shop* were scripted across a freestanding chalkboard with an arrow pointing up the steps.

I dropped my hands at the sound of a snapping twig. I didn't want to be caught peeping into the window or eaten by an alligator who'd wandered over from the marsh or sound. I especially didn't want to be spotted by Eloise, the teahouse owner.

The lights blazed to life inside the home, and I jumped. Another quick look inside revealed a figure in the dining area. The curvy, grandmotherly woman carried a tray of teapots to a table near the door, only a few feet away. Her face lifted as she drew closer. As if she sensed me there.

I ducked, then ran down the steps and around the corner, hoping not to be spotted.

A small white convertible slid against the curb a few feet away, and the driver waved a hand overhead. "Excuse me," she called.

I stopped, heart still racing, and attempted to mentally switch gears. I didn't recognize the driver or the car and wasn't convinced she meant to speak with me. I checked over my shoulder, to see if she was possibly waving to someone else. "Hi."

"I am so sorry to bother you," the pretty brunette called,

pushing sunglasses onto her forehead. "I'm kind of lost. Any chance you know your way around?"

"A pretty big chance," I said, feeling my natural smile return.

"Great!" She paused, then tilted her head over one shoulder. The faint look of recognition hit her deep brown eyes a moment later. "I think I recognize you. You're from Charm, right?"

"Born and raised," I said, stepping onto her side of the vehicle. "I'm Everly Swan, I own Sun, Sand, and Tea. It's an iced tea shop in the historic Victorian home at the beach."

"Nicole Homes," she said. "I run a stationery shop in Manteo. That's actually why I'm here. I have an order to deliver, but this town is unexpectedly confusing."

"Who are you looking for?" I asked, fairly sure I could get her to most neighborhoods and businesses by memory.

She bit her lip, looked around, then motioned me closer. "Tara Larsen."

I felt my eyes widen, and I worked to be cool. "Oh yeah?" I asked. "I'm happy to help."

She freed her phone from the cupholder and turned it in my direction, revealing the address where she was headed. "I've been trying to find this place for twenty minutes, but it's as if my GPS can't decipher these streets. I'm trying to turn at intersections that don't exist, like Charm is in some kind of cosmic void the satellites can't read. The Bermuda Triangle of the Outer Banks." She laughed. "I'm sorry. I'm frustrated. Let's go with whatever theory makes me look less ridiculous for not being able to follow directions."

I looked up from the phone and smiled. "Your luck has

officially improved. I know this place," I said. "It's a rental on the beach. Other side of the island. Take Middletown to Ocean Drive, turn left, then follow that until it seems to dead end at a public parking area. From there you kind of scoot around the bend." I made a snaking motion with one hand as I explained. "It only looks as if the road ends. It's really just a tight curve. You'll find yourself on Sea Spray from there. This house is the biggest on that street by far, and sits above the dunes, so you can't miss it."

Nicole chewed her lip, as if she might still be lost. "Thank you. I think I can do that. I should also come clean." She lifted her palms in surrender. "I recognized you right away from the local papers and that blog your town keeps. I should've just said that. You've been so nice, and it's weird to pretend I don't know who you are. I do. Sorry."

I wrinkled my brow then laughed. "It's no problem. I'm a local celebrity for all the wrong reasons some days." I cringed internally at the memory of the morning post, one-hundred-percent wrong and knee deep in my personal business. "Most of the stuff on the blog is totally sensationalized," I said. "I'm not nearly as interesting as the posts make me sound."

"But you are going to look into Kai Larsen's murder. Aren't you?" she asked, a hopeful lift to her words. "I've followed your progress on similar things in the past. You do a good job. And Kai deserves justice."

My stomach tightened. "Why? Are you a fan of his? A reporter?" I crossed my arms and narrowed my eyes, feeling suddenly incredibly stupid. "Is that why you're looking for Tara?"

"No!" she squeaked. "I'm a fan of surfing. I grew up in

Rodanthe. I'm just a woman with a little shop and a delivery to make. Trying to enjoy the island life. You and I are a lot alike. Except I don't solve crimes or date hunky detectives. Lucky." She threw the last word on a whisper.

I grinned at the reminder of dating Grady, then relaxed my rigid muscles. "What are you delivering?" I asked, making sure not to be duped by a friendly face and likely story. Why would the wife of a murder victim need a stationery delivery so soon after his death? It wasn't as if she could've known about it in advance and ordered memorial invitations. I hoped.

"I shouldn't say," Nicole said. "Considering what's happened, the event is off, but I still need to get paid." She winced. "I know that sounds awful, but it's a big order, and I can't afford to eat it. I have rent to pay."

"Absolutely." I nodded, mentally rehashing our conversation so far. "Did you say you're from Rodanthe? Any chance you saw Kai around earlier this week?" I asked. "I heard he was here doing promotional work."

"He was at Surf Daddy for a photo shoot, and he did a breakfast thing on our pier. My shop was flooded with visitors both days. It's nice to have a celebrity in town."

"Everything went smoothly at the events?" I asked. "No fighting or protesting? No stalkers? Crazed groupies? Attempts on his life?"

Nicole looked confused, then horrified before bursting into laughter. "No. It was all very chill. Good vibes. Great weather. He looked happy. Hamming up the attention, like he's known for."

"Flirting with the ladies," I guessed.

"And the cameras," she said. "His whole team was there, not just Kai. Plus a man in a golf shirt, who I assume was his manager." She frowned. "Or his dad. I don't know, he stayed in the wings." Her gaze jumped to the knots and clusters of people lingering on curbs and corners nearby.

I realized Nicole and I were being watched. "I should let you make your delivery." I stepped back and smiled, releasing her to drive away, and making silent plans to visit Tara Larsen myself later. If anyone knew who might want to hurt Kai, surely it was his wife.

"Wait." Nicole put her phone away and pulled a sheet of cardstock from the bag beside her. "You were really helpful, and I know you get a bad rep, but you do great things." She scribbled on the paper, then passed it my way with a Cheshire cat grin, before sliding dark glasses over her eyes once more. "If you ever need a special, high-quality stationery order, let me know."

The little convertible slid into traffic and rolled smoothly away.

I waved pointedly to the collection of ogling eyes, and the little crowds dispersed. Then, I hurried back to the crosswalk. I only had a few hours to prepare for my first on-site cooking class tonight, and there was much to do.

I stopped at the light and fiddled with the paper in my hands as I waited to cross. A hearty breeze threatened to take the thing away, and I held on more tightly, then turned it over in my fingers.

A fresh smile spread across my face as I read the beautifully embossed text on the back. Nicole had slipped me one of Tara Larsen's invitations.

-Goodbye to You-

Hosted by Tara Larsen

JOIN ME IN SAYING GOODBYE TO MY CHEATING HUSBAND
AND HELLO TO THE FREEDOM I DESERVE.

1128 SEA SPRAY DRIVE, CHARM, NORTH CAROLINA

BRING YOUR SUITS AND A BOTTLE OF CHAMPAGNE
TO CELEBRATE MY NEW LIFE AND IMMEDIATE WEIGHT
LOSS OF ONE HUNDRED AND SIXTY-FIVE POUNDS.

A wild bubble of laughter burst from my lips before the darker, more sinister thoughts rushed in. Kai Larsen's wife, a known diva and lover of all drama, had been planning to leave him! And she was throwing a party!

CHAPTER

SEVEN

I nearly ran back to Sun, Sand, and Tea as my mind whirled with theories. A scorned wife with a known temper had planned to publicly dump Kai by having a party!

Maybe he'd gotten wind of it and argued with her.

Maybe she'd caught him with another woman and hadn't been able to control her anger a moment longer.

Maybe there was a big life insurance policy, and she realized it was more lucrative to kill him than to leave him.

The possibilities were endless, and I was giddy. Respectfully. The best way to give mourning family members and friends peace was to help them get closure. So, finding the truth and saving Matt's behind before Grady hauled him off in cuffs was good for everyone concerned.

Charm loved Matt now, but would they view him the same way if he was arrested for murder? I wasn't sure, and that frightened me. If Grady made the arrest, the charges wouldn't stick, because he'd eventually realize he was wrong, but the black mark on Matt could be permanent. And that wasn't fair.

The only problem with my theory about Tara possibly killing her husband, a problem Grady was sure to point out and use against me, was the arrow. That longbow seemed unwieldy in the hands of anyone other than Matt. But, if the murder had been planned, like Tara's party, she could've learned to use the bow in advance, setting the stage before ever arriving in Charm.

My breath came faster, burning my throat and chest. I wasn't sure when I'd started jogging, but my body was beginning to protest. I had to force my feet to slow before I collapsed.

The buzz of my cell phone drew my attention as I sucked down ragged gulps of air. I turned the phone over in shaky hands, then tilted forward to slow the spread of black dots in my vision. I hoped the text was from Matt so I could reply with the good news. A reasonable suspect had presented herself!

Unfortunately, the incoming message wasn't a text at all. It was a notification from the web page I'd made to communicate with cooking class participants. Either someone was trying to get a last-minute reservation or someone was canceling.

I swiped the message to open it, then gaped at the screen. A small video accompanied three pointed words.

Stop asking questions

The five-second video played on repeat. A volley of arrows arched through the sky, then landed on the head of a cartoon woman who looked disturbingly like me. Her head wobbled, then fell off, taking the arrows with it.

My stomach lurched, and this time, I broke into an intentional jog. I didn't stop until I was home.

The sight of Grady's truck was enough to slow my steps. I knew exactly what he'd say about the little cartoon threat, and I didn't like it. He'd say I brought the threat on myself.

I waved feebly to a set of exiting guests with pastry bags and hearty smiles. Then I dragged myself up the short flight of steps to the front door. I took a minute to catch my breath in the foyer before making an appearance in the café.

Denise smiled at the sight of me, distracted by an order she was taking at a table near the window. Her expression fell as my distress registered.

"Everly?" Grady asked, swiveling on a barstool at the counter. "Everything okay?"

I shook my head quickly, heat blazing in my cheeks from fear and exhaustion as I took the seat beside his. "No."

His brows furrowed. "What happened?"

I unlocked my phone and passed it to him, the cartoon GIF playing on its horrific animated loop.

Grady's expression darkened. "You got this while you were out?"

I nodded.

Denise rushed around to the business side of the counter, quickly pulling together a set of glass jars, ice cubes, and teas to fill her most recent order. "What's going on? Why do you look like that?" she asked, flicking her gaze from me to Grady, then back. "You both look like you just stubbed your toe."

Grady turned my phone to face her.

She watched intently, her expression moving from mild amusement to shock when my cartoon head rolled off. "That's awful!" she gasped. "Who made that?"

"I don't know," I said, hating the quiver in my voice. "It was sent through my cooking class website. The user's name is Leave_This_Alone."

"Original." She frowned. "Can you identify the user's identity through the site?"

I lifted my shoulders, then had to force them back down.

Grady tapped the screen, navigating to the threat-maker's profile page. "This account was created today, and based on a phone number made of one repeating digit, and the cuss words used in all the contact information, I'm assuming Leave_This_Alone had no intention of being found."

I took a seat on the stool beside Grady's, then rested my forehead on the cool countertop.

"I'll be right back," Denise said, presumably taking the teas to the guests who'd ordered them. She set a glass near my head when she returned. "Strawberry mint, extra ice," she said. "Drink. You'll feel better."

I obeyed, and she was right. My heart slowly stopped thundering, and by the time the tea was gone, all the sweat I'd worked up by racing home had dried. "Who do you think did this?" I asked, pressing the remaining jar of ice to my pounding head.

Grady set my phone on the counter with a look of exasperation. "Could be my badge and ten years of experience talking, but I'm thinking this is the work of someone who doesn't want you poking into this murder investigation. Someone besides me," he clarified.

"Funny," I said, flatly and with a glare. "Sarcasm looks terrible on you, by the way."

His cheek ticked up, fighting a smile.

"Maybe the threat itself is a clue," I suggested. "Assuming the message was from Kai's killer, this person somehow knew about my cooking class site."

"And that you tend to mix yourself up in these matters," he added. "So we can add everyone with internet access to your suspect list."

Denise cocked a narrow hip and shot him a hard look. "That person would also need to be in the Outer Banks last night and know Kai. That he was in town. And where to find him."

"The killer used Matt's phone, which he forgot at the amphitheater, to ask Kai to meet them there," I said. "So the killer would've also needed to know Matt's phone was left behind."

Grady groaned and rubbed his forehead.

I looked from him to Denise, then back again. "What?"

He fixed me with a no-nonsense stare. "What have you been up to? Don't say, 'nothing,' because I know that expression and that voice. And I've got a gory little cartoon that disagrees."

"I haven't done anything," I said, frowning deeply. This was the part where Grady would suggest the threat was somehow my fault. But I hadn't done anything to provoke the killer.

Sure, I'd spoken to a few friends about what had happened. Lou, Denise, Aunt Clara, and Amelia, but none of them would say a word. The only other thing I'd done was a little research at home. And I'd made a quick, unrelated trip to Subtle Teas. Where I'd run into Nicole. Was it possible our meeting wasn't a coincidence?

"I've been sitting over here trying to figure out why you

are being threatened. You didn't know the victim, and he's barely been dead twelve hours."

I did my best to look innocent while I mentally explored the possibility that Nicole had killed Kai for a reason I didn't yet understand and had been following me all morning. Because I was sure someone had been, at least while I was outside the teahouse. Moments before I met her.

Grady's eyes narrowed. "So, you think Kai Larsen's killer somehow heard about your previous involvement in similar situations, and was so concerned that he or she went through the trouble of finding your cooking class web page, made an account, then a little cartoon, and sent it to you. Just in case you tried to get involved again?" He raised an eyebrow. "Completely preventative measures?"

Denise backed up a step.

My mouth fell open, and I had to work to shut it.

"Everly?" he pressed. "The message says, Stop asking questions? Why?"

I puffed out my cheeks, then released a long, exhaustive breath. "Who can guess what goes on in a killer's head?"

Grady turned his stool to face mine, then he reached for my seat and turned me too. "Who have you discussed Kai Larsen's death with? When and where did those conversations take place?"

My muscles tensed, and my chest constricted. "Friends," I said. "I talked to Amelia about it last night via text, then Lou this morning over coffee."

He nodded. "And?"

"I talked to Denise when she arrived, then to Amelia again this morning."

"Where?" he asked quietly.

"Outside her shop."

Grady's eyelids drifted briefly shut. When he opened them, the blank cop face I hated was in place. "Who else?"

"Aunt Clara."

"By phone?" he asked.

I shook my head. "Outside her shop."

Grady's jaw clenched. "Anyone else?"

I stole a look at Denise, who had immersed herself in cleaning the counter as if her life depended on it. When I turned my eyes back to Grady, he was waiting. "Nicole."

"Nicole who?"

I chewed my lip. I couldn't remember. "She runs a stationery shop in Rodanthe."

"Why were you in Rodanthe?"

"I wasn't," I said, thankful I hadn't left town to question anyone. "I ran into her while I was checking out the new tea shop."

"How do you know her?"

My cheeks heated, and I stole a look at the exit, contemplating how far I could get before he cornered me again. "We met this morning. Near the new tea shop."

Grady's face turned red.

"I thought someone was watching me while I was there," I said. "None of the people in my line of sight seemed to be paying any attention at the time, but I had that same creepy feeling I get when there's someone staring holes through me."

Grady worked his jaw. "How long was that before Nicole appeared?"

"Not long," I said.

"How many people could've overheard you talking about the murder to your aunt, Amelia, or Nicole, the alleged shopkeeper from Rodanthe, whose last name you can't recall?" he asked, interrupting my thoughts.

I blinked my way back to the moment, wrestling the tidal wave of ideas building in my mind. "Quite a few, but I was always quiet when I spoke." I forced a smile. "Aunt Clara and Amelia were too, and Nicole was careful because she wanted to be professional."

Grady looked as if I'd grown a pelican's bill.

"She was looking for directions to a rental home because Kai's wife had placed an order for delivery today," I added, eager to prove my new friend was who she said she was, and hoping I was right.

I dug the invitation from my bag and turned it to face Grady and Denise, who'd stopped pretending not to listen.

Denise whistled long and slow. "She was throwing a party to dump him? That really is dramatic."

I nodded.

"And this Nicole just gave you one of Mrs. Larsen's invitations?" Grady asked.

"No, she gave me her contact info," I corrected, turning the paper over in his hands. "Which she happened to scribble on the back."

Grady inhaled deeply, then released the breath to a silent count of ten. I knew he counted because he'd told me once. This was one of the ways he tried to manage his temper where I was concerned. I hadn't seen him do it in months.

Not since the last island murder.

"Did you know Tara Larsen was in town?" I asked Grady, changing the subject slightly.

"Yes," he answered. "I spoke with her last night."

I tried to hide my frustration. I hated when he made progress ahead of me, even if he was the cop and I was the tea maker. "Did she say what she's doing here?"

Grady frowned. "Why wouldn't she be here? She's his wife."

"But she didn't want to be," I said, giving the card in his hand a hearty flick.

Grady slid the card onto the counter, away from me. "Have you considered the possibility that Matt might've sent you this warning?"

"Matt wouldn't try to scare me," I said, feeling the certainty of it in my bones. "And he didn't kill anyone."

"Well, the crime scene evidence is all pointing to him," Grady said. "And Matt knows you. He knows you love to meddle, and he's familiar with your café and your upcoming cooking class."

"He is also innocent and clearly being framed," I said. "Any decent framer would know all of those things about Matt too."

"Don't do this," Grady said suddenly, slumping slightly and switching gears. "You know what happens when you get involved, and I'm not sure I can take seeing you in the kind of danger you always wind up in. Not now. After we've..." He snapped his mouth shut and straightened, scanning the café for lookie-loos. There were plenty—and all about to topple out of their seats from craning their necks so hard. "Begun dating," he finished with a sigh.

I smiled. We'd been dating for months, but we never called it that. We didn't call it anything, and we never responded to prying questions. We'd never denied it either, so most folks just accepted what they saw happening for what it was, confirmation or not.

But he'd said it. And they'd all heard. And that made me feel ridiculously like the prom queen.

I watched as his expression firmed up, giving nothing away. His Adam's apple bobbed, and he ran a finger along his jaw, a tell indicating he was stressed. I'd picked up on the habit a while ago while trying to decipher his otherwise blank cop face.

"Let me handle this case on my own," he said finally, a pleading look in his eyes. "Stop asking questions. Stop trying to help. Stop digging for information. Trust that I will find everything I need to arrest the killer without any assistance from you."

"What if I say I'll try?" I asked. "And for the record, I didn't go looking for that information." I flicked my gaze to the invitation he'd pushed away. "That information found me. I can't exactly stay at home and hibernate until you catch the bad guy, afraid someone who knows something might accidentally tell it in my presence."

Grady stared. Patiently evaluating until his phone buzzed. "I've got to go, but you and I will talk later," he said, making the words sound more like a threat than a promise. "Try real hard to stay out of this until then."

He kissed the top of my head, then made his way through the door.

I ground my teeth, hating to be told what to do. And

completely incapable of allowing myself to be bullied by some cartoonist.

But for now, I had a cooking class to prepare for.

CHAPTER
EIGHT

I closed the shop at seven sharp, then placed my little chalk-board easel on the porch beside the front door. Amelia's dad had painted the blackboard with seashells, tiny sweets and scones, plus two lines of perfect curling letters informing visitors there was a private class in progress. Those who'd registered for the class received emailed instructions letting them know the door was unlocked and they should come in.

I'd dimmed the lights in the café to emphasize the fact Sun, Sand, and Tea was closed, then I turned music on in the former ballroom, which was now my private event space. I'd selected a playlist of classical music as a distinct switch from the peppy beach tunes and golden oldies I typically bobbed around to in the café.

I'd arranged a series of rectangular tables in a U formation, with chairs and supplies every few feet. Guests needed enough elbow room to work and also a place to rest and enjoy.

My little card table was stationed at the open end of the U, allowing me to move freely around and check the progress of my friends and students as they worked. I'd covered my table in a white cloth I'd pulled from a trunk at my aunts' home, also known as the Swan Homestead. The property that had been in our family's possession since the founding of Charm and was filled with a bevy of things, many which were better suited for a museum. All tangible links to our past.

I'd set out aprons logoed with my shop name and planned to take as many pictures as possible to post on my blog. I'd established a solid following on my baking tutorials, so I wanted to livestream the class and see how it impacted my viewing numbers. Guests had been asked to sign waivers upon registration so I could use their images. Aunt Fran's Corker friends had confirmed within hours of being invited, and I appreciated that to the moon and back.

I took a last-minute spin through the space, evaluating the décor and wondering what my guests would think when they saw it. Banners featuring the *Lost Colony* play hung between my large windows, and I'd covered the refreshment table in a fancy linen cloth, with old pieces of china for my serving plates and bowls.

In honor of the upcoming opening night, I'd chosen a recipe from the family archives that would represent the Roanoke colonists' pasts as well as their, albeit temporary, futures here. A Southern Tea Cake.

The seashell wind chimes jangled, and I hurried out to meet my first guests. "Welcome!" I called, rounding the corner in time to see Amelia and several women, two of which I recognized as the eavesdroppers from this morning. The ones who'd been pretending to talk to Aunt Clara.

"Hey," Amelia said, pulling me into a hug. "Look who I ran into on my way up the steps. This is Henrietta and Pearl. They belong to my Sassy Sixties book club."

The ladies had nodded as their names were called, then waited patiently at Amelia's side.

I offered a hand to Henrietta first. "Welcome."

"You can call me Henri. Thank you for having us," she said, giving my hand a weak squeeze.

Henrietta wore thick round glasses and tight gray curls. She had a cane and stooped slightly over it. What I hoped was a faux fox fur circled her shoulders, biting its tail to stay in place. I couldn't help thinking Henrietta had likely been eligible for Amelia's Sassy Sixties book club at least twenty years ago, had it existed.

She shuffled past me toward the refreshments, and I turned my attention to Pearl.

Pearl extended her hand with a look of expectant curiosity on her gaunt face. "How do you do?"

"I'm well, thank you," I answered, taking her small, cold hand in mine. "I'm glad you could make it."

"As am I." She grinned and a mass of wrinkles gathered at the corners of her mouth and eyes. She wore a sleek white bob that fell against her fair cheeks, and cat-eye glasses hung on a silver chain around her neck. "You're quite the enigma, aren't you," she whispered. "The last of a powerful, historic line of women. An ancestry packed with mischief and mystery."

I looked to Amelia for help.

She smiled warmly at Pearl, and I wondered if the latter was getting senile.

"We're just a really old, very nice family," I said with a wink.

Pearl giggled. "That you are. I've known four generations of Swan women," she said, raising three fingers. "I like you best. You're not in any hurry to take your place in the legacy. You don't garden or tend bees. Or sew or dabble in local history. You're just over here, making good food, having a grand time and dating like there's no tomorrow. Well, I say, good for you. Life is for living."

Beside her, Amelia mimed drinking.

Pearl leaned forward and gave a slow wink. "Unless you're one of the unlucky fellows. Am I right?"

I had to think back to understand her meaning. I gasped when I realized her intent. The unlucky fellows she referred to were all my dead male relatives: uncles, grandpas, and my dad. Men who'd been unlucky enough to be loved by a Swan woman.

Amelia took Pearl's arm and ushered her away. "We'll chat again soon."

"Great," I said, not sure I meant it.

The wind chimes pulled my attention to the door. Aunt Clara bustled in, eyes wide and looking slightly disheveled. "The wind!" she gasped. "If I had a sail, I'd be halfway to the Keys!"

I hugged her while she smoothed her hair. "Good thing you don't have a sail."

"No doubt!" she said, hurrying toward the group of women selecting refreshments.

I stayed to wait on the rest of my guests, until it was time for class to begin.

Through the archway, I watched as women oohed and

aahed at the renovations to the ballroom. I'd done my best to return it to its former glory, on a budget, and with my own, sometimes thin, elbow grease. All-in-all, I was proud of the results.

Fully restored and highly polished hardwood floors and trim. Painstakingly repaired and repainted ornate plaster ceiling. Fresh robin's-egg-blue paint on the walls. White wainscoting from baseboard to wall switches. Billowy white curtains on each of the multitude of windows.

Not too shabby for a tea maker who'd never done much DIY before.

Henrietta inched past me on her cane as I headed for my table. "Beautiful. Just beautiful," she repeated to no one in particular.

Other voices carried the same sentiment, and many said they'd always wanted to see the inside of my home. It was, after all, a large part of island history, and yet another local legend. Rumors of ghosts, hauntings, and everything in between had been hitched to my property. I tried not to think about any of it more than absolutely necessary, for a plethora of reasons.

"Everly?" Pearl asked, settling into a chair between Aunt Clara and Amelia. "I'm so glad to be here. Thank you."

I nodded magnanimously as the group seemed to take her cue and head for their seats. "I'm really looking forward to getting to know each of you better and seeing how your cakes come out!"

"Yes," Pearl said, regaining control of the room. "Before we get started, I wonder if you'd do us the kindness of answering a question or two."

I scanned the room, unsure of where Pearl could be going with this. "I'll do my best," I said when Amelia and Aunt Clara failed to intervene or indicate I should flee.

"What have you learned so far about the surfer who was killed last night? Do you have any reasonable leads or suspects that can help draw speculation away from that nice young man, Matt Darning? And is there anything that any of us can do to help?"

My jaw dropped. I'd been sure Pearl would press me about my family after the big to-do she'd made in the foyer. Questions about murder rocked me back on my heels.

"Well?" she asked. "We all know Matt is innocent, and the two of you are friends, so obviously, you won't let the accusations stand."

Around her, heads began to nod. Amelia and Aunt Clara scanned the room too, then turned warm eyes on me.

Pearl tented her brows, still waiting. "You aren't alone in this, you know."

"You never were," Genevieve from the local patisserie added.

My throat tightened, and my eyes stung from the unexpected outpouring of support.

"We are here for you," Aunt Clara said.

Amelia smiled. "Whatever you need. Even if it's completely ridiculous."

The group broke into smaller discussions about all the trouble I'd gotten myself into while investigating local crimes, as reported by the *Town Charmer*. I gave them a minute to gossip while I pulled myself together.

Eventually, I cleared my throat, "We should get started so we don't run out of time."

"Of course," Pearl said. "Just remember you have plenty of available hands, if you ever need assistance. More than just the pretty faces you see here."

The whole room supported me? Would help me if I needed? And there were more like them? I couldn't help wondering how many and who they were. Though, I would never intentionally drag anyone else into my investigations. Mostly because, though I'd never admit it to him, Grady was right. I frequently found myself in danger. I wouldn't risk anyone else's well-being, but the idea this support team existed hit me hard in the chest.

A round of raucous laughter erupted across the room, and Mrs. Waters covered her mouth with both hands.

Henrietta looked my way in express faux innocence. "I didn't know."

"Know what?" I asked.

Pearl shook her head. "That you can't fake a stroke with a medical professional."

Henrietta shrugged, as if this might've been something she'd tried.

Mrs. Waters burst into laughter again. "Or call 911 and request a specific medic like you're ordering a pizza!"

"She called for an ambulance last summer after we went to that play," Pearl tattled. "Just so the longbowman would have to try and resuscitate her!"

I smiled as the story began to take shape. "You didn't."

Henrietta frowned. "A woman showed up. Apparently the caller doesn't get any say in who comes."

The room erupted again, and I clapped my hands once. "Okay," I said, breaking the word into long syllables. "This is a respectable cooking class, and we aren't here to objectify the men of Charm. Let's start baking instead."

Mrs. Waters wiped her tears, trying in vain to stop her giggles. "I'm thinking of buying my husband a longbow."

The room exploded into laughter.

"Or an EMT uniform," she added.

Aunt Fran appeared in the archway, and I made a show of welcoming her to redirect the class's attention. "The mayor is here! I'm so glad you could make it! Come in! How was your day?"

She cocked a curious brow at my over-the-top greeting, but thanked me, then handed me her coat. "The whole town is taking sides on whether I should've agreed to bring Back to the Beach back to Charm. Today was a public relations nightmare, and I'm exhausted."

"Of course you should have brought it back," Pearl said. "The last regime took away all our fun. We've been stuck at Crooked Oaks making our own itineraries for years! People retire to beach towns expecting there will be things to do. We've been playing shuffleboard and bingo for a decade. Taking the same hikes and inviting the same rotation of public speakers is killing us faster than our age alone. If it wasn't for Amelia's book club, we'd never have a thing to do after dark."

Aunt Fran nodded. "I know, and I'm trying. It's just been more difficult than I'd imagined, getting everyone in the same boat. A murder related to the first big event isn't helping. Especially when the event hasn't happened yet. It feels a little foreboding." She crossed the room to take the last available seat.

"If there's anything I can do to help," I said.

"Same to you," she said, and my heart swelled with thanks once more.

Grady might've had the power of a police force behind him, but I had an amateur army.

I went to stand near the tripod I'd erected in the corner. "I'm going to livestream tonight's class for those at home who enjoy my tutorials but couldn't make it out to join us. Are you ready?"

The group nodded.

"Great!" I said brightly, adjusting the angle of my phone on the stand, then pressing the button to go live. "Tonight we're making my family's Southern Tea Cake recipe, with a little lime drizzle, in honor of the *Lost Colony* play." And the fact I'd overbought on limes when the sale had been too good to pass up. "We'll begin with our dough."

I motioned to the laminated recipe cards before them, then read the ingredients list for the camera's benefit. "This recipe makes three dozen three-inch cakes, so you might want to wait for a party, or divide that in thirds. If not, you should know the dough and the cakes freeze well, so no worries."

When I signed off from the livestream forty minutes later, I thanked the group for their willingness to be my first ever live-baking-class guinea pigs. "If you have any questions about the video we made, I'm happy to answer."

Pearl snorted. "We know all about livestreams," she said. "We've been bored to death for years. The internet is our nighttime and winter sanity. Henrietta keeps a blog about buttons. She even has a YouTube channel."

Henrietta smiled. "I call it Henri's Happy Buttons."

"I'll have to check that out," I said, a little stunned but tickled.

"Please do," she said. "And while you're there, don't forget to hit that Like button then subscribe so you won't miss my latest updates. Things are really getting good on my button-hunting road trips."

"Told you we've been bored," Pearl said.

Henrietta leaned back in her chair, shooting eye daggers at Pearl, then she poked at her with her cane.

I clapped again. Loudly. "Well, that's it for my class. I think it was a success, so I'll put another one together soon, then post a sign-up on my blog and at the front counter."

I followed the group toward the foyer, where they stopped to collect their wraps and jackets from hooks along the wall.

Aunt Fran and Aunt Clara stayed back a few paces, presumably to help me clean up and chat a while before going home.

"How was Subtle Teas?" Aunt Clara asked softly.

I nearly broke my neck getting to them in time to hear Aunt Fran's response.

"Fine, I suppose," Aunt Fran responded. "Eloise kept going on about a Peeping Tom she'd seen at her window this morning."

I bit my tongue, suspecting I was that peeper.

"I was too upset to eat a thing," Aunt Fran continued, "but the Earl Grey was lovely."

Pearl edged her way into our little circle, apparently drawn by the mention of the teahouse. "Did you get a chance to talk to Eloise?" she asked. "She's an absolute delight, isn't she?"

Aunt Fran nodded politely. "She seemed very nice."

"The ladies and I made reservations for tomorrow," Pearl said, locking one of her arms with one of Aunt Fran's, leading her toward the other waiting Corkers and our town's only taxi. "Tell us everything before we have to go."

Aunt Fran reluctantly agreed, moving away slowly and with a soft sigh.

Aunt Clara stepped close and slid an arm around my back. "I'm worried about her. Being mayor is stealing her zip."

"She'll be okay," I promised, hoping the words were true. "No one's tougher than Aunt Fran."

"You're probably right."

"I'm a little jealous everyone's getting a look inside the new teahouse," I said. "I'd like a chance to see what all the fuss is about."

"It would be interesting," Aunt Clara agreed. "I haven't been to a proper tea in decades. No one takes the time to do that anymore. We're all in such a hurry these days."

"Maybe we shouldn't be," I said, an idea flickering to life in my soggy brain. "Maybe I should call and see about making a reservation."

"Oh?" She seemed to inflate at my side. "That sounds nice. Do you think we can get a reservation?"

"Maybe," I said, hating the possibility of rejection even more. "What if we don't go as ourselves? It might be better if she doesn't know I'm there to see how my café measures up," I said. "And if I sound important when I make the request, she might find room to get us in."

"Important?" Aunt Clara asked.

"Like we're businesswomen who might go home to wher-ever we're from and brag about the teahouse. Maybe even send others her way or create some kind of buzz."

Aunt Clara grinned. "We should go in disguise."

"I like it," I agreed. "Where should we be from?"

"Surprise me, dear."

That wouldn't be a problem, since I had no idea what I might say next, even as I excused myself to look up the venue's number and dial.

"Hello," I told the after-hours recording. "My name is Millicent Harlow Abernathy," I improvised, giving the name of the heroine in my favorite historic romance novel. "I would like a reservation for two at your earliest convenience because I will only be in town another few days before returning to Boston for a very important conference for fine ladies." I rattled off my phone number for a return call, then hung up with a satisfied smile.

Maybe now I'd finally get to see what all the fuss was about.

CHAPTER
NINE

I jogged down my interior staircase the next morning, eager to start the day. The proffered camaraderie of the women in my cooking glass had buoyed me through the night and given me great clarity. Even if I never literally called on any of last night's students for help with my investigation, just knowing there was a large group of locals who believed in me felt incredible.

I pumped up the volume on my beachy playlist inside Sun, Sand, and Tea, then danced barefoot as I prepped the café for business. Today would be a great day. And I, like the whitewashed wooden sign hanging over my sliding glass doors, was accepting Good Vibes Only.

Motion on the deck caught my eyes, and I smiled at my newly landed visitor.

"Morning, Lou!" I called to the stout gray gull perched on my deck railing. "I'll be right there!"

I stowed my broom in the closet, then grabbed a plate of raw shrimp from the fridge and hustled to the sliding doors.

Warm, salty air whipped over me as I stepped onto the deck, sending delicious chills across my skin. I savored the moment, the humidity and the sensation of belonging that always accompanied the sweet island air.

Lou preened at my appearance, fluffing his feathers until he doubled in size, then cocking his head to stare at my breakfast offering. One beady eye followed the plate to the railing a few feet away.

I carefully slid the crustaceans onto the wood, then stepped back to enjoy the view and company.

A thin row of white clouds raced along the vibrantly colored horizon, which was still slightly pink from the sunrise. Early risers peppered the beach, carefully choosing the best spots for their blankets and sandcastles, or combing the surf for unblemished shells and bits of sea glass.

I rubbed gooseflesh from my arms, then paused as the prickles over my skin began anew.

Lou ogled me, ignoring the meal he normally loved.

"I don't suppose you feel that too?" I asked, slowly scanning the smattering of distant beachgoers in the surf or on blankets tucked into the shade of a few flimsy tents.

"Squawk!" Lou did a little two-step back and forth on my railing. "Squawk!"

I shivered.

Like the day before, no one seemed to be paying any attention to me, yet the instinct to flee and possibly hide was nearly overpowering. The air around me was suddenly jittery and charged, like a million spindly spider legs dancing across my skin.

Lou raised his head and stared at the widow's walk on my roof, a long, flat space where the wives of sailors could look out across the sea in search of their husband's ship.

It was also a place where some very bad and eternally unsettling things had happened to me last fall, and I wasn't ready to follow his gaze.

Instead, I listened to my instinct and fled. "Enjoy your meal, Lou. Be safe today."

I darted back inside, making the same wish for myself.

I gave one more hasty peek in each direction as I secured the sliding door, then spun away on my toes. And screamed.

Denise screamed back.

She pressed a hand to her heart and set the salt shaker she'd been refilling on my counter with a clatter. "You nearly scared the tea out of me!"

"Me?" I gasped. "You! What are you doing here?"

"I work here," she said, slowly dropping her hand to her side. "You were with Lou when I came in, so I just got busy."

I glanced at the clock, astonished by the time. "Sorry. I'm jumpy."

"Apparently." She frowned. "Any particular reason?"

I thought of the way my intuition had spiked outside, then I worked to let it go. My plans for the day had likely made their way into my subconscious, dredging up latent fears. I'd gotten myself into trouble in the past, digging into local murders, but I'd learned a lot since then. I was more careful now. Wiser. "I think yesterday's cartoon threat is wreaking a little havoc," I said.

As were my morning plans.

"Understandable." Denise went back to filling salt shakers, then loaded them onto a tray. "Anything on your agenda this morning? Or are you hanging out here with me?"

"I've got one quick delivery, and I'm all yours," I said, collecting the bag of cookies I'd put aside after class.

"Who's the delivery for?" she asked, a little too casually to be truly casual.

"Tara Larsen," I said with equal faux breeze.

Denise stilled, tray in hand as she ferried salt shakers table to table. "Tara Larsen ordered cookies this morning?"

"No. I'm just being cordial. I don't know her well enough to take a proper casserole, so I thought a few cookies would do."

"Not to split hairs," Denise said. "But you don't know her at all. So, what are you really up to? Or do I even need to ask?"

"Taking a grieving widow a little sugary comfort just seems like the right thing to do," I said. "She should know Charm cares."

"Uh-huh." Denise hooked a hand over one hip. "You think the woman who was throwing a goodbye party to leave her husband is over there in tears? Or that she's the one who killed him?"

"Only one way to find out," I said.

Denise rolled her eyes and went back to distributing salt shakers. "Just be careful. This sort of thing is exactly why you should've made time for those self-defense classes. You said you wanted them, then never had time to take any."

"I do want them," I said, already on my way to the foyer. "I'm just not sure I'm ready to be sweaty, clumsy, and weak in front of Grady." At least, no more than could be helped.

I stopped at the front door to stuff my feet into sneakers. "You didn't even ask about my class last night," I accused weakly, desperate to change the subject.

"Didn't have to," she said, leaning casually against the archway to the café behind me. "I read all about it on the *Town Charmer* this morning over breakfast. So did Grady."

I examined her expression as I tied my shoes. The words had been benign, but her tone was definitely not. "What did the *Town Charmer* say?"

"Only that your class went well, and you're recruiting locals into some sort of network you'll use as a mystery-solving militia."

A bark of unexpected laughter burst from my lips as I imagined the kind of nutty story that went with that many bananas. "I'll bet Grady loved that."

"He didn't," she said. "Now he thinks he'll have to clone himself fifty times to solve this murder while keeping you and the unnamed numbers of your militia safe."

"That's ridiculous," I said, straightening and taking a few steps in place to check my laces.

"Is it?" Denise asked, a hint of fear in her sharp blue eyes. "You're saying there wasn't any talk of adding helpers to your ranks?"

"I mean, they offered, but I said no." I forced a tight smile as I opened the door and let myself out. "I won't be long!"

I hurried down the boardwalk toward the public parking area and slowed at the sight of a small crowd. A group with serious-looking cameras on neck straps called out to someone I couldn't fully see, but suspected, from the glimpse of a red Surf Daddy hat, it was someone connected to Kai Larsen. Maybe a fellow surfer or that slick-looking manager, Mr. Osier.

I picked up my pace and quickly confirmed my theory. The entire Goodwin family braced themselves against a crush of reporters.

"What do you think of the death of Kai Larsen?" one man called.

"Are you afraid his murder will reflect poorly on your brand?" another asked.

I pushed my way through the crowd. "Excuse me. Pardon me. Break it up," I called to the throng of faces I didn't recognize.

They raised their cameras and began to snap away.

Meanwhile, the Goodwin family stood in a huddle, with James at the front, his wife and children tucked protectively behind. All were in their swim gear. The youngest of the children had clearly been crying.

My protective instincts grew claws.

I spun back to the pushy pack of photogs with a sudden need to make them disappear. "Charm has a strict rule against unregistered gatherings on public streets," I said sternly, raising my voice above the din of accusations and chatter. "We also have no-tolerance policies for loitering and harassment. If you want to set up camp here, you're going to have to file a permit request at the courthouse or be ticketed and fined."

The crowd exchanged disbelieving looks, and several members disbanded.

I pulled my phone from my pocket and pressed it to my ear. "Hello, Officer Franks, this is Everly Swan. That's right, the mayor's personal assistant. I have a collection of reporters at the beach, loitering in public parking. No, they don't have permits." I shook my head disapprovingly. "And they're harassing a very nice family. Can you please send someone out to pick them up? Better send a few cruisers."

The remaining clutch of men with cameras schlumped away.

I pushed my phone back into my pocket. "Sorry," I told the Goodwins. "Charm is usually a great place to enjoy the beach in peace."

The family visibly relaxed, and James extended a hand. "Thanks," he said. "They came out of nowhere."

I accepted the handshake and smiled as his wife moved to his side.

"I'm Cindy Goodwin," she said warmly. "This is my husband James and our children, Tate and Josephine."

"Nice to meet you," I said. "I'm Everly Swan. I own Sun, Sand, and Tea. I recognized you from your store's advertisements."

Cindy blushed. "Surf Daddy. That's us."

I nodded. "The brand has really grown. I think it's amazing, and it's been great for bringing attention to the area. I'm a huge supporter of that. Good job."

James beamed. "Thanks. It's all because of these guys." He motioned to his family. "I couldn't do it without them."

"Are the police really coming?" Cindy asked.

"No." I laughed. "There's a law on the books forbidding unregistered gatherings, but I didn't actually call anyone."

She belted out a delighted laugh. "You bluffed! I completely believed you."

"Mommy," Tate tugged Cindy's hand. "I want ice cream." His pale-blond hair swelled in windblown tufts and curls around his deeply tanned face. He seemed to be younger than Denver, but not by much. A preschooler or kindergartner maybe.

Cindy swung him onto her hip, then tousled his fluffy hair. "Maybe we should ask Miss Everly for recommendations."

"Sandy's Sweet Shack is fantastic," I said. "They have every topping you can think of plus six more, and the owner is really funny."

"The Sweet Shack it is," she said. "We're making our way up the coast, checking out the beaches and towns along the way."

"That sounds nice," I said.

"It has been. Reporters aside." She rolled her eyes. "We're staying in Corolla for a few nights. I think the kids need some time away from the hoopla in our town. I probably do too."

"I can certainly understand," I said. "I won't keep you. Stop by my tea shop anytime. I've got twenty flavors on tap and a view like none other." I turned my eyes to James as Cindy began to usher the children away. "I want to thank you for sponsoring Back to the Beach this year," I said. "What happened to Kai Larsen was tragic, but my great-aunt is the mayor here, and she worked hard to bring the event back to the islands. I'm sure that having a local sponsor like you was a cinching factor."

"Don't mention it," James said, looking a little troubled at the change of subject. "I'm glad to be a part of such an incredible event."

"Daddy," Tate called. "Ice cream."

James lifted a palm in my direction, and I stepped away, releasing him from my company. He smiled as he reunited with this family, but I couldn't help wondering about the flash of regret in his tone.

❧

I made it to Tara Larsen's rental home twenty minutes later, a hefty sheen of sweat coating my skin. I pressed the doorbell, already imagining the polite way to ask for a gallon of iced water. Half to drink and half to pour over my head.

The door swept open, and a woman in a bikini and sarong stared out. "Can I help you?"

"Mrs. Larsen?" I asked. "I'm Everly Swan from Sun, Sand, and Tea, the iced tea shop and café down the beach."

"Oh," the woman said, sipping from the salted rim of her frozen margarita. "No. I'm Darcy, Tara's sister. We get mixed up all the time. Tara's out on the beach. She didn't tell me she placed an order for lunch already."

I looked at the bag in my hand.

"What does she owe you?" Darcy asked.

"Nothing," I said. "It's all taken care of."

"I can take it," she said. "Unless she needs to sign the receipt or something."

I nodded. "Point me in her direction?"

Darcy stepped aside, one arm extended toward the open sliding doors across the space. "Beach."

"Got it. Thank you!"

I hurried onto the rear deck, scanning the sand for signs of Tara Larsen as I moved.

A large teal and yellow umbrella was arranged a few yards from the home's private pool, and I headed that way.

"Mrs. Larsen?" I moved in a wide arc, careful to approach in clear view, so as not to startle her.

A pair of lean, tan legs came into view first, stretched out on a white lounge chair beside a small table and tote bag. The closer I got, the more unreasonably perfect she appeared. I'd seen her in multiple videos online, but in person, she was even more gorgeous. Her long, wavy locks had been gathered in a loose bun on top of her head, and the yellow polka dot bikini she wore coordinated perfectly with her bright red lipstick and nail polish.

It was hard to believe I'd thought she was Darcy, the merely beautiful woman suddenly paling in comparison.

Her eyes opened as I arrived in the shade of her enormous umbrella. "I'm not giving autographs," she said. "I'm mourning."

I gave her beachy setup a judgmental look, then scolded myself for thinking it.

"I'm not here for an autograph," I assured. "I live in town and run a café on the beach. I heard about what happened to your husband, and in the South, we comfort folks with food. So, I brought you some sweets."

The blond bombshell turned curious brown eyes on the bag. "What kind of sweets?"

I hesitated, wishing I'd brought a selection and hoping she liked tea cakes. "A special family recipe."

Her narrow brows furrowed. "How much sugar is in them?"

"A lot," I answered honestly, certain it was the wrong answer.

Her lips curled into a tiny smile, and she scooted up in her seat. "Maybe just a bite."

I passed the pastry bag into her hands, and she opened it immediately.

I plucked the fabric of my shirt away from my chest, attempting to cool my overheated skin and contemplating a run into the ocean.

Tara's eyelids fluttered as she sank her teeth into a lime-drizzled tea cake. "Mmm. These are amazing."

"Thanks," I said, evaluating her with curious distrust.

For starters, as grieving women went, Tara didn't seem very sad.

"I'm really sorry for your loss," I said, carefully broaching the subject. "It must be hard to be here now, away from your family and friends when you need them most."

"It's awful," she said, finishing off the first cookie, then opening the bag once more. "But not surprising. Kai had a way of ruining everything in my life, so I shouldn't be surprised he'd mess things up with his death too." She sucked icing from the tip of her thumb and shook her head. "He was so manipulative and self-serving. Now he's gone, and it's over. On his terms. Like everything else. At least I have my sister with me to get through this."

I bit my tongue against the idea that murder happened on a victim's terms, and I tried to remember everyone grieved differently.

"It's my fault," she said, dusting crumbs from her lips.

"Your fault? How?"

"For trusting him," she said. "I was the other woman once. I should've known it would only be a matter of time before he cheated on me too."

I wiped a red-hot forearm across my sweaty head. "Kai was cheating?"

If that was true, a whole other line of possible suspects

just opened up. The person Kai was seeing might've been tired of waiting for him to leave his wife. Or maybe the other woman's spouse or boyfriend didn't like Kai interfering with them. "Are you sure?" I asked. "Do you have evidence? Or was it just a suspicion?"

"I'm right," she said, nodding as she chewed. "What goes around comes around. Right?"

"Sometimes." I blinked dry, gritty eyelids at the apparition of heat hovering over the sand. My head went light with dehydration, and I deeply regretted not bringing a water bottle along.

"Are you okay?" Tara asked. "Here. Take this."

I accepted the offered glass without hesitation, thrilled at the clink of ice cubes as I raised it to my lips and gulped, deeply and repeatedly. My eyes opened, and I choked against the burn of liquor in my throat and esophagus. I coughed painfully, gasping for air. "What is this?" I croaked.

"Vodka on the rocks," she said, bored. "Light on the rocks."

"You're drinking straight vodka?" I gasped.

"I'm mourning. Are you okay?"

"Water," I croaked, regaining myself from the long, ignorant gulps of hard liquor.

She handed me a bottle of water from the small cooler beside her chair.

I sniffed it before sipping, just in case.

"I should've listened to Matt," she said, watching as I chugged the entirety of her second offering. "He was such a good guy. I really screwed that up."

"Matt Darning?" I asked, slowly finding my mental

footing. When she nodded, I dug deeper. "How do you know Matt?"

Tara looked heartbroken for the first time. She swept her gaze across the horizon, then said, "He was my first husband."

I dropped the empty bottle, ready to sample the vodka again.

CHAPTER

TEN

I rushed back down the sidewalk, head spinning. I'd nearly drained Tara's drink in those big gulps, and the bottle of water I'd chased it with hadn't kicked in. The sun was out in full force, but I was glad to be walking.

Tara Larsen had been Matt's wife. The words circled nonsensically in my brain. Matt had been married before. And he'd never mentioned it. Or the fact she'd left him. For another man. His enemy. The weight of it was nearly too much. I wanted to sit down and sort it out, but I was still blocks from home.

Worse than my frazzled thoughts and slightly numbed face from the vodka was the fact the case against Matt was practically building itself. And if I didn't share my newfound information, I would find myself on the other side of this investigation. The shady side. And that wasn't who I was. I had to tell Grady, but first I needed to hear from Matt. Two sides to every story and all that.

I hated that these things usually came around to the simplest explanation. Because this time, the most obvious suspect was a man who'd saved my life with his expert medical intervention multiple times. Unfortunately, he was also a man who'd quit a sport he loved after his known nemesis had stolen his wife and his professional spotlight. Add the arrow from Matt's longbow in the victim's back, and it was no wonder Grady thought I was on a wild goose chase.

I probably owed him an apology. But despite the fact whatever was going on here walked like a duck and quacked like a duck, Matt absolutely wasn't that duck.

I sent him a quick text while I was thinking about it, requesting he swing by Sun, Sand, and Tea as soon as possible. Hopefully he wouldn't be in a hurry when he arrived, because the number of questions I had for him might keep us busy through dinner.

The phone buzzed before I could slide it back into my pocket, but it wasn't Matt or a text. Instead, Ryan's face appeared on the screen.

Guilt sprang to the forefront of my messy mind, and I moved into the shade of a nearby tree to answer. The world swayed a little when I stopped. "I am so sorry!" I said, skipping a traditional greeting. "I never meant to put you off so long. Is everything okay?"

"It's better now," he admitted, "since you finally decided to answer my call. I was getting concerned. My next attempt would've been a singing telegram. Or a carrier pigeon."

"Lou wouldn't have tolerated the pigeon," I said, smiling as I leaned against the tree. "What's the big emergency? You never call, and your texts are usually just silly memes you make about my café."

"The memes are getting good, though, right?" he asked. "I've been working on them."

I thought of the awful cartoon I'd recently received and shivered. "There's been a murder," I whispered, in case anyone was listening. "It's hit close to home and thrown me for a major loop."

"I've heard." Ryan's tone turned uncharacteristically glum. "It's too bad about you and Grady. Half the island waited on pins and needles for the two of you to get together, but you dragged the whole thing out for years, only to break up after a few months."

My spine stiffened and my feathers ruffled. "We didn't break up. Where did you hear that?" I silently cursed the *Town Charmer*, Ryan's most likely source of local gossip.

"Haven't heard it yet," Ryan said. "Though I suspect it won't be long. You know what happens when you start digging into his investigations."

I bit my tongue, not wanting to fight and knowing Ryan had been around for more than one of the situations he described.

"You're fighting," he supplied when I didn't respond. "Aren't you?"

"No."

"But you are meddling," he said.

"Maybe."

Ryan laughed. "Then trust me. You're fighting."

I blew a ragged breath into the phone. "What do you want, Ryan? It must be important for you to try three times in two days. Let's talk about that instead."

"Right," he said. "I need your help. Amelia's turning

thirty next month, and I want to throw her a big party to show I care. I want it to be a surprise, and I can't plan it from New York. I need you as my liaison. And I really want to wow her. Something terrific and completely over-the-top. Theatrical," he said. "Something she'd never expect from you or her dad."

"Offense," I said. "I throw big parties all the time."

"You throw big island parties, with seafood buffets and seaside views. They're quite lovely. A+ jobs, really. But that's not what I want to do this time. This party is a gift from me, and I want to dazzle her. Show her I pay attention."

I frowned. "Okay. What are you thinking? Examples, please."

"Cirque du Soleil in an enchanted library," he said. "And I'm thinking it can be a surprise after-party to follow one of your buffet numbers."

"Offense," I repeated.

Ryan chuckled. "Can I send you the details? I promise to cover all the costs, and I'll pay you as the liaison, of course. That is, if you think you're up to it."

I rolled my eyes at his juvenile attempt to challenge me into doing his bidding. If he knew me at all, he'd know I'd never say no to anything that would make Amelia smile. "Fine. Send the details."

"If not, I'm sure Mary Grace Chatsworth—"

"Do not," I interrupted, and Ryan laughed again. "I'm having a complicated enough day without being provoked."

"Investigating something that's none of your business is like that," he said.

"I'm hanging up now."

"Let me know when you read my email!" he called as I disconnected.

I pushed away from the tree, pausing briefly to catch my balance before heading to the crosswalk.

The series of endless questions I'd had for Matt were suddenly shuffled with images of floating books and acrobats. Cirque du Soleil in an enchanted library sounded exactly like Amelia's dream come true, playing both on her lifelong love of theater and books. But could Ryan pull it off? Could I?

I was at the center of the road when I noticed the massive light-colored SUV barreling down on me, its knobby tires eating up the pavement faster than my addled mind could process. Sun gleamed from the shiny silver grill, blinding me and shifting my fight or flight response belatedly into gear.

A horror-film-worthy scream tore from my throat as I leaped for the curb, throwing myself into the air. The collision that followed, though thankfully not with the SUV, was brutal. My knees crashed against the curb, and my palms skidded across the sidewalk, embedding sand and pebbles into my skin as it tore.

Behind me, the vehicle careened around a corner and out of sight. I hadn't seen the driver and didn't get a look at the license plate.

I dragged upright with a whimper, and though I could clearly hear the faint peal of laughter and bass of a radio over the low drone of waves on the beach, there wasn't another soul in sight. I considered calling the police, but decided there wasn't anything that could be done. The SUV was long gone, and I had nothing to tell them that would aid in their identification of the vehicle or driver. I sent Grady a text with the little details I had, then moved away from the scene of the crime, eager to get home in case the nut returned.

I forced my shaking limbs to cooperate, biting my lip against the sting of fresh scrapes and bruises. Then I headed for the boardwalk, where no vehicles could attempt to mow me down. I rinsed most of the blood and gravel away with the outdoor shower in the public access beach parking lot. And by the time I made it home, the more shallow scrapes had stopped bleeding.

My heightened emotions had twisted themselves into a sharp point, but my mind and body had gone strangely numb.

I wondered if Tara had accessed a vehicle, then come at me in the time it had taken me to reach the corner and talk with Ryan. Maybe. Did she own, or had she rented, a large SUV? I wasn't sure, but that wouldn't be too hard to find out.

Kai's manager was another possibility. He surely knew where the Larsens were staying. And if he'd already issued me a cartoon threat, seeing me questioning Kai's wife couldn't have made him happy.

The same was true for anyone who'd been following me. Kai's girlfriend, his competition on the circuit, or another enemy I'd yet to uncover. If they all drove, or had access to, a large SUV, my only clue was out the window.

I climbed the front steps to my home slowly, going easy on my thoroughly banged up knees.

My ex-boyfriend, Wyatt, met me on the porch. "What on earth happened to you?" he asked, holding the door open for me to pass. "I was on my way out, but I've got to hear the story behind this. I'm hoping you tripped and fell so I don't have to go hunt down whoever did this to you and give them some trouble."

"I fell," I muttered, pausing in the foyer so he could loop one arm around my back.

He sniffed the air indelicately. "Have you been drinking?"

I groaned, then retold my story while he helped me into the café.

"Good thing you called Matt, then," Wyatt said. "He just got here. What did Grady say?"

"I haven't spoken with Grady yet." And I'd texted Matt before my near-death experience, though Wyatt was right. It was a good thing I had.

Matt was on his feet as we crossed the threshold, already headed in our direction.

I waved at a handful of startled patrons. "I'm fine. Just took a little spill."

"What happened?" Matt asked.

"We should go onto the deck," I said, certain no one wanted to see me triaged over lunch.

Matt opened the sliding door, while Wyatt helped me onto a chair.

"I want more details on this story when you come back inside," Wyatt said, before turning to leave us alone.

I offered Matt a weak smile. "Thanks for meeting me here."

"Start from the beginning," he said. "And please tell me you wiped out on a skateboard, because I can't think of anything else that could cause this much overall damage. Unless you were alligator wrestling." He paused. "Were you alligator wrestling?"

His rueful grin and the comfortable gleam in his eye brought on all the tears I'd been working so hard to hold back.

"Oh, hey," he said, recognizing my emotional shift immediately. "Don't cry." He crouched before me on the deck and wrapped me in a hug. "It's okay. Whatever happened, you're going to be fine. I have my medical kit in the truck, and all these cuts look superficial. What really happened? Did you fall on your walk?"

"No," I croaked and sniffled against his shirt. "Someone tried to run me over after I left Tara Larsen's rental home."

Matt pulled back slowly. "What?"

I wiped my steadily leaking eyes. "Why didn't you tell me you've been married before? Or that Kai stole your wife? Or that she was in Charm?"

Matt hoisted himself into the chair across from me, visibly daunted. "I didn't know it mattered."

"The man you're accused of killing married your wife," I said, my emotions zigzagging recklessly. "You had to know that was important."

"Ex-wife," he corrected.

"Squawk!" Lou swooped through the air in our direction, wings spread wide. He landed on the deck railing beside us. "Squawk!"

I lifted one hand in a little wave.

"Squawk!"

Matt offered the bird an encouraging smile. "I'm not going to hurt her. She's injured, and I'm going to help." He pressed onto his feet, then motioned from Lou to me. "Will you keep an eye on her until I get my medical bag?"

Lou puffed his chest and ruffled his feathers.

Matt pointed a finger at me, indicating I should stay put. He was gone and back in a minute with his bag.

"Why didn't you ever tell me you've been married?" I asked again.

Matt crouched before me once more. He opened his medical kit and selected a pair of gloves, sterile gauze, and a small bottle of something I assumed would sting as he cleaned my cuts. His face flushed and he averted his eyes, concentrating instead on the work at hand. "I didn't tell you because I've never told anyone," he said. "Not since I moved here for a new start. Somehow, the paparazzi didn't latch onto that story, probably because they spent so much time following Jamal's recovery and waiting for his story about what happened. Regardless, no one in Charm seemed to know anything about my previous life, and I liked it that way."

"You could've told me," I said. "You can always tell me anything."

His eyes met mine, looking suddenly vulnerable and many years younger. "Tara knew what I thought of Kai. I told her everything. She knew exactly the kind of person he was, and she still chose him."

I set my hand on his arm as he finished cleaning and bandaging my shins and knees. "I'm sorry this is happening to you," I said, "but none of it is your fault."

Matt worked diligently until the scrapes on my hands had been treated, then pulled in a long breath and returned to the other seat at the table. "Why did you visit Tara today?"

"I took her condolence cookies."

"And?" he asked.

"I wanted to see how she behaved when I brought up her husband."

Matt sighed. "Have you told Grady?"

"That the man you're accused of killing also stole your wife?" I asked. "No. I wanted to talk to you first."

"I meant that someone tried to kill you," Matt said slowly.

"I sent him a text."

He folded forward on his seat, resting an elbow against each knee. "He's not going to like that, and he'll think it's my fault. You keep sticking your neck out for me. Everly," he waited for me to turn my gaze to him. "I'm not asking you to do that."

"I know, but this new information just makes you look guiltier."

"Doesn't matter," he said. "I'm innocent, and I know Grady will figure that out, if he doesn't know already."

I leaned forward, matching his posture. "Tara thought Kai was cheating on her. That also makes her a suspect, so at least you aren't the only one anymore."

"Tara isn't a murderer. She's high maintenance and demanding, but she's not cruel."

"She was going to leave him," I said. "And she was throwing a party to do it. She even ordered fancy invitations."

He frowned in distaste, but didn't rush to defend her again.

"She was mad enough to want to humiliate him in a big way. She'd set a plan, and I'm sure the anticipation was brewing. It's possible they argued and she lashed out."

Matt rubbed his palms against his thighs. "Man. What happened to the quiet, normal life I built here?"

"That's what I'm trying to find out."

CHAPTER
ELEVEN

An emergency put an end to my chat with Matt, but I'd learned over the past year that he was always on call, regardless of what the official schedule said.

He hugged me tight and kissed my cheek before reluctantly jogging away.

I couldn't help wondering if the call was initiated by one of the women at Crooked Oaks again. If so, at least the caller would finally get the EMT she wanted. And as a significant bonus, this possibility would mean no one in Charm was having a true medical emergency at the moment. I liked that thought a lot.

I said my goodbyes to Lou before stepping into the cool air-conditioned café and tugging the door closed behind me. He'd kept a close watch on Matt as we talked, listening intently, as if he understood every word. Sometimes I wondered if he might.

My throbbing knees and stinging palms reminded me I had more pressing mysteries to solve, and I willed myself to focus. I squared my shoulders and raised my chin in response to the sensation of curious eyes on my back. Then I pasted on a sweet smile before turning to face the handful of patrons and onlookers.

Grady's sharp gray gaze was the first to catch my attention. He hadn't been there when I went outside with Matt, but he was seated next to Wyatt now, and he wasn't smiling.

If there was a silver lining to the moment, it was that most of customers who had been present upon my earlier arrival were now gone. Fewer witnesses to whatever came next.

I wiggled my fingers in a hip-high wave as I reached Grady, then tried to hide the wince as my palm burned in response to the movement. "When did you get here?"

"Just in time to watch you hug Matt, let him wipe your tears, and tend to your wounds. You want to tell me about that?" Grady asked, expression blank and voice flat.

My hackles rose. "Matt's a medic who was giving me medical care. And he's a friend, so he was comforting me." I crossed my arms, prepared to let him know what I thought of jealous men.

Grady stared, wholly unaffected. "I was talking about your injuries. You sent me a text, letting me know someone tried to kill you. Or did you forget?"

I wasn't sure if he thought I'd forgotten sending the text or nearly being killed, but I didn't ask. I gave the room another careful look, then slid onto the stool beside him. "I asked Matt to meet me here before that happened."

"What happened?" Grady asked. "Try adding details."

"I fell." I wet my lips, feeling emotions press against my eyes as I prepared to elaborate. I needed to tell him everything, but I didn't want to do it while crying.

"After you were nearly hit by a car," he said. "Why didn't you stay there until I could get to you? Or call emergency services?"

"The SUV rounded a corner and was gone," I said. "What was I supposed to wait for? I can't tell you who was driving or what the vehicle even looked like. It was a big SUV. That's all I remember. And I didn't need emergency service. Matt bandaged me up in less than five minutes. I probably could've done it myself," I said, raising my bandaged palms in evidence.

Denise returned from one of the tables and began to assemble chicken salad sandwiches with fruit. "I can't believe this happened," she whispered. "This is awful. You could've been killed."

I batted back a deluge of hot tears, willing myself to keep it together.

"Why were you at Tara Larsen's rental home?" Grady asked.

"I brought her cookies," I said, voice slightly wobbly.

"Why?"

"I wanted to see how she was doing after her loss," I said. "I was being hospitable."

"You were being nosy," Grady returned. "And you broke your promise. You said you'd stay out of this."

My heart sagged, knowing he was right, but he obviously didn't understand my lack of self-control in these matters. "I promised I'd try."

"And did you?" He tented his brows in challenge.

"Yes?"

His stomach growled, and my gaze dropped to his middle.

"When was the last time you ate?" I asked.

Denise shifted her attention to him. "He skipped breakfast."

I heaved a sigh, then slid off my stool. "Well, you can't yell at me properly on an empty stomach." I limped around to the business side of my counter, sidestepping Denise as she ferried her finished tray to a table of guests near the windows.

"What'll it be?" I asked the men before me. "Food? Sweets? Both?"

An oversized blackboard hung on the wall behind me, with the day's menu scripted neatly in brightly colored chalks, but those limitations didn't apply to Wyatt or Grady. They were welcome to whatever they wanted, as long as I had the necessary ingredients. The same was true for any of my family and friends.

Wyatt glanced at Grady, then tipped his cowboy hat back on his head and looked at me. "I'll take one of your famous grilled cheese sandwiches, if you're offering."

I smiled. My "famous" grilled cheese sandwich was made the same way as every other grilled cheese sandwich in history. Wyatt was just a sucker for the simple things. I knew him well, maybe even better than he knew himself. I'd spent years as his girlfriend, traveling around the country on his rodeo circuit. I'd juggled our relationship with culinary school and the slow breaking of my heart as I realized the thing he loved most wasn't me. In hindsight, I could see things turned out exactly as they should have. I'd gotten to know him better since he'd given up the rodeo and returned to Charm—more than I ever had while we were dating. And I much preferred our new relationship to the old.

From the look on Grady's face, I needed as many members of Team Everly as possible. "Grilled cheese sounds nice," he said.

I set two sandwiches on my griddle, Wyatt's with American Cheese and Grady's with gouda and a slice of ham. I served Grady a preemptive dessert. One hefty piece of lemon cake. Notes in my ancestor's recipe book indicated the cake had been created to bolster a hero's heart, and I hoped it would also soothe his soul. He and I both needed a little calm amidst the current storm.

I presented Wyatt with a bowl of munch mix, then made a tray of sliced fruits, cheese cubes, and hunks of bread to share with Denise. When she returned, we discussed the events of my day as a group, and I filled them in on all the details I could remember. I added my current theories for good measure, then listened as Denise and Wyatt tossed the ideas around.

"I can't believe he was married before," Denise said, tucking a tiny pillow of bread between her lips. "He doesn't seem the type."

"What type?" Grady asked, a small frown returning to his face. "I was married before."

"Yeah. You seem the type," she said.

Grady looked to me, then Wyatt for explanation, but we deferred to Denise.

"You're more serious," she said. "And kind of intense. It's just easier to imagine you in that kind of real, grown-up role. Matt's so carefree and easy. He *seems* single. Not at all weighted down."

"Marriage doesn't weigh people down," Grady said, his frown deepening. "Not if you're doing it right."

The air grew heavier, and we each forced a small smile.

Grady's marriage had been nothing like Matt's. Grady's relationship had been strong and good. And it was evident, at times like these, how deeply he missed that life.

Wyatt wiped his lips, then set the napkin on his empty plate. "I think this whole secret marriage thing is a great illustration of how much we don't know about one another. We all have some skeletons in our pasts and private dreams for our futures. Plus other parts of us we want to keep for ourselves."

I instantly wondered what all those things were for him, Grady, and Denise. I wondered what my secrets were as well. Did I hide parts of who I was? How would I feel if those things were revealed?

"Well, maybe it's the cop in me," Grady said, "but this revelation makes me wonder what else Matt hasn't told me, and what I'm likely to uncover next."

I pushed a chunk of cheese into my mouth and fought the urge to argue Matt's innocence. Everyone in my little group knew where I stood.

All that mattered now was that whoever had set out to frame Matt for murder was succeeding, and I was failing. Hard.

CHAPTER
TWELVE

I wrapped a soft blanket around my shoulders, then carried my mug of steaming chamomile tea to the deck outside my private quarters. Lou had waited patiently while I changed into comfy pajamas and fuzzy socks.

"It's been a day," I said, folding onto the chair across from him. I curled my bandaged palms around the mug, sipping its contents and stealing its heat. "I think Grady's mad at me," I confessed. "And the whole case against Matt keeps getting stronger. I don't know what to do."

Maggie sauntered through the open door before Lou could respond. She paused to arch and preen before curling at my feet.

"Hello," I said, reaching to stroke her downy white fur. The responding purrs began immediately. "I'm glad you're here. Three heads are better than two. Right, Lou?"

"Squawk!"

I smiled warmly at the bird who always seemed so genuinely concerned. "What would I do without the two of you?"

My phone buzzed, and I shifted on my seat, taking the

mug in one sore hand so I could fish the vibrating device from my pocket with the other. I'd fielded concerned calls from my friends and Aunt Clara all evening, each wondering if I needed to talk now that the café was closed for the night or if there was anything they could do to help. I'd assured everyone I was fine, and for the most part, they'd seemed to believe me.

I was actively trying to convince myself.

The new text from Amelia made me smile. A simple snapshot of her nightstand with its pile of books and a little note saying Sweet Dreams. I returned her well wishes with a sleepy face emoji, then checked the time.

It was my bedtime too, but my mind was far too restless to sleep. Hence the blanket, animal entourage, and chamomile. All things that calmed me, like the salty night air.

"If I had a little more energy, I'd go bake or clean something," I told my feathered and feline audience. "But I'm beat and a little sore." It was too bad, really, because I thought most clearly when my hands were busy. "Maybe I'll spend tomorrow on the third floor," I said, referring to the thoroughly cluttered, but otherwise unused level above my living quarters. The open space had likely been a music room or entertaining area at one time, but it was currently full of junk. The previous owners had left things over the years that I'd never bothered to sort or explore. A number of my mom's and grandmother's things from the homestead were housed there too. Until I found the right place to display them.

My phone buzzed on the small table at my side. I groaned. "Can't anyone sleep tonight?"

Maggie blinked luminous green eyes at me.

Lou stretched his wings.

I lifted the phone for a better look at the caller ID.

"Hello?" I answered quickly, startled by the sight of Aunt Fran's image on the screen. "Is everything okay?"

"Everything is fine," she said smartly. "Why would anything be wrong?"

"It's after ten," I said. "Don't you have to get up early tomorrow? Run the town and all that."

"Yes, and I'm exhausted. I just wrapped up a completely drawn-out call with a council member who thinks he knows best, and I wanted to talk to you before I fall asleep at my desk."

I listened patiently to the shuffling of papers, then the creak of her wooden desk chair as she got comfortable or maybe got up to go to bed. I braced myself for whatever was to come. Those same sounds had often been the precursor to lectures when I was a teenager, caught sneaking in late or hooking up in the driveway. Nothing ever got past Aunt Fran, Aunt Clara, or Grandma.

Whoever said old people went to bed early obviously never met a Swan.

"First, tell me how you are," she said. "I haven't had a chance to speak with you since Clara told me what happened. I'd like details and to know why you didn't call me yourself."

"I didn't want to worry you," I said guiltily and knowing it was a lame response. My aunts worried about everyone in Charm, especially me, and if I hadn't been afraid of bursting into tears like a child, I would've called.

Avoidance and denial were my super powers.

"Not calling didn't stop me from worrying," she said gently. "How bad were you banged up?"

"Some minor scrapes and bruises," I said. "Matt was here when I got home, so he bandaged me up. I wasn't actually hit by the car," I clarified. "More like I saw a speeding car, and I threw myself headfirst onto the sidewalk in response." I grimaced at the painfully accurate description, suddenly thankful there hadn't been any witnesses.

"Well, whatever the case, you terrified me. And Clara. And half the town for that matter," Aunt Fran said. "I've always encouraged your enthusiasm and embraced your go-getter attitude, but days like today, I have to wonder if I've done you a disservice. You aren't invincible, Everly. Not like Dharma."

I puzzled over her last few muttered words. "Who?"

"Hmm," she said, ignoring my question. "I have an idea. How's your carriage house looking?"

I pulled the phone from my ear to frown at it. Why was she changing the subject again? And who was Dharma? I set the phone back on my shoulder, half wondering if Aunt Fran had fallen asleep at her desk after all and was sleep talking.

"The carriage house could use a cleaning," I said. "Why?"

In truth, that space was more cluttered than the third floor of my house. I'd been meaning to clean it since I moved in two years ago, but had only managed to make enough room for Blue, Bicycle, and Wagon.

"I have something I'd like you to store there," she said. "Any chance you can make a little room?"

"Sure, I guess," I said, not feeling very sure at all. "What is it, and how soon do you want to bring it over?"

Aunt Fran groaned loudly. "I'm getting another call from that stubborn Stewart Crane on the council. He's going to be the death of me," she said. "Or me of him, if he doesn't look at his clock and realize whatever he wants can wait until morning." She sighed. "I have to take this. I'll be there first thing tomorrow, and I'll see if I can get you some help with the clutter." She disconnected before I could press her for any additional information.

I set the phone beside my now tepid tea with a sigh.

"I'd better get some sleep," I told Lou and Maggie. "Sounds like I have a bunch of work to do before I open the café tomorrow."

❧

I woke to the alarm I'd set only three hours before. As it turned out, going to bed and telling myself I had to get up early hadn't done anything to help me fall asleep. Instead, I'd researched online, obsessing over details of the surfing industry and looking into the top three competitors. Kai Larsen, Locke Suarez, and Ava Hyde. All were managed by Ted Osier.

The Rodanthe newspaper showcased a number of local promotional events leading up to Kai's death, and I scrutinized the photos. Each surfer appeared happy, confident, and completely at ease. If there was hostility brewing among the teammates, it wasn't evident in the photos. Or in any online articles. Everything I read felt like another dead end.

Tara was the only possible lead I still had to explore, so I planned to visit her again as soon as possible. This time, I'd walk the beach to her place from mine and avoid the roads for my safety.

If I was lucky, I'd also run into Kai's manager soon. Apparently he'd been Matt's manager too. I had no idea why Osier might want to kill off a source of income, but I was still hung up on the fact he'd been the one to find Kai's body. More than that, he would have known about the rift between Matt and Kai, making Matt the obvious scapegoat from where he stood. And he would've known Kai's number, so he could have easily sent the phony text from Matt's phone.

I bounded down my staircase in yoga pants and a T-shirt, thoughts swirling. I'd wrangled my wild hair into a messy bun and skipped my morning shower. If Aunt Fran wanted me to make space for something in the carriage house, I'd be filthy in no time.

I could only imagine what she wanted to store. With Aunt Fran, it could be anything. A weaver's loom? Steamer trunks? A dozen artificial pine trees for the town square at Christmas?

My phone bellowed with an update from the *Town Charmer*. I'd applied a distinctive foghorn sound to the notifications so I wouldn't miss any news. I just hoped the newest headline didn't feature my love life.

I paused on the porch to check the post. An image of the crime scene outside the amphitheater gave me hope for something good. Maybe even something I could use to help Matt. The headline set me back a step, and I leaned a hip against the railing to ponder.

SURF HERO STABBED IN THE BACK

What did that mean? Had the *Town Charmer* discovered Tara's previous marriage to Matt on the same night I had? Were my internet searches being recorded?

"Preliminary reports suggest national surf champion and recent murder victim, Kai Larsen, wasn't shot with an arrow as originally suspected," I read softly to myself, unable to make sense of them. I'd seen the arrow in his back. I'd been there while the coroner made his initial report, but the *Charmer* was rarely wrong.

I read faster, eager and hungry for whatever the blogger was trying to say.

"While the longbow, wielded masterfully by Charm's beloved EMT and most-eligible bachelor, Matt Darning, was initially believed to be the murder weapon, that theory has now been refuted. According to our source at the coroner's office, Dr. Dray has confirmed the width and depth of the fatal puncture wound doesn't match the arrow found in Larsen's back, thus eliminating it as the murder weapon. The true murder weapon has not yet been revealed." I gasped, skimming to the bottom line as I marveled at the news. "Lab reports suggest the arrow was placed into the wound, post-mortem, as a means of misdirect."

I dropped my hands to my sides and breathed in deep lungfuls of blessed island air. This was exactly the kind of news I wanted to start my day with. This was a wellspring of hope.

Now it didn't matter that Matt was an expert marksman with the longbow. Anyone could've killed Kai, then used the arrow to temporarily cover the truth.

But the jig was up.

My smile widened as I slowly danced down the porch steps, ignoring the protests of my bruised knees. "Wait a minute," I muttered, raising the phone once more.

I dialed Grady for confirmation of the news, then listened intently as the call began to ring. Irritation tightened my gut as I waited. Grady knew I was looking into this, trying everything I could think of to point authorities away from Matt. So, if the article's revelation was accurate, why hadn't Grady told me?

"Hays," he answered sharply, frustration and fatigue deepening his voice.

"I just saw the blog," I said, rushing to the point and assuming by the distance in his tone he was distracted or already busy. "Is it true?"

Grady groaned. "I don't know how they got ahold of this information, but it's leaked, and I'm trying to get the post taken down. Details to an ongoing murder investigation can't just be thrown around like this. It's careless and unprofessional. I'm sure whoever did this knows better, and they've caused me all kinds of unnecessary trouble. I'd prefer the killer not know we have this intel yet."

"Sorry," I whispered, no longer upset he hadn't told me the news himself. Grady had bigger problems than a protest from me. No one knew who owned or operated the blog, so it wasn't as if he could stop by their home or give them a call. And by the time he went through the legal hoops to remove the post, everyone in town would have already seen the information he wanted buried. "I wish I could help."

"Don't help," he said. "I'll figure it out."

"Okay," I said brightly, not bothering to fight the smile that bloomed. "At least this proves Matt isn't the killer." Now, I could go back to my life in progress, and Grady could stop being so grouchy. The invisible, but tangible strain on our relationship could go kick stones. "This is great news."

"It's not great news," Grady complained. "And it doesn't prove anything, other than Kai Larsen's murder weapon wasn't an arrow. Matt could surely still wield whatever object the killer used first."

I opened my mouth to protest, or scream, but Grady interrupted with a laborious sigh.

"I love your enthusiasm," he said. "Everyone does, but you have to slow down. Think critically. If you're going to keep doing this, you're going to have to start doing it better."

My cheeks heated with the sting of his words, then the implication slowly registered. "You're not yelling at me."

"I never yell," he said, his voice going softer.

"Maybe not as defined by decibel," I said, "but you yell. Just quietly. Like now."

I heard him sigh.

"So, you're not demanding I make some tea and butt out?" I smiled. "You're not going to lecture me? Or go stomping around Charm like a big, handsome Godzilla?"

"I do not stomp around," he said.

"Then what are you doing?"

"I'm trying something new."

I waited, but he didn't expound. And my heart began to soar. For the first time since we'd met, Grady wasn't telling me to mind my own business. He was giving me a tip. *Slow down. Think critically.* "The change in murder weapon doesn't prove Matt's innocence, but it does support my theory Matt is being framed."

"It *appears* to support that theory," Grady corrected. "Yes."

I smiled. "Things aren't always what they appear?" I guessed.

"Exactly. Which means it's important to scrutinize facts and avoid theories. Do you remember why?"

I chewed my lip. "Yeah." Grady had told me once that people with theories usually found a way to prove them. Not necessarily because the theory was right, but because investigators tended to find evidence to support their belief, often overlooking details that didn't fit their narrative.

"I have to go now," Grady said, "but let's talk later. For what it's worth, I really do wish you'd leave this alone. My job would be a lot easier, and I'd sleep better."

"I know," I said, apologetically. "I get it."

"Good. And Everly," he added, a little more firmly. "Be safe."

I warmed at the sound of the words and the emotion packed into them. "You too."

CHAPTER

THIRTEEN

We disconnected, and I finished my trip to the carriage house, which sat to the side of my home with easy access to the drive. The building was adorable, and coordinated fabulously with the house, right down to its delightful gray shake siding, white trim, and ancient weather vane.

A big blue pickup truck pulled in behind me, and Wyatt climbed out. "Morning!" he called, jogging to my side, a tray with two takeout cups of coffee in one hand. "I thought you could use a little liquid pep."

"Always," I said, accepting the offered cup, while casting him a curious look. He'd dressed in his usual cowboy boots and hat, faded jeans, and a fitted T-shirt, but he also had a pair of work gloves tucked into his pants pocket. And his gaze flickered pointedly to the closed door behind me. "You about ready to get started?"

I frowned. "In the carriage house? How do you know about that?"

I hoped my phone wasn't tapped, then wondered when I'd become so paranoid.

Maybe it was when I'd nearly become a human hood ornament.

Or when I watched my cartoon head roll off.

"Fran," Wyatt said, before taking a long pull from his cup. "She gave me a call this morning. Said you could use some help. It's my day off at the nature center, so it worked out pretty well."

I tapped my coffee to his in cheers. "Well, she did say she'd try to find me some help. Any idea what she plans to put in here?" I asked "Or how much room she wants us to make?"

"Nope." He set his coffee on a large rock near my flower bed, then tugged the work gloves over his hands. "Might as well get started. Let's see what you've got."

I opened the carriage house doors, and he made a disappointed sound. The place was stuffed to the gills with castoff belongings from countless previous homeowners. More than one-hundred-seventy years of people's abandoned things, and it was all in desperate need of a good purge and sorting.

"Yikes."

"Yeah." I nodded in agreement.

"Well, I brought my truck," he said. "And plenty of empty boxes." He sauntered forward, hands on hips, formulating a game plan. "Let's just dive in. One item at a time. Stuff for the trash over there," he pointed to the gravel-covered space alongside the carriage house, then swung the same finger a foot to the right. "Things you're donating can go over there. I'll toss all that in my truck before I leave and drop it off at Charmers Helping Charmers on my way home. Stack whatever you want to keep on your porch, so it doesn't get mixed up with the rest. Then, we can haul all that up to your place or put it back in the building once we're done."

I let my head drop back and my eyelids close.

"It won't be that bad." He nudged me playfully. "Come on. You've got all this strapping muscle to help you out. We'll be done in no time."

I raised my face and found him flexing like a body builder while admiring his changing shadow on the ground. I laughed despite myself. "Dork."

He grabbed a box of old books, then carried them immediately to my porch. He knew me well. "Only one way to move a mountain," he said, heading back for more.

I collected a stack of china dolls I was certain would murder me in my sleep and set them gently in the gravel for donations.

"One stone at a time." Wyatt lifted a box of rusted tools that looked like they belonged in a serial killer's playroom. "What should we do with antique gardening equipment?"

I wrinkled my nose. "Is that something the nature center might want to display?" I asked.

"I'm not sure." He dug carefully through the aged box. "I'll take it for now, and bring it back if it doesn't work out."

Wyatt's position at the Nature Center focused on the island's wild horses, tracking and monitoring as well as educating others about them. He'd fallen in love with the job and staff immediately, even starting a Little Cowboys club for boys and girls each summer. If there was a place for the creepy old tools there, he would be the one to find out.

"No hurry," I said, eyeballing the box as he passed.

Wyatt loaded the box into the bed of his truck. "It would help if we knew what we're making room for. If it's not bigger than a breadbox, we're practically done."

I smiled as he returned, appreciating him for his dedication and hard-working ways. "Thanks for being here," I said. "I wouldn't have known where to start."

He dazzled me with his handsome smile, then added a wink for good measure. "Fran said you needed help. Where else would I be?"

I ignored the butterflies lifting off in my stomach. My head and heart were on the same page, but my body sometimes had an agenda of its own. Especially when faced with my devastatingly handsome first love. Who had, unfairly, grown up and settled down two years too late to rekindle any flames. No amount of romantic history, good looks, or southern charm would change that. But I dearly appreciated his friendship.

We worked companionably until our coffees were gone and my back ached, then took a little break to evaluate our progress.

Wyatt wiped sweat off his forehead with the back of one arm. "How are you and Grady getting through this mess with Matt?" he asked. "You taking the other guy's side has to be bucking at the good detective's ego."

"Grady and I are fine," I said. "And I'm not siding with Matt. I'm just trying to protect a friend."

"A male friend you went out with once," Wyatt added. "Grady's a professional, but he's still a man, head over heels for you. And Matt's viable competition."

"That's ridiculous."

"Have you seen him?" Wyatt asked. "I go home and do

pushups every time I spend more than five minutes with that guy. He's hot."

I laughed. "Maybe you should ask him out."

Wyatt rocked his head side to side. "I wouldn't mind getting to know him better. He seems like a stand-up guy."

"He is," I said. "And you should. He could probably use another friend right now."

Wyatt grinned. "Can I have his number?"

"Yes," I laughed, bumping my shoulder against his arm. "Now, stop being weird."

I enjoyed the twinkle in his easy blue eyes, then thought of something else I'd been wondering. "Whatever happened with you and Denise? You were quite the thing for a while."

He shrugged. "We're probably going to agree to be just friends."

"Why?" I asked, genuinely curious and realizing it didn't feel awkward to ask about his love life. We really had come a long way.

"She's a little younger," he said. "She's not ready to be tied down, and I think I could be." He peeked at me from beneath his lashes. "I'll bet you, of all people, would never have expected to hear me say that."

I smiled. "I'm glad to hear it. You're going to make the right girl real happy."

He laughed. "This time," he promised, "I'll try."

I hugged him, proud for the way he'd grown and thankful to have him in my life. Which was probably something he never would've expected to hear from me not too long ago.

He stiffened briefly before hugging me back. "What's this for?" he asked.

"I appreciate you," I said.

He sighed into my hair and rearranged his grip on me. "I know."

The peaceful moment was interrupted by a blaring Beach Boys tune.

Wyatt and I stepped apart as a bright yellow Volkswagen convertible pulled up beside his truck. Aunt Fran was in the driver's seat, and there were large hippie flowers painted on the hood, roof, and door.

I covered my ears with my palms.

The music silenced when the engine settled, and Wyatt socked my arm. "Slug bug."

"Ow!" I hit him back, but probably hurt my hand more than his bicep.

Aunt Fran creaked out and gave the door a hearty slam. "Good! You're making room," she boomed, removing her sunglasses, then pulling squishy-looking orange plugs from her ears. She surveyed the chunk of space we'd cleared in the carriage house with obvious approval. "How long until there's room for Dharma?"

I suppressed a grin as the name registered in my mind. This was the Dharma she'd mentioned last night.

Wyatt folded his arms, bemused. "She sure is pretty."

"She's fierce," Aunt Fran reported proudly. "I bought her in 1965, then took an epic road trip with two of my best girlfriends, Gina and Rose. We went all the way to New Mexico where Gina's boyfriend was stationed on an Air Force base. We got in at two a.m., and he proposed to her on the spot. Rose and I had to drive home alone and draw straws for who would tell Gina's folks. I lost, but they weren't even mad," she said wistfully. "It was a different time then."

I was a little surprised to hear Aunt Fran had left the island, given her vehement belief in our family curse, and I suspected the base she visited might've been in Roswell, but I forced myself to focus. "Is something going on at the homestead?"

"I don't think so," she said, her thin gray brows furrowing. "Why do you ask?"

"I'm trying to figure out why you want to store Dharma here," I said. "I don't mind making the room, or having her," I clarified. "It just seems odd that you've decide to relocate her after all these years."

Her expression clouded in confusion for a moment, then she barked a laugh. "No, silly girl." She dug into her oversized handbag and pulled out a pale blue certificate. "Dharma's all yours. I'm signing her over to you today."

"You can't do that," I said, wholly stunned. "It's too much!"

"Pish." She waved the paper between us. "You need a car, and I have two, so this works out perfectly."

"You have two cars?" Wyatt asked, looking at her as if she'd grown two heads. Though, to be fair, it had been rare to see either of my aunts without their bicycles until Aunt Clara bought the Prius a few months back.

"I bought Mom's Bel Air from Clara," Aunt Fran explained. "Clara bought the Prius." She handed me the paper. "And Everly gets Dharma. See? It makes perfect sense."

I accepted the paper, and Aunt Fran folded her hands in front of her.

Her gaze slid over my shallow and healing scrapes. "Dharma's small, but she's mighty, and she'll offer you some protection in the face of oncoming vehicles. We can have the title transferred this morning, if you don't mind driving me to work."

"I can't accept this," I said, staring blankly at the car title in my hands. "She's your car."

Aunt Fran straightened at my flimsy attempt to decline her offer. "I have no heirs, so everything that's mine will be yours eventually. You might as well have some fun while I'm still around to enjoy it," she teased.

I hated that she was right about the inheritance part. One day I really would be alone. And I wished more than anything that I could somehow trade all the centuries of Swan possessions for a lifetime with my aunts instead.

Emotions overcame me, and I wrapped her narrow body in a tight embrace. I'd never owned a car before, and the milestone felt utterly monumental. Knowing my first vehicle had belonged to Aunt Fran, and had been in my family for more than half a century, seemed exactly right. "Thank you." I sniffed. "I love it so much. It's the absolute nicest thing you could've done for me."

Aunt Fran softened under the weight of my words and lowered her mouth to my ear. "Dear girl, there is nothing I wouldn't do for you."

She released me, then cleared her throat. "Try to be patient with Dharma. She's middle-aged, and she has her quirks. Some things can probably be fixed. Others, you'll have to live with. But whatever you do, don't remove the bouquet hanging from her rearview mirror. My mother put it there to protect the car and all her passengers. So far, Mom's flowers have done a mighty fine job. Let's not jinx it."

I nodded, wiping tears and smiling at the sun-bleached leather strap hanging inside the window. Dried and crumbling stems and buds were encased in what appeared to be a plastic sandwich bag to keep them from disintegrating in the wind. "I promise."

Wyatt stepped to my side and set a hand on my back. "I guess we're going to need to make more space in the carriage house."

I laughed and nodded. "Dharma is definitely bigger than a breadbox."

Aunt Fran clapped her hands, then passed me the keys. A fuzzy, hot-pink pompom dangled from the ring. "First, I'm going to need that ride to work."

I followed her back to the car, then parted ways at the grill. She went for the passenger door, and I climbed behind the wheel.

Fran fastened her safety belt, then inserted her ear plugs, rested her handbag on her lap, and arranged her sunglasses over her eyes.

I waved goodbye to Wyatt, then buckled up and turned the key in the ignition.

The engine purred to life, and a moment later, the opening chords to "I Get Around" by the Beach Boys began. At full blast.

I jumped, then slapped at the dashboard, attempting to turn the music down. Or off.

"That won't work," Fran yelled from two feet away. "Radio's busted. Volume is stuck."

I frowned at the offending radio, where the butt end of an eight track cassette protruded from the space beneath an old AM/FM dial. I jammed my thumb against the eject button until it hurt, then attempted to grip and remove the tape by force.

Fran watched, as unmoved as the tape.

I sagged as I twisted the volume back and forth again. Nothing happened.

"What is going on?" Denise yelled, hands over her ears as she arrived for her day at work.

Wyatt went to her side. His mouth moved, but all I could hear were the blaring lyrics to a 1960s beach song.

I assumed, by the shocked and highly entertained expression on her face, that Wyatt was filling her in on the situation. "I'll be back," I yelled, shifting into gear and pressing the gas gently to get a feel for the car.

Dharma responded easily, carrying us back across the boardwalk at the end of my driveway and onto Ocean Drive. She was easy enough to maneuver and impossible to miss, judging by the blatant stares of everyone in sight. And probably within a four-block radius. "Maybe if we put the top up, it will smother some of the sound," I screamed at Aunt Fran, hoping to be heard over the music and through her ear plugs.

"What?" she asked, popping one plug free.

"The top!" I yelled. "Maybe we should put up the top!"

"No," she shook her head, then replaced the ear plug. "It won't stop. When the tape ends, it just starts over."

I blanched, thoroughly disheartened by this news. Nothing in Charm was more than a few minutes' drive.

Which meant the Beach Boys would be eternally searching for a place where the kids were hip. And I had to listen. "The top!" I hollered again, pointing frantically to the sky overhead as I spoke.

Aunt Fran watched my lips, then shook her head again. "Stuck."

"What?" I yipped. "The top is stuck?"

"Has been for years." She nodded. "I think it rusted that way."

I stopped at the next red light, then dropped my head against the steering wheel, rethinking my life choices.

I jerked my head up when the car behind me honked. The light had turned green.

I pulled into the lot at the town hall with an extra punch of gas, then snuffed the engine as quickly as possible and considered a lifetime supply of ear plugs and aspirin.

"A family of squirrels lived in the trunk for nearly a decade," Aunt Fran said, stuffing her ear plugs into her handbag and straightening her windblown hair.

I turned slowly to stare. "What?"

"It's true. I relocated them to the oak tree out front after I found them, but they still come around sometimes, maybe looking for a nut," she said nostalgically before climbing out and heading for the sidewalk. "I think they must smell their former lives here," she said, patting the bulbous fender lovingly as she passed.

I followed her with ringing ears, certain there would only be one nut in that car for the foreseeable future.

Me.

CHAPTER
FOURTEEN

Transferring Dharma's title only took a few minutes. Then, I was back on the street and deciding where to go next. My mind turned immediately to Tara Larsen. My gut and ears suggested I find the closest mechanic and hope he had experience with 1960s Volkswagen radios.

Before I could decide, I spotted Ted Osier, seated alone at an outdoor café on the next block, a laptop open before him.

BE MORE ACTIVE!

My little fitness bracelet flashed a stick figure in the run position as it buzzed against my wrist. I glared. What had my bracelet been doing while I'd worked nearly two hours in my carriage house this morning? Clearly not paying attention. I'd bent, stretched, and lifted things until my back, thighs, and arms screamed in protest. I stifled the urge to flick the flashing stick figure with my opposite hand, then looked at Dharma. My quest to reduce noise pollution by finding a mechanic would have to wait.

I pocketed my keys and turned on my toes in Osier's direction. I tried to make my strides purposeful and strong, but the sidewalks were sprinkled with pedestrians buzzing in and out of restaurants and shops. I smiled and nodded, taking uneasy notice of their clean clothing, combed hair, and proper makeup.

My clothes, hair, and makeup, on the other hand, were none of those things. A glancing peek in a passing shop window and a discreet sniff in the general direction of one armpit confirmed my worst suspicions. My deodorant's promise of all-day protection had fallen woefully short.

I dusted my shirt and hands as I closed the distance to the café, then reminded myself to stay upwind from Mr. Osier.

He looked up as I drew near. My fun-house-quality image reflected in the mirrored lenses of his wire-rimmed aviators.

"Hello," I said, doing my best to look confident and congenial, rather than how I actually looked. "Ted Osier?"

He nodded slowly. "That's right." His dark-brown skin gathered in creases across his brow.

He'd aged visibly in the few years since he'd been photographed as Matt's manager, and I couldn't help wondering if the added grays and wrinkles were a direct result of four more years with Kai Larsen.

I supposed it was also possible Mr. Osier had simply stopped coloring his gray, or using a good sunblock, but the difference was blatant, nonetheless.

"I remember you from the amphitheater," he said, his lips twisting low on each side.

I hoped the negative response was caused by the awful memory and not by my failed deodorant.

"That's right," I said. "I'm Everly Swan. I'm a friend of Matt Darning's. I was with him at the amphitheater that night. I'm very sorry about the loss of your friend. If there's anything I can do, please let me know. This is my town, and I think I speak for everyone when I say we'd like to make your stay as comfortable as possible."

"Thanks," he said, looking slightly more at ease. "It's a nice town."

I beamed despite myself, warmed by his kind evaluation of Charm. "I run Sun, Sand, and Tea," I said. "It's an iced tea shop and café on the beach. You should stop by anytime. Tea's on me."

He nodded, kicking back a bit and resting a forearm on the table. His hand curled into a fist. He rubbed his thumb against the crook of his first finger. "I might do that. Thank you for your kind words, Miss Swan. Kai will certainly be missed."

"He was definitely a fan favorite," I said, quoting an online article and hoping it would spawn new words from Osier. "The alleged bad boy surfer." I smiled warmly, not yet ready to leave and completely unsure how to ask all the things I wanted to know without seeming as if I was cold-hearted or nosy.

Osier's frowned turned thoughtful. "Kai was a handful," he said. "He loved the spotlight, whatever the cost, and I hate to say it, but his antics made him more enemies than friends in the years I've been working with him. It was probably only a matter of time before his behavior came back to bite him."

I felt my eyebrows rise, and I forced them back down, trying not to look as accusatory as I suddenly felt. I'd assumed he would at least put on a show for me and pretend he was torn up over Kai's death. "It must've been difficult to be his manager."

"It wasn't easy," he said. "I was constantly covering up his messes. Representing Kai was an exhausting, full-time job, and he wasn't my only client."

I shook my head, feigning disappointment on Osier's behalf. "That sounds awful."

He leaned forward with a humorless chuckle. "You have no idea. Kai set a bad example for everyone else. All my other surfers eventually started acting up just trying to get a piece of the spotlight. I've dropped more clients than I've kept in the last four years because of him."

I chewed my lip, mentally connecting the dots. I'd come into the conversation assuming it wasn't in Osier's best interest to get rid of his most famous client, but the benefits of Kai's death were beginning to clear up. No messy breakup. No more drama. No more frustrated sponsors or misbehaving Kai wannabes.

"Figures he'd go out like this," Osier grouched. "Whatever causes me more work."

I took my silent theory a step further and wondered if there was more Osier wasn't telling me. For example, what if Kai was actually losing Osier money? What if his bad boy ways had begun to push the biggest and best sponsors away? Taking their fat financial support with them? My mouth dried and my intuition spiked. "I bet the sponsors hated seeing him acting out while wearing their gear," I said. "That must've felt like he was smearing their names."

Osier stretched, then flexed his fingers before curling them back into the loose fist. "And guess who those companies look to for an explanation every time Kai was hauled out of a club by bouncers or caught fighting on the street with his nutso wife by a hundred photographers?" He extended a finger, then swiveled the fist to point at himself. "Me."

My thoughts began to pick up speed. "It's understandable," I said, imagining someone like Kai wearing one of my logoed Sun, Sand, and Tea shirts while being belligerent in public or hauled off to jail. "No one wants to become the brand of drunk and disorderly," I said, as much to myself as to Osier.

He grunted. "Why do you care so much?" he asked, his tone going suddenly accusatory. "I thought you didn't know him."

"I didn't," I said, immediately on the defensive.

He cocked a brow, and I scrambled mentally for a better answer.

"I was just curious." A nervous chuckle bubbled out, and I looked for witnesses in each direction. There were dozens. And my cheeks heated. "Small-town curiosity," I said, backpedaling. I waved a palm dismissively. "I just can't seem to help myself."

His lips curled into a smile that verged on a sneer. "I heard that about you."

"You did?" I stepped backward, my heel finding the edge of the curb. "Where did you hear that?"

Osier scanned the scene around us, maybe buying time to make something up or deciding how quickly he could get in his SUV and mow me down.

Given the options, I'd prefer the lie.

"It's on the website where the waitress told me I could check the tide schedule for the week." He adjusted the lid on his laptop against the sun. "The *Town Charmer*," he read.

"They like to joke," I said. "You can't believe anything you read on there. Except the tides," I amended, then chuckled nervously. "So, Matt told me he was a professional surfer before moving to Charm," I said, changing the subject gracelessly and without apology. "But I didn't realize he'd been one of the best. Or that you were his manager."

Osier tented his brows. "I'm surprised he told you I represented him. We weren't on very good terms when he left."

"Because of Kai?"

"Because Matt thought I should sort his problems for him, but it wasn't my fault Kai was so difficult or that Tara changed teams. And it wasn't up to me to fix any of that. All I'm contractually obligated to do is to keep track of my surfers and get them to events and promotions. Which was hard enough to do with any success."

"So, you literally started tracking him," I said, recalling Osier's admission at the crime scene.

He lifted and dropped his hand on the table. "Desperate times and desperate measures."

"Did you track Matt too?" I asked.

"I never needed to. Matt was always the yin to Kai's yang. The three of us could've made a fortune as a trio, but Tara ruined that. I think her betrayal was the last straw for Matt. Something else he thought I should've known about and reported back to him. I wish things had gone differently. Sponsors loved Matt, especially the wholesome, family ones."

"Like Surf Daddy," I supplied.

"Exactly." He pulled his sunglasses off and rubbed the bridge of his nose.

"The Goodwins are very nice," I said. "I wouldn't blame them for not wanting their brand or logo associated with Kai and his antics."

"Then you understand," Osier said, sounding mildly defeated. "When Kai showed up drunk for that public relations breakfast, it didn't go over so well. He scared half the kids and disgusted the parents with his behavior. Thankfully it was a private event. No press allowed. I told everyone Kai was trying out a new medication for an old surf injury and needed to cut the morning short for a medical evaluation, but anyone within three feet could probably smell the alcohol on his breath."

I thought again of the Goodwin family and their little getaway. The way they'd been circled by the press, and their eagerness to escape. They were humiliated by Kai's behavior at the ruined Surf Daddy event, no doubt, and the piranhas had come to feed. I felt so sorry for them in hindsight. No wonder they'd decided to leave town until the dust settled. Reporters were intimidating. To the Goodwin kids, the situation must've been downright frightening.

Then another, more puzzling observation rose to mind. Nicole from the stationery shop had specifically told me Kai's publicity breakfast event had gone smoothly, but Osier said his client had shown up drunk. Which meant one of them was lying. But why?

"I'm trying to get a meeting with some sponsors and my next best surfer," Osier said, lifting and wiggling his cell phone. "If you don't mind, I should get back to work. The

S-Curves is expected to have some nice breaks today, and they'll make for great promo if I can get things set up."

I considered that a moment, then nodded. I was familiar with the area. The S-Curves was one of the island's most popular destinations for serious surfers. Only a few minutes north of Surf Daddy in Rodanthe, the S-Curves was the place to go when big swells came in. Cars and SUVs, often lined up along the highway for miles, were a testament to the area's popularity among surfers.

I thought of the billboards along the highway and the trio of glossy muscled bodies. Two men and one woman, but who had the most to gain? Locke was considered second in performance by serious surf blogs, but Ava had been the clear favorite among fans and one of very few women doing as well in the sport.

According to Matt, there were hundreds of thousands of dollars at stake. What young person didn't want that?

I opened my mouth to ask Osier who was next in line for the throne, but his phone rang, and he lifted a finger, indicating I should put a cork in it.

I waited, impatiently, as he pasted on a false smile and chatted with the caller. "Yes, of course. No. It's no problem. I was just enjoying a little coffee and the beautiful day."

Within thirty seconds, he seemed to have forgotten I was there.

The good news was that, thanks to Aunt Fran, I now had my own wheels and could pop down to Rodanthe and ask around whenever I wanted. No more looking for rides and divulging my secrets.

I checked my watch, debating how long I could wait

before heading home to take a shower. It was already after eleven. There was no way I could make it to Rodanthe before Denise's shift ended, but maybe I could pop in on Tara Larsen for a do-over interview.

I leaned into Osier's line of sight and waved goodbye.

He lifted his chin a fraction in acknowledgement, then laughed at whatever had been said on the other side of his phone call.

I didn't mind leaving him there. There was something unsettling about him. Maybe it was the way he hadn't bothered to pretend he was grieving Kai's death. Or the way he spoke of his surfers, as if they were the life-size equivalent of pieces in a board game instead of actual people. Or maybe I'd simply begun to suspect everyone. Because since Grady had told me to think critically, I couldn't stop imagining everyone as a killer.

CHAPTER

FIFTEEN

I cut through the knots and clusters of shoppers on my way back to Dharma, then froze as an old woody station wagon rounded the corner. The Surf Daddy logo clung to its side. And James Goodwin sat behind the wheel. Had he left his family in Corolla to meet with Osier? Perhaps about a less troublesome replacement surfer to be his brand ambassador?

Before I could imagine any truly sinister intentions for either of the men, James noticed me staring and honked. He smiled broadly, then stuck his arm through the open window and raised his fingers in a wave.

I waved back, then moved more quickly toward my new car. It was time I visited Tara again. If anyone would have the inside scoop on Osier's relationship with Kai, and possibly any recent drama between them, it was her. If I played my cards right, maybe she would even share the name of the person she suspected Kai had been having an affair with.

And if Tara turned out to be homicidal, I'd use my two new dress sizes against her.

I jumped behind the wheel and motored over to Sea Spray Drive wearing enormous, black-framed sunglasses I found in the glove box and smiling apologetically at folks who stared. It was nice that Aunt Fran wanted to protect me from hit and run drivers, but Dharma was the opposite of stealthy. She was a single-song concert at full blast, and once the killer knew that, he or she would be able to pinpoint my location from half a mile away based on volume alone.

I swung the Volkswagen into a parking space outside Tara's rental, then hopped out and headed for the porch. The front door swung wide before I could knock or ring the bell.

We both startled.

"You," she said, blinking slowly as she regained herself. "What are you doing here?"

I stepped back to add a little space between us and fumbled to find my words. The gurgling sound I managed wasn't even close to the confident, hospitable local I'd planned to be.

Her expertly makeup-ed eyes scanned me with concern. "Are you hurt?"

I glanced down at my dusty work clothes and bandaged hands, then belatedly recalled my ratty hair and failed deodorant. "No. Sorry, I was cleaning." I smiled, ready to start over. "I was just thinking of how I reacted yesterday, to news of your previous marriage. I thought I should come over and apologize for leaving so abruptly. I didn't know Matt had been married before, and it threw me. I didn't realize how little I knew about him."

She shrugged, hiking the strap of a designer handbag higher on one shoulder. "Well, that's just Matt," she said.

"He's a private person, which is probably why he moved here." She fluttered one hand in an arc before her, as if to say, there was obviously no reason anyone would come here unless they wanted to be alone.

I ignored the jab on my town and focused on her instead. A pop psychology book I'd recently borrowed from one of Amelia's little libraries had suggested that most of what people said told us more about the speaker than the target. And I knew enough about Tara from online articles to realize she'd be miserable anywhere she wasn't stalked or worshipped.

It took me another minute to register her overall appearance. A fitted white sundress. Purse. Heels. Silk scarf tied over perfectly arranged hair. She was on her way out!

I cursed myself for not getting there sooner. A third visit on my behalf would definitely seem like stalking.

"Excuse me," she said, stepping onto the porch and locking up behind her. "I have lunch plans."

"Lunch plans?" I repeated, admiring her perfect figure and impeccable style. She wasn't exactly the picture of heartbreak and grief, but she looked fantastic.

I immediately wondered who she was meeting.

A friend? A date? Matt?

"Maybe we can talk on the way?" I suggested, following her back down the porch steps. "Where are you headed?"

Tara stalled and stared. "I'm having lunch at the new teahouse on the sound. I've called a car, and I don't need company while I wait. My ride will be here any second." She lifted her phone, the GPS app open and likely tracking the car.

As if on cue, the town's only cab stopped on the street before us.

I waved to the driver. "Hi, Mrs. Cress."

She leaned across the passenger's seat and smiled. "Hey, Everly. How are you?"

"Good." I tried to return her cheerful expression, but the effort didn't take.

Mrs. Cress was the local children's librarian, and a good friend of Amelia and her dad. I'd never gotten to know her. My reading addiction hadn't taken hold until I'd discovered cowboy romance novels in high school.

Tara opened the back door and let herself inside.

I couldn't bring myself to ask her any of the myriad questions I had for her, not with her lunch date waiting and Mrs. Cress at her side.

Instead, I handed her my business card, in case she wanted to get in touch later, then watched in defeat as she rolled away. Off to lunch at the teahouse that was my new competition.

～

By closing time that night, I'd already packed a selection of themed sweets into bags for the *Lost Colony* cast and crew. Apparently, Manteo's police had given the play's director a green light to move forward after determining the amphitheater was not a crime scene. Kai had been killed several yards behind the stage and twice as far from the seating, so rehearsals were back on track, and the island thespians were good to go.

I planned to surprise them all with delicious, unexpected refreshments, and maybe talk to a few folks about what they saw or heard the night of Kai's death while I was there.

I rushed through my set of evening rituals, shutting the café down in a hurry, eager to get one more look at the first and last place I'd seen Kai Larsen in the flesh.

"Thank you," I told my final set of customers, smiling warmly as I walked them to the door and flipped my window sign from *Come on in, Y'all* to *See Y'all Tomorrow*.

The couple returned my smile, then joined hands and went on their way.

I darted across the driveway to my carriage house, bags of treats in each hand. I set them on the floorboards of Dharma's back seat, then hurried back to collect the tea dispensers I'd earmarked for the trip.

A note in Wyatt's familiar scrawl caught my eye atop a pile of boxes beside the car.

> *Trash at curb.*
> *Keepsakes in boxes.*
> *Found an injured sandpiper in the garden.*
> *Taking him to the wildlife rescue.*
> *Wish us luck!*
> *~ W*

I sent up a round of healing thoughts for the bird, then tapped out a text for Wyatt, thanking him for all his hard work. Afterward, I tucked his note into my pocket, then toted the stack of keeper boxes to my porch.

I was certain the local historical society or museum

would want to put at least some of the things on display. A diary documenting life in Charm during the early twentieth century. Antique traps for crabbing. A trunk of women's clothing. Several hat boxes, complete with hats and enough knickknacks to open a consignment shop.

I set the final box against the wall beside my front door and checked my watch. I didn't have the time or energy to carry the boxes to my third floor. I was already running behind, and the task would take four of five trips. My home was air conditioned, which would keep me from sweating as if I'd been to the gym, but I was often winded after one trip up the steps. Repeating the process four times was out of the question. And taking all the boxes up an additional flight, seemed like a stroke in the making.

An angry voice wafted to my ears on the wind, and I stilled to listen.

Through the blowing wind and steady roar of waves, the voice came again. Muddled but angry, and evidently not too far away.

I edged around my porch to the gardens, then moved slowly toward the point where my property broke sharply away, leaving a jagged cliff of earth and rocks between myself and the sea.

Locke Suarez, the young man from the billboards with Kai and Ava, their female teammate, shuffled through the sand below, a cell phone pressed to his ear. "It was his," he bellowed. "And it passes to me!"

I stiffened, and a cold shiver reverberated down my spine.

Locke was the next in line for stardom and stood to gain the most from Kai's demise. But was he capable of murder? How far would he go to get his hands on fame and glory?

I covered my mouth and shuffled backward, racing mentally through the facts. It seemed more than possible that a client of Osier's—and a teammate of Kai's—would know about Kai's tense history with Matt. His phone had been conveniently ripe for the picking at the crime scene. Along with the arrows used for the play. And Locke would know Kai's number, enabling him to send the phony text. But could he have known Matt's password somehow?

I'd originally assumed the killer had set out to frame Matt, but what if the location had simply made the setup convenient? My foot hit a stone, and my ankle wobbled, sending a rock and hunk of loose earth sailing over the hill's edge.

I held my breath and watched as the rock landed soundlessly on the beach below.

A cluster of seagulls squawked and took flight.

The man with the cell phone turned to look at the birds, then at the place where the stone had landed. A moment later, he raised his eyes in my direction.

I ducked, then turned and ran.

I doubled back to my porch and yanked a box from the top of the keeper pile. If anyone knocked on my door, they would see I'd been busy working. For hours. Cleaning the carriage house, and therefore nowhere near my property's edge, eavesdropping.

I hit the stairs at a clip, box clutched to my middle, forcing my feet forward. My heart hammered and my lungs burned as I jogged the steep interior staircase to my private quarters. From there, I hustled up another flight to the third floor, then slid the box onto the floor with the others and ran away.

I hadn't been able to spend any time in the cluttered space since my strange run-in with...something...last Halloween. And I didn't have the time or desire to think about it now.

My heart and pulse hammered from fear and supreme lack of fitness as I clomped back down to the foyer, hoping the coast was clear. Anyone who saw me now, and the remaining boxes on my porch, would understand I'd been too busy to be listening in on a private, and apparently heated, conversation.

I took a quick detour through my café before heading to the door. I peeked through my windows toward the beach, confirming the man was no longer there. My heart began to settle at the confirmation. The world had lost what little light it had clung to earlier. The setting sun had sunk into the horizon over the sound, leaving my side of the island in darkness. Though it was hard to say for sure, there didn't seem to be any obvious tracks headed in my direction. I considered that a win.

I decided the rest of the boxes could wait to be dragged upstairs, and I opted to leave them in the foyer instead.

I opened my door with purpose and nearly broke an ankle stopping short.

A line of arrows lodged in the sandy ground at the bottom of my porch steps, like a line I'd been forbidden to cross. A single word had been carved into the earth before them.

STOP

CHAPTER SIXTEEN

I texted Grady a photo of the threat, then looked at my dark, empty home and made a run for the carriage house. I drove away like a lunatic, watching my rear view mirror as often as the road ahead of me.

My phone lit and vibrated on my lap before I reached the first red light in town.

"Hello?" I yelled into the receiver as families sharing ice creams outside the Sweet Shack gaped.

"Everly?" Grady asked.

"You got my text?"

"I can barely hear you. Where are you?" he hollered back.

"In my car. It's the radio!" My heart hammered, and my eyes made a steady circuit, scanning the world in every direction. The car might protect me against another vehicle, but with the top down, I felt exposed. As if someone could simply walk up to me at the light and stab something into my back too.

"Turn it down," he growled, clearly losing patience.

"I can't!" A frustrated tear stung my eye as the light

changed, and I pressed the gas with purpose. "I'm on my way to the amphitheater with refreshments. I'll call you when I get there."

Grady tried to continue the conversation, but I yelled an apology and my goodbyes, then disconnected. I dropped the phone onto the passenger seat in favor of getting both hands on the wheel. The last thing I needed was a ticket for distracted driving. Or a noise ordinance violation.

My arms shook as I gripped the wheel and headed for the highway connecting island towns. Hopefully by the time I reached Manteo, Grady would've had time to evaluate the situation at my house, maybe find a clue I was too frightened to look for, and arrest the killer.

I tipped my chin up and squared my shoulders as determined tears plucked at my eyes. I would trust Grady to handle the threat, and I would concentrate on what I did best. I fed people. And I made them smile. Tonight, my treats would be a fun surprise and a great way to show Aunt Clara and her history group, plus the *Lost Colony* cast and crew, how much I appreciated them.

The tension fell away as I added distance between myself and the arrows outside my home. My thoughts grew less fearful and more positive, mile by mile. And all I wanted in the world was a hug from Aunt Clara.

Soon, I swung the Volkswagen into a parking space beneath a security light and cut the engine. I unloaded Wagon, then filled her with my handled bags and tea dispensers. Her pretty blue paint and Sun, Sand, and Tea logo shined under parking lot floodlights.

I rushed toward the amphitheater, desperate to be with

people and excited to surprise them with my offerings. The anticipation of their smiles warmed my chilled skin from head to toe.

The stage was empty, but I spotted a mass of folks in period costumes gathered in the grass. My heart leaped. I was just in time for their break.

The thrill settled as the table came into view, and I got a look at the spread.

Crisp, white linens covered the table. A royal blue satin cloth was draped at an angle over the white. Fancy, gilded plates and tiered trays had been arranged on top. Each generously filled with tiny sweets and mini-sandwiches. Pinwheels and tarts. Crostini and caramels. Taper candles added ambience to the already remarkable layout, and rows of teapots sat on hot pads along one side. Not a single, sensible paper plate or disposable cup in sight.

The guests carried adorable mismatched teacups and actual plates, each piece equally as pretty as those displayed on the table.

"What is happening?" I whispered to myself.

Aunt Clara darted into my line of sight, then hustled over to greet me. "Oh, dear," she said, dragging her gaze over Wagon and her load. "I didn't realize you were coming."

I turned accusing eyes on her. "I thought I would surprise you."

"Good job," she said, turning her eyes to the posh table and gourmet selection.

A few cast members took notice as we drew near. They nodded and smiled, hands and mouths full of fancy plates and foods.

I refreshed my smile and returned their nods. "This was all provided by the new teahouse. Wasn't it?"

That was why I hadn't been asked to cater tonight. And why I'd only learned play practice had resumed after reading about it on the *Town Charmer*.

"Mm-hmm," Aunt Clara responded softly, "but for what it's worth, no one asked her to cater. She just sort of volunteered, then showed up."

I fought the urge to complain about Eloise's presumptions when I remembered I'd shown up without being asked as well.

"Oh!" A young woman in twin French braids and a frilly blue dress hurried in our direction. "Hello!" She smiled politely as she flitted to our sides.

I raised a hand in a small, hip-high wave.

"Welcome!" Her eyes were the cornflower blue of her dress, and she'd tied a ribbon at the end of each braid, reminding me of Dorothy from *The Wizard of Oz*.

"Look at all this!" She motioned to Wagon while exuding over-the-top energy. "Is this more food?"

"It is," I said. "And you are?"

"Kate!" She rolled onto her toes, then back down. "I work for Subtle Teas and was lucky enough to be sent by Eloise on this refreshment-delivering mission. I'm also a theater major at the College of the Albemarle, and it's my goal to one day play a role in this production."

"Ah." I slid my eyes to Aunt Clara. "Nice to meet you."

"You as well!" She beamed without asking my name in return. Which was just as well.

Aunt Clara smiled kindly. "Can we make a little room on the tables for the incoming treats?"

Kate nodded eagerly, then looked at her perfectly set tables and frowned. "There doesn't seem to be any room."

"Well," Aunt Clara said, raising an arm overhead and gaining the attention of a man in a stage crew T-shirt. "Maybe we can make some."

The man nearly threw his snacks aside to get to her. "Clara? Is there anything I can help you with?"

"I hoped we could borrow a set of saw horses and a piece of plywood. Make a little table for all this lovely food," she said.

He winked, then hurried off and returned in the space of a few minutes. He did as Aunt Clara had asked, then came to help me with the refreshments.

"Thanks," I said, reluctantly setting out my offerings.

I poured a cup of sweet tea from my dispenser, then went to mingle.

Kate trailed me with her eyes but thankfully didn't follow.

After a few minutes of small talk with the men and women dressed as soldiers, royalty, and colonists, I eased into my reason for coming.

Everyone had seen Matt's argument with Kai before he died, but only a few had heard what was said. One colonist thought she'd heard the words *money*, *Tara*, and *Surf Daddy*, but the wellspring of new information ended there.

I spotted Matt sitting on the edge of the stage and headed in his direction, eager to cheer him up and hoping he wasn't alone because the group had shunned him.

He stiffened briefly when he saw me, then visibly relaxed. "Hey," he said, forcing a smile. "I thought you might be another cop or reporter, coming to ask me if I really killed Kai Larsen."

I grimaced. "Nope. It's just me, coming to see if you're okay. Not in the mood for fancy snacks and hot tea?"

He shook his head. "I just got here. I talked to the director earlier today to see what she thought about me coming to practice. I didn't want to draw any bad press for the play. Turns out we aren't running any of my lines tonight, so it was up to me. I came anyway, to support the others and see if I could help the Queen and boat captains with their lines, but I got here right after the tea arrived. I haven't gotten a chance to dive in yet."

I climbed the steps to the stage, then sat on the edge beside him, dangling my feet beside his. "I'm sorry you're going through this."

He groaned. "I'm sorry you've gotten hurt because of it."

I leaned closer, bumping my shoulder with his. "What are friends for, if not to help one another beat a murder charge once in a while?"

Matt laughed again. The sound was more genuine this time. "Right."

"I wish I knew what happened that night," I said softly. "Not just for you, but for Kai and his family too. Victims deserve justice." And killers deserved to be punished.

"I know," he said softly. "Me too. How are your scrapes and bruises healing?"

"Okay," I said. The memory of a charging SUV sprang to mind, then combined with the threat outside my home tonight, and I cringed.

"What's that face?" Matt asked. "Did something else happen?"

I considered lying so he wouldn't feel worse than he already did, but I didn't want to lie to Matt. Instead, I took a deep breath, then told him about the arrows I'd left for Grady to clean up.

"Oh, man." Matt wrapped one strong arm around my back and pulled me closer. "I'm so sorry."

"It's not your fault," I said, leaning into the lean muscle of his side.

"I hate to see you go home alone. Have you considered staying with your aunts at night?" he asked. "At least until the killer is found? I hate the thought of you in that big old house all by yourself. I'd offer you my spare room, but I think your boyfriend might take issue."

I rolled my eyes. "I don't think my boyfriend is very happy with me right now." I felt the weight of the words as they fell from my lips. "Grady hates when I get involved in this stuff, but I can't seem to help it. Or I don't want to. Maybe both." I still needed to call him and let him know I'd arrived safely, but the little chicken parts of me were avoiding the discussion that would follow. I wasn't ready to hear more about my most recent threat.

Matt tipped his cheek against the top of my head.

Warm ocean air whipped around us, blowing the scents of salt and distant bonfires our way. It would've been the perfect moment, if not for the looming threats to Matt's freedom and my life.

"Grady worries," he said. "Believe me. I get that. I don't know how well I'd deal with someone threatening my girl all the time. But he handles it. He steps up. Protects you. Cuffs the bad guy and keeps his cool. I'm sure he'd stay with you if he could, to keep you safe."

"Maybe," I said, "but Denver needs him there every night. That poor kid's already been through so much. It wouldn't be fair to make him worry about his dad too."

"I wonder," Matt said, almost to himself as he shifted away.

"What?" I turned to look at him when he released me.

"What if I stayed with you?" he asked. "Then you, Grady, and I could all breathe a little easier. I wouldn't get in your way, but I'd be available if you needed me. Maybe having me around would keep whoever's threatening you from coming back onto your property."

"Maybe," I said, not hating the idea.

"At least then, when they haul me in again and keep me, someone will know I'm gone." He offered a small smile. "Eventually, one of these trips to the station will be the one where I don't get released with a warning. At least if I had a roommate, someone would know I was gone."

My jaw dropped. "You've been formally questioned more than once? At the police station?"

Matt rubbed the back of his neck. "Yeah. My prints are the only ones on the arrow found in Kai's back and on my phone. Everyone knows about my past with Kai now, and Tara's role in our feud. Everything points to me, and I don't even have a solid alibi." He rubbed his palms together and averted his eyes. "The evidence is pretty damning."

"The evidence is circumstantial," I said.

"My boss suggested I take some paid time off today. A couple weeks." Matt sighed. "I'm not sure I can say no. I just hope I'll get the chance to go back when this is over. If I'm not in jail. I can't really blame him right now," he said.

"Most folks needing medical intervention don't want a killer sent over."

"Stop," I said. "Don't talk like that. You'll get your job back, and this mess will all be sorted. You've just got to hang in there."

Matt stood, but didn't make eye contact. "I should probably get some tea before break is over. Want anything?"

"No, thanks. I'm not staying much longer. I have to get back. Grady's at my place with the arrows."

He nodded, then raised a hand in goodbye.

My phone buzzed, and Grady's face appeared on screen "Hello?"

"You didn't call me when you got there," he said, a note of relief in his voice. "I worried."

"Sorry. I was talking with Matt." I sighed when he bypassed the refreshments and headed for the parking lot instead.

"So, you didn't call as promised, and I've been worried whoever left this threat followed you, because you were talking with Matt?" Grady asked.

"I wasn't thinking about the arrows once I got here." I glanced at the fancy tea tables in the distance and frowned. "I got distracted. Then I saw Matt and wanted to see how he was doing," I said. "I worry."

"I worry," Grady snapped back "Another nut was right outside your door an hour ago. A killer, Everly. Do you get that?"

"I am fine," I said, emphasizing each word and not appreciating his tone. "Matt's going through a lot right now. No thanks to you," I added. "When were you going to tell me you've hauled him down to the station more than once for questioning?"

"I was doing my job," he said. "Like right now."

The pang of terror in my chest jerked back into place, picking up where it'd left off in the car. I reminded myself that I was safe. There were dozens of people just a stone's throw away. "Are you at my place?"

"Yes."

"What did you think about the arrows?"

"I think you've peeved off another killer," Grady said. "You didn't cool it after he sent the little cartoon, then tried to run you down, so he or she is coming to your home now."

My stomach sank then rolled. "Maybe Matt really should stay with me," I whispered to myself more than Grady. I looked for Matt's truck in the lot, but it was gone.

"I'm sorry. What?" Grady asked, voice going low and rough.

I returned to myself, hoping Matt was okay and that Grady would try to be a little more understanding. "Matt suggested he could stay with me," I said. "To protect me from whoever is taunting me or at least discourage them from coming back to my home."

Grady did a slow, humorless chuckle. "Is that right?"

"Yeah," I said. "You have to admit, it's not the worst idea."

Grady didn't respond. I changed the subject. "Find any useful clues?" I asked. "Maybe the culprit dropped his ID?"

Grady snorted. "You'd be surprised how rarely that happens."

"Bummer."

"We'll just have to wait for the lab," he said. "I photographed and bagged the arrows as evidence. With a little luck, we can pull a few prints."

"Will you erase the message in the dirt?" I asked. "I don't want to see it again."

"Already done," he said. "How soon will you be here? Do you want me to wait? See you in safely? Or does Matt have that handled?"

I bit into my bottom lip, wanting to ask him to stay, but also not very impressed with his gruff responses. "Matt left," I said. "I didn't ask him to come over, but you can wait for me and come in, if you have time." I knew it was a long shot, he had plenty of work to do, and I didn't want to take him away from it. "I'll understand if you get a call or a lead and have to take off. Catching the bad guy before he scares me again is job one."

"Yeah." Grady chuckled darkly. "Maybe if you scared a little easier we wouldn't be in this position again."

My spine stiffened and my eyes narrowed. "What position?"

Grady sighed. "Never mind. I'll hang around as long as I can. Be safe, Swan."

I pocketed my phone and marched toward the crime scene with renewed purpose. Someone knew something about what happened to Kai Larsen. I just had to find the right person to ask. And if I couldn't find them, then I needed to find a clue I could work with. I turned in a small circle as I walked past the place I'd last seen Kai with the coroner. I gave the area a wide berth, then looked closely at everything in sight.

The shadows were deep and thick along the buildings.

I ignited the flashlight app on my phone and scrutinized the area's nooks and crannies, searching for anything the authorities might've missed. Or places where the killer could've hidden. If Kai hadn't been shot by an arrow from two-hundred yards away, then where might an attacker have tucked themselves out of sight and waited to make their move?

The strike had to have been quick. Something Kai hadn't seen coming. He was in prime physical condition, and based on the shiner he'd given Matt, the guy could throw a punch. There probably weren't many people in the area he couldn't have fought off. So, the attack must've come fast and without warning.

I tried squeezing into spaces between buildings and behind wooden fences, checking my view of Kai's murder site from each and imagining how I could reach him without being seen. The soft sounds of sobbing interrupted my calculations.

I crept from behind a small dumpster and followed the sounds toward the sea.

A small memorial had been erected on the beach several yards away. Beside it, a woman sat on the sand, her bent knees pulled up to her chest and narrow arms wrapped around them. Wind off the water tossed her hair in a halo over her head, which she'd bent to rest against her legs.

I inched slowly in her direction, attempting not to startle her.

She looked up when I lowered myself at her side, and I recognized her as Ava Hyde, the third surfer from the billboards. The pain in her puffy red eyes was nearly enough to seize my heart.

"I'm Everly," I said, bending my knees and attempting to match her posture. "I heard you crying. Thought you could use some company."

"Sure," she said, turning her attention to the sea.

I evaluated her profile a moment before following her lead. She looked smaller in person than she did in the posters and ads, and significantly less formidable. At the moment, she seemed incredibly young and vulnerable. I doubted she'd been out of high school more than a few years, and I sensed her utter heartbreak was about more than a lost teammate.

"Did you know him long?" I asked quietly.

"Yeah." She sniffed. "Almost a year."

I smiled, suspecting I was right. Ava was young. The years went much faster after twenty-five in my experience, and I'd place her at barely twenty. "You're the surfer from the promotional campaign."

She nodded without taking her eyes off the darkened sea. "Ava."

"You were Kai's teammate."

"Kai was more than a teammate," she said. "He was my mentor. My hero. He taught me everything."

My heart broke a little for hers, and I hoped Kai hadn't taken advantage of her youth and sincerity. I hoped he hadn't crossed a line. "I heard him arguing with Matt that night," I said, pulling her eyes to mine.

"You were here?"

"Yeah. So was the play's cast and crew. A lot of witnesses. Any idea what they were fighting about?"

She shook her head. "None."

"Someone thought they heard Matt or Kai say the words

money and *Tara*," I said. "They also heard the name Surf Daddy. Does that mean anything to you?"

She frowned. Her freckled face was red and tear stained. Her pale brows crowded between her eyes. "Tara was Kai's wife. Surf Daddy's a sponsor."

"Sponsors pay the surfers," I supplied. "That explains the word *money* too."

She turned back to the distant breaking waves. "Surf Daddy might've paid, but they were an enormous drag. The morality clause in their contract practically demanded Kai become a monk."

My intuition tingled again. "I guess that was a problem for the bad boy of surf," I said in my most teasing tone.

The effort fell short.

Ava turned to me, eyes hard as the rising wind pressed lush, sun-streaked locks against her cheeks. "Kai was a good man. He was so much more than those awful gossip articles and online photos made him out to be. He worked hard, and he was the best for a reason. He deserved so much better."

"Than what?" I asked without thinking. So much more than a gorgeous wife and posh Malibu home? More than his title as champion? More than the lion's share of sponsors and all the money that came with them?

Or did she simply mean he deserved better than murder?

She didn't speak. Didn't move. Didn't appear to breathe.

"Ava!" a familiar voice called, snapping her from her reverie. She shot to her feet as Ted Osier appeared down the beach.

He moved swiftly in our direction, one arm extended, as if he could collect her from thirty yards away. "Let's go."

She wiped her eyes frantically, then dusted the sand from her hands and legs.

I lifted my hand in goodbye as her manager latched onto her, then turned her away, leaving an icy chill in their wake.

CHAPTER

SEVENTEEN

Grady wasn't at my house when I got there, but the arrows and threat outside were gone as promised. My shoulders sagged in relief.

I hurried to the porch, then pointedly ignored the stack of boxes still waiting to be dragged inside. I sent a text to Grady after I was safely in my living quarters, letting him know I appreciated him.

When he didn't respond after a few minutes, I began to wonder if he was upset about the threat left outside my door or Matt's offer to stay at my place for a while. He hadn't seemed happy when we spoke earlier, and I was sure he blamed me for both.

I faintly missed the days before we started dating, when there was nothing at stake if he didn't like something I said or did. Now, there was a constant internal pressure to be a good girlfriend, and a growing sense of vulnerability I didn't like. My deeply rooted but thinly veiled insecurity left my heart tender and afraid more often than not. And I hated it.

I changed into sweats and fuzzy socks, then made a cup

of hot tea, checking repeatedly for signs of a text from Grady. My message to him had been delivered and opened, but he hadn't responded.

I sent a text to Wyatt next, checking on the sandpiper.

Wyatt responded with a selfie. He gave the camera a thumbs up, and the bird was in the background, inside a cage at the wildlife rescue facility, its wing wrapped awkwardly. The text he sent next simply said:

He's a fighter!

I smiled and relaxed a little more knowing the bird was going to be okay.

The house was still but not quiet, as I moved through the living space toward my bookshelves. Reliable ocean winds played gently around the windows and ancient rafters, causing muffled groans overhead. I nudged the baseboard with my toe, then slid the built-in shelving away. I'd discovered a small, hidden room behind the shelves last fall and presumed the space had originally been used to hide rum during prohibition. I'd slowly transformed it into my secret hideaway and safe space.

I'd spent long winter nights making the room my own. My grandmother's golden velvet armchair now stood before the ancient desk that had already been inside. I'd added a teal throw pillow to the chair and a plush cream rug to the floor. Family keepsakes lined antique shelves and accent tables.

I twisted the knob on a gilded floor lamp with a hot-pink shade I'd placed near the door, illuminating the space. I'd tucked the lamp's cord stealthily under the bookshelves, then beneath the living room carpet along the baseboard, and plugged it into an outlet I'd hidden with a plant stand for good measure.

Framed photos from my life on the island were arranged in decorative clusters on the walls. Wild horses on the beach. High school graduation. And sweet moments with Grandma.

I set my mug on the little desk, then sat and crossed my legs on the comfy chair. My gaze sought the shoebox-sized chest where I kept my greatest treasures, and I flipped the teak lid to peek at the contents. Hundreds of handwritten letters from my grandma to her best friend lay neatly inside. I'd inherited them all when her best friend died, and I cherished every scripted word. I felt drawn to them some days, especially when I was down. I traced Grandma's elegant script with my fingertips, remembering her at her desk, writing letters while I trudged through homework on the sofa.

Grandma had loved writing letters. And she had loved me. Flaws and all.

It wasn't easy to take someone at their worst. I knew that. And I thought of how much I put Grady through in the past few days. Things had been going swimmingly before Kai Larsen's death, but Denise was right: we'd had nothing to argue about then. Now, our mutual love of finding answers to questions, which had brought us together, threatened to pull us apart. I could hear the growing tension and distance in his tone when we talked and feel it in the vibe settling over me, day by day. Grady had to be careful who he loved, because his life wasn't about him alone. He had Denver to think of. And they'd both lost the first woman they'd loved. Now Grady was with me, and I'd nearly been killed by four homicidal maniacs in two years. I wasn't honestly sure I was the best woman for their lives. Though, I selfishly wanted to be.

I never meant to make his life more difficult when I snooped. I didn't intend to worry him or cause him undue problems. But I also couldn't sit politely aside while someone I knew was in danger, or in this case, being framed for murder. And changing who I was for Grady, or anyone else, didn't seem wise.

"I wish you were here, Grandma," I whispered, knowing she would tell me to trust my instincts and let the rest work itself out. Grandma had had an unparalleled sixth sense about everything from people to the weather. If she were here, she'd know exactly what to do about Grady, and she'd probably have already fingered the killer.

If only I could channel a little bit of her right now.

I set my face against my hands and clung to the notion that the universe was in control, a stance I regularly wavered on, according to my best interest.

My phone buzzed and I started, then flipped it over immediately.

Grady had finally responded with a tiny, two-word text. **Breakfast tomorrow?**

I smiled as I replied, hoping he wanted to see me because he missed me, and not because he wanted to yell at me in person. My thumbs dashed over the little keyboard.

My place. Lemon cake and coffee.

And his timely response: **See ya soon Swan**

Then one more. **Sweet dreams**

I set the phone on the desk, then tucked Grandma's

letters back into the little chest. When I closed the top, a framed photo of Grady, Denver, and me at Christmas came into view, previously blocked by the raised lid. I'd set the old family frame in my line of sight months ago so I could sneak peeks at it when I curled in the chair with a good book.

We'd taken Denver to see a massive holiday lights display on the mainland and bought matching hats with giant stuffed elf ears sewn to their sides. We looked like a family, and that night, we'd felt like one too. I'd marveled at the notion, while smiling at onlookers and holding Grady's hand. I'd never felt more anchored or at home in my life.

My instincts said it wasn't time to let that dream go.

I stretched onto my feet with a yawn and collected my tepid tea. If Grady was coming over for breakfast, I needed a good night's sleep and plenty of time to prepare.

A shadow box I'd filled with treasures from the man who'd commissioned my home caught my eye, and I paused in the doorway. Folks from all over the world had hunted high and low for the priceless items in that box. One individual had even killed to get their hands on them.

I extinguished the lamp, then slid the bookcase back into place, an old idea blooming in my tired mind. *Follow the money.*

The details of Kai's death rolled around in my head as I went to my bedroom. There were only a handful of reasons for murder, and most of them led back to money. Money was security, and it was status. Enough money granted power and influence. A scorned wife, for example, stood to gain the whole of the marital empire, instead of dividing it in divorce. Teammates who gained notoriety in the reigning king's absence would receive money too. They'd also gain the status and visibility associated with becoming top banana. And of course, there was the manager, who'd likely get a lot more sponsorships for a surfer willing to behave.

I tried hard to shake my feelings about Mr. Osier, not wanting to create a theory I would, possibly incorrectly, become focused on solving, and as a result, overlook more important clues. But it bothered me deeply that Osier tracked his clients. That he'd been the one to find Kai's body and that he'd shown up to take Ava away tonight.

I slid beneath my comforter and set my alarm for five-thirty to get a jump start on the day. After I had breakfast with Grady, I'd find a way to orchestrate a meeting with Tara and possibly make a trip to Rodanthe afterward.

∾

I jolted out of bed a few minutes before my alarm sounded. The world was dark outside my window, but unlike the sun, I had lots to do and no time to delay rising. I hustled into the shower to get started.

By the time Grady arrived, I'd dried my hair into a manageable mess, applied my aunts' Bee-Loved lip balm and a little mascara. I'd slipped into my best-fitting jeans, meaning I could button them and still breathe, and a periwinkle polo shirt with the Sun, Sand, and Tea logo.

I answered the door with a tight smile, unsure if breakfast would go well—or incredibly poorly. "Hey."

"Morning," Grady said, stepping inside, cowboy hat in hand. His gray eyes twinkled at the sight of me. "You okay?"

"Yeah," I said, taking my first full breath of air since I'd woken. "You?"

"Yeah."

"Is this stuff coming in or going out?" he asked, nodding to the last three boxes stacked beside my front door.

"In, but I'll grab them later."

"Or," he said, bending to lift the stack with ease. "You can hold the door, and I can help you now."

I slipped past him in the threshold and onto the porch. It would've taken me three trips to carry the boxes, and I might've blacked out by the third. "Were you able to pull any fingerprints from the arrows?" I asked, tugging the door shut behind him, then leading the way upstairs.

"Yeah." He followed on my heels, then set the boxes on my kitchen counter. "All Matt's."

I hung my head momentarily, then headed for the coffee pot. "Well, at least he has an alibi. He was at play practice when I got there." Though, he hadn't actually spoken to anyone yet. I chewed my lip, knowing Grady probably had this information by now.

"Whoever delivered the arrows left your place before you," Grady said. "Seems likely that person would've also reached the amphitheater before you. Anyone speak to Matt last night before you? Can someone give an estimated time for his arrival?"

I growled. "This is madness. You know that, right?"

Grady took a seat at the island. "I will admit, Matt doesn't strike me as homicidal, but my job isn't to determine his mental state or emotional capabilities. I'm here to follow facts."

I slid a mug of coffee in his direction, then poured one for myself. "Any idea who might really be behind all this?"

"Maybe." Grady lifted sharp gray eyes to mine over the rim of his mug. "I was promised lemon cake."

I smiled, and he took a long pull from his coffee. I retrieved the cake I'd been saving, then sliced two thick pieces and plated them for us.

Grady reached for his with greedy hands. "Thank you." He sank the tines of his fork into a chunk with icing, then closed his eyes as he brought it to his mouth and chewed.

I waited, hoping the cake would work its magic and soothe his soul.

"Tell me about your new car," he said, digging in for another bite and looking more relaxed by the second. "Where did that come from?"

I set my mug down with a small clatter. "Did someone complain? Because I can't help it. I plan to get to a mechanic as soon as I have some time."

Grady laughed. "No complaints yet, but it was pretty loud when I called. You said you can't turn the radio down?"

"Nope, and there's a Beach Boys eight-track tape that won't eject. The darn thing rewinds and starts over every time I start the car. I have to listen to the same song at top volume whenever I leave the house." I lifted my mug again, recalling his other question. "Aunt Fran gave me her old Bug, Dharma."

Grady's lips quirked and twitched as he chewed, obviously suppressing a laugh. "Which song?"

"You heard it."

His eyes twinkled. "Yeah, but tell me."

"'I Get Around.'"

Grady barked a laugh, and the story was almost worth the frustration when his dimple sank in.

"New subject," I said. "Who are your suspects for Kai's killer?"

Grady shook his head. "New subject."

I ground my teeth a minute. There wasn't a point in pressing him on the investigation directly, so I altered my question. "Were you able to get the blog post taken down last night?"

"Yeah." Grady paused, and something flitted across his expression, there and gone before I could name it. He went back to his cake. "It took a little longer than I would've liked, but I think we handled it before any real damage was done."

My intuition spiked. "Good." I nodded, watching him for clues about what he was hiding. "How?"

Grady rubbed a finger across his jaw, and I gaped.

"You are hiding something! What is it?" I demanded. "Is it about this case?"

He turned a droll expression on me. "Everly. I am hiding everything I know about this case."

We stared at one another while I backtracked over the conversation and pointedly ignored his statement. An intended distraction.

A total impossibility occurred to me. I rolled it through my mind a few times before speaking the words aloud. "You know who runs the *Town Charmer*."

His eyes narrowed by a fraction, confirming my guess.

"Shut. Up." I slapped a palm onto the counter between us. "Tell me everything immediately."

He grinned.

I inched into his personal space, my smile growing with each step. "Tell me. Tell me, tell me, tell me."

Grady shook his head. "I can't," he said, lifting both palms in surrender. "I promised."

My phone rang, and I cast a sideways look at it, already hating the caller for the untimely interruption. I didn't recognize the number, but I'd given Tara Larsen my card the last time I saw her, and there was a slim chance it was her, ready to confess.

"Don't move," I told him, then I reached for my phone. "Hello?"

"Ms. Abernathy?"

I blinked. "Who?"

"Oh, dear," the voice spluttered. "My apologies. I was trying to return a call to Ms. Millicent Harlow Abernathy. She left a voice mail message requesting a reservation for tea."

"At Subtle Teas?" I asked, stepping away from Grady.

I ran for the pen and paper, attached to my refrigerator by magnets. "Sorry. That's me. I must've misunderstood. I'm a little hard of hearing."

Grady raised his brow, then lifted his mug to smiling lips.

"Well," she yelled into the receiver, apparently believing my lie. "I have a teatime available for two at eleven o'clock today. Will you be able to make it?"

I pumped a fist. "Yes! Perfect! I'll see you then."

Grady grinned as I disconnected and checked the time. "Should I even ask?"

"Depends. Are you available for a reconnaissance mission

at Subtle Teas around eleven? That Eloise and her fancy two shoes are my new competition. I'm going undercover so I can see what I'm up against."

Grady abandoned his last bite of cake, rounding the island instead to pull me near. "That teahouse has nothing on you, but I like this as your new focus. Any chance I can convince you to give up my investigation fully and immerse yourself in this one instead?"

I frowned at him as he clasped his hands behind my back. "So, that's a no for tea?"

"I would if I could, but I promised Denver I'd have lunch with him on the playground today. The school's having a Date with Dad at eleven-thirty, and since not all the kids have dads, I signed up to stand in for whoever needs one. Which brings me to my next question."

I warmed impossibly further to him as I stared into his sincere, unreasonably handsome face. "You need lunches to impress a dozen first graders?"

"Yes, but if it helps, you should know I'm willing to pay any price."

"Is that right?" I asked, and my heart fluttered as I leaned in to collect.

CHAPTER
EIGHTEEN

"How do I look?" I asked Denise, adjusting my hat and glasses.

She slid her disbelieving gaze to Aunt Clara, at my side, then dragged her attention slowly back. "You look like a middle-aged librarian. Remind me why?"

"I have reservations for two at Subtle Teas." I tugged the hem of my navy suit jacket and pencil skirt, then jammed another bobby pin into my too-tight bun for good measure. The suit was more than a little snug, but it was something I'd never normally wear, so I considered that a win. The pillbox hat and wire-rimmed glasses were icing on my not-so-subtle disguise. "I don't want to be recognized," I said, lowering my voice and checking the café for obvious eavesdroppers. "I just want to see what her place is all about, hopefully ebb my worries, and maybe enjoy a few scones. I don't need any more of my insecurities exposed while I'm at it."

Denise softened. "What's the plan?"

"I'm going to be polite but discreet, and avoid eye contact

and unnecessary conversation with the servers and staff whenever possible."

"I see," Denise said, not looking convinced. "Well, I can't wait to hear about it in an hour or so."

"Make it two," Aunt Clara said, nudging me toward the door.

"It was nice of Aunt Fran to watch the store for a while," I said, as Aunt Clara piloted us down Middletown Road in her Prius. "Are things improving for her?"

"A bit," she said. "Fran seemed glad to be back behind the counter at Blessed Bee. I'm sure it's a welcomed change of pace."

"Sometimes we all need a little break," I said. "How about you? How are you doing?"

"I'm planning a weekend off after *The Lost Colony* wraps up," she said. "I thought throwing a couple of fundraisers for the play would be easy exposure for my new branch of the Society for the Preservation and Retelling of Unrecorded History. Turns out, supporting a play as big as this one is incredibly time-consuming. And I'm exhausted." She hit her turn signal outside the teahouse parking lot, then looked at me with keen interest. "Matt resigned from his role as longbowman this morning."

I gaped. "You're kidding. I thought he loved doing the play."

"He does, but you know Matt. He wasn't thinking of himself. He said he didn't want the negative press surrounding him to make a black mark on the play this year or on its long and respected history."

I sighed inwardly. He'd said as much last night. "How will they find a replacement?"

"I'm not sure they can," Aunt Clara said. "Matt's very good." She parked the car, then dropped her keys into her purse. "Are you ready?"

"Absolutely."

We marched along the walkway at a slug's pace while Aunt Clara admired every bush, tree, and plant. "Marvelous," Aunt Clara repeated, impressed with every bud. "These aren't easy to grow," she mused. "I wonder what her secret is?"

I focused on the door ahead of me. I had similar plants in my gardens that didn't look half as vibrant or full. The green thumb gene had skipped me. Even my houseplants looked as if they'd like to move.

I waited impatiently on the welcome mat while Aunt Clara played with the adorable whirligigs on her way to join me.

Then I opened the door and led the way inside.

Subtle Teas was impossibly warm and inviting, and apparently everyone had gotten the memo. Every table in sight was filled. Couples, friends, and families shared tea, smiles, and laughter. The gentle clink of silverware on plates and clatter teacups on saucers echoed in the sweetly scented air. And I was annoyingly excited to be there.

Aunt Clara stopped at my side with a little gasp. "Wow. She's really busy."

"Yep," I agreed, gaze settling on an empty table overlooking the sound.

"Welcome!" A middle-aged woman strode confidently in our direction. Her cream blouse was tucked neatly into wide-legged black dress pants with a cinching gold belt. She was tall, but not lean, and evidently trying hard to make a good impression. Her kitten heels clicked briskly across the refinished hardwood floors. "We're so glad to have you with us today," she said, reaching the wooden podium before us.

Aunt Clara beamed. "Well, thank you. We're excited to be here."

The woman scanned her paperwork, a broad smile fixed in place. "Ms. Millicent Harlow Abernathy and guest?" she asked, looking from Aunt Clara to me, then back.

"Clara," my aunt said, with an odd expression. I wondered if she'd considered giving a fake name too.

"I'm Eloise," the woman said. "Owner and sole proprietor of Subtle Teas. I'll show you to your table, then give you a few minutes to settle in and look at the menu. Follow me."

Aunt Clara and I obeyed, eagerly falling into step behind her as she led us across the first floor toward the table I'd spotted at the window.

Classical music lifted from carefully hidden speakers, raising the mood and setting a lovely ambience.

The decor was profoundly white, with elegant accents in muted shades of pink, mauve, sage, and gray. Paintings of the English countryside and floral arrangements lined the walls. The tables boasted crisp white linen cloths and small vases with fresh lilacs and roses or tulips and daffodils.

"This home was built nearly one hundred years ago," Eloise said, stopping at a beautifully set table. "It was commissioned by Jon and Mary Deeter who lived here for more than fifty years. They were lifelong residents of Charm, who raised their son, Mark, right under this roof." She smiled, then extended an arm, as if we might suddenly see Mark run past.

I hoped we wouldn't.

"The property transferred to Mark following the deaths of Mr. and Mrs. Deeter. Mark was married to his job in Dallas and never had children. He planned to retire in Texas, so after holding onto this place for years, he put it on the market," Eloise said. "A young couple saw the listing online and knew it was meant for them, so they went out on a limb and purchased it. They had big plans and a small budget, but they were resourceful and determined. They sought state and federal grants to fund some much-needed updates, and in the process, the wife discovered she was a distant relative of the Deeters." Eloise paused for maximum effect. "Mark was so pleased to discover his childhood home had found a way to stay in the family that he instructed the couple to send him any bills the grants wouldn't cover. He vowed to support their efforts, regardless of cost."

Aunt Clara and I lowered into our seats, enraptured by the story.

Eloise beamed back. She pushed a swath of sleek salt-and-pepper hair behind one ear, hooking it around the stem of her tortoise shell glasses. "When the couple listed the renovated home as available for rent, I snapped it up. The new mayor allowed the property to be used commercially, and that is the story of how the Deeter estate became Subtle Teas."

Aunt Clara clapped silently. "Bravo. You have a real knack for storytelling."

Eloise smiled, then took a bow. "I've always had a bit of a flair for the dramatic."

"How are you with a longbow?" Aunt Clara asked.

I pressed my lips tight to stop my mouth from falling

open. Bringing up anything related to Matt could draw too much undue attention and keep Eloise around. I just wanted to sample her foods and get out.

"Are you talking about *The Lost Colony*?" Eloise asked, suddenly looking less like a proper tea shop owner and more like a run of the mill gossip. "I've been following that story. Half the island was in love with that hunky, shirtless bowman. Can you believe he turned out to be a murderer?"

"Untrue," I muttered, fixing my eyes on the views through the window.

"He killed a surfer with his bow from the play," she said, excitedly filling me in. "It only took a single arrow to knock him right off his surfboard, midwave. The coroner doesn't even know if it was the arrow that killed him or if he drowned."

I bit into the sides of my cheeks and nearly swallowed my tongue trying not to set her straight.

Aunt Clara watched me as if I might explode. "That's not exactly how it happened," she said. "Matt's a wonderful person. Definitely not a killer, and I'm afraid this was all an unfortunate mix up."

I peeked back at Eloise, hoping she'd accept Aunt Clara's truths and spread those around like she was spreading the lies.

Eloise's eyes widened. "You know Matt Darning?"

Aunt Clara nodded. "Quite well."

I lifted a waiting menu as a distraction, then poured myself into reading every word. The single-page list was neatly printed on high-quality linen cardstock with embossed golden script. The choices were impossible, each sounding better than the last. I'd have to try everything to form an educated opinion on my competition's abilities in the kitchen.

"I heard that Matt and Kai had a huge blowout in front of an audience that same night," Eloise went on. "Their fight completely disrupted the play's practice, then Matt stormed off with a black eye."

Aunt Clara's frown deepened. "That's not wholly accurate."

"No, it is," Eloise said. "My hostess, Kate, was at the amphitheater last night, talking to folks about how they're doing after witnessing something so traumatic. I sent a ton of food and tea to the cast and crew. Kate was generous enough to handle setup and teardown for me. I'm always saying how important it is to reach out to folks when they're hurting. People just don't care about one another like that anymore."

I dropped my menu and my hands to the table. "I'm ready to order."

Eloise blinked, then regained herself, morphing back to the tea shop proprietor who'd welcomed us. "Of course. What can I bring you?"

I ordered the full service tea for two, then sent Eloise away.

"Did you hear that?" I asked Aunt Clara, seething, as I leaned across the table toward her.

Aunt Clara's thin brows knitted. "Yes. Fascinating. This house found its way back to the bloodline who built it. I've heard rumors that island properties did that, but I've only known of one for sure." Her eyes sparkled as she looked to me.

Magnolia Bane, the young woman my home had been commissioned for, was a distant cousin of mine.

"Quite magical," Aunt Clara mused.

I dipped my chin and fixed my most serious expression on her. "That was your takeaway from the conversation? That old island houses somehow convince specific people to buy them?"

"Well, that," she said quietly, her gaze sliding to the hall where Eloise had disappeared. "And the fact Eloise has a lot of faulty information regarding the details of the crime."

"Yes," I said. "Because she is obviously a shameless gossip. She probably only sent food to the amphitheater last night so her server could find fuel for the rumor mill." Heck, Eloise had probably only opened Subtle Teas to get the town tea, not serve it.

"Well, I'm not sure I disagree," Aunt Clara said, "but isn't that good news for you? You're currently collecting details on the situation with Matt, and there's usually a nugget of truth in every lie."

Eloise reappeared with our tea, and Aunt Clara and I stopped talking. She set two teapots, cups, saucers, and a delicate looking pitcher with creamer on the table between us, then added a small bowl filled with sugar cubes. "Your teas today are honeysuckle lavender and ginger strawberry." She pointed to one pot, then the other. "Pots are bottomless, so let me know if you need more. The food will be out shortly. My staff is working on that right now. If there's anything else I can get you, just let me know."

I chewed my lip, then lifted a finger.

"Yes?"

"I was just wondering if you know anything about that poor surfer," I asked, busying myself with pouring and fixing a cup of tea while I asked. "I mean, it must be awful for his family, not being here when he passed."

Eloise's eyes flashed with mischief. "He was married," she said, a coy smile on her lips. "His wife's actually in town. I invited her and a guest for tea yesterday. When she got here, she wasn't even wearing black."

Remembrance sparked in my mind. I'd totally forgotten Tara had been on her way here when she'd blown me off.

"She met a man," Eloise said, without waiting for me to ask. "He was handsome. A little older than her, but he didn't seem to be related. They smiled a lot."

"Flirting?" I asked, bringing my jealous boyfriend idea back from the theory pile. Maybe Tara was seeing someone too? Maybe he'd gotten tired of sitting on the sidelines?

Eloise's wrinkled lips curved slightly upward, as if savoring the fact she knew something I didn't, and clearly enjoying that power. "They certainly seemed amiable," she said finally, her voice lifting with pleasure.

I wasn't sure how many people Tara knew in town, but Mr. Osier was more than a little older than her, and Locke, the second male surfer, was definitely younger. "What did the man look like?" I asked.

"Midthirties. Brown hair and eyes. Clean cut."

I pulled out my phone and searched for Surf Daddy.

"Oh," Eloise whispered, throwing her hand over my phone. "No phones." She pointed to a tapestry on the far wall.

A sprinkling of colorful flower petals floated over pretty

red letters that spelled out, *Leave Your Phone Alone*. Followed by an *X*, an *O*, and *Thank you!*

I rolled my eyes, then pulled my phone against my chest, shaking away Eloise's hand and warning her with my eyes. "Is this the man?" I turned the screen to her, and she looked instantly.

"It is!" she said.

I set the phone aside and pondered. When I'd seen the Surf Daddy station wagon, I'd assumed James was on his way to talk with Osier.

The front door opened, and Eloise scurried away, meeting the next guests.

I sipped my tea, which was unquestionably delicious.

Aunt Clara poured a second cup. "This is excellent." She dropped a sugar cub into the steaming contents and swirled it with a tiny spoon. "Fran and the ladies from Crooked Oaks really enjoyed the service when they came. I'd never thought of retiring until I met them, but they sure make it look like fun."

"What would you do with all your time?" I asked, smiling at the idea.

"I'm not sure. Probably dive into my role with the unrecorded history society. Maybe travel the islands, speaking with other local historians, sharing legends and tales. Or visiting schools and nature centers with one of our hives. I miss teaching the occasional class about our precious American honeybees."

"You'd be great at all those things," I said. "I think you should go for it, when you're ready. So long as you don't sell the homestead and become a Corker."

She laughed. "I couldn't keep up! Those ladies are busier than any of my bees. They have daily itineraries, and when they can't find something to do, they bring in speakers to entertain them. It's not the kind of place where old people go to die," she added seriously. "There's simply no time." She set her teacup aside and smiled brightly, clearly struck by inspiration. "You should offer to present one of your cooking classes there! It would be a wonderful gift for those who couldn't get out to come see you earlier this week."

Eloise reappeared with her tray and our goodies before I could respond. "Strawberry soup," she said, placing a bowl before each of us. "And hand-tossed greens with homemade vinaigrette." She positioned the small salad plates beside the soups. "Be right back."

We barely finished the delicious offerings before she returned to collect the bowls and plates.

Next, she set two three-tiered serving towers between us. "For your savory tastes, we have mini ham and leek quiche. Smoked salmon, goat cheese, and dill with shaved onion, truffle mushroom choux and, of course, a traditional cucumber sandwich on crustless white."

I felt the drool begin to form.

"On the second tier, we address your sweeter side," she said. "There are mini meringues, raspberry tarts, and lime cheesecakes, along with an assortment of chocolates, including chocolate mousse shots. Homemade scones and cream are on the bottom."

The door opened again, and Amelia waltzed inside.

Her cheery smile faded at the sight of me and Aunt Clara.

"I'll be right with you," Eloise called over her shoulder.

I lifted a finger to my lips, indicating Amelia shouldn't give me away.

Eloise spoke with her briefly, then vanished into the kitchen.

Amelia hurried to our table, an apologetic and somewhat confused expression in place. "I am so sorry," she whispered. "I know how bad this looks, but I swear it's not what you think."

"You're getting your tea from somewhere else?" I asked, trying not to sound hurt.

Her eyes went round like saucers, and her lips tipped low at the sides. "Not tea," she said. "Never tea."

"Then what?"

Amelia's shamed gaze flickered to Aunt Clara, then back to me. "Eloise brought some samples to my shop last week, and I couldn't help myself. I only meant to have a taste, but things got out of hand."

"How?" I asked, unable to rein in the shock of seeing her here. "What does she have that I don't?"

"Nothing." Amelia shook her head definitively. "It's not like that with her, and I was planning to tell you. I just didn't know how."

"Tell me what you ordered," I said, more quietly this time, choked by unexpected emotion.

"Chocolate hazelnut and strawberry sandwiches," she whispered. "I've never had anything like them before. There's a hint of jam against the chocolate spread, and the berries are so thinly sliced."

A pang of betrayal and jealousy moved through my heart. "I would've made those sandwiches for you."

"I know, and I'm so sorry."

Eloise reappeared, and Amelia rushed back, pretending not to recognize me once more.

I watched her walk away a moment later, carrying another tea maker's takeout bag.

NINETEEN

CHAPTER

NINETEEN

Aunt Clara dropped me off at home on her way to Blessed Bee. I changed into my usual ponytail and jeans, stuffed bare feet into white sneakers, and tugged a logoed Sun, Sand, and Tea shirt over my head. But I wasn't ready to go to work.

All the radical gossip Eloise had proudly delivered on the topic of Kai's death made my stomach churn. How many other people did she share her false information with each day? How many of them didn't know she was wrong? And how were those people treating Matt after hearing the lies?

I'd been on the receiving end of Charm's suspicions before, and it felt nearly as awful as being wrongly accused in the first place. Our town was loving, inclusive, and loyal, but it was also composed of humans, and some were easily deceived.

I trudged downstairs, distracted, and according to my watch, I had three hours before Denise's shift ended and I needed to take over. I locked the door to my interior staircase then sneaked a peek into the café. The seats were half full, Denise was laughing with a couple near the window, and the blessed sounds of busy silverware on plates made me smile. I inhaled and savored the heady scent of sizzling jerk chicken. The mixed aromas of pineapple, sweet tea, and sugar cookies. Then I turned for my front door.

I had the life I'd always wanted, because my name had been cleared of murder when I was in the crosshairs. Now, Matt needed every hand on deck, fighting for him. And I had two good hands.

I hopped into Dharma, inspired and ready to take action. I sang along with the music as I got around to the highway and jetted toward Rodanthe. The thrill of independence was intoxicating. Never before had I been able to leave town on a whim. And I loved it. The urge to learn more about Kai's time in the Outer Banks weighed heavily on my right foot as I cruised along the highway. What had the days leading up to his death been like? Who had he spoken to? Argued with? And seen?

I didn't have a solid plan for the trip, but a visit with my new ally, Nicole, seemed like a good start.

Signs and billboards for Back to the Beach grew more plentiful as Rodanthe drew near. Cars lined the highway near the S-Curves, and the beach brimmed with blankets, small nylon tents for shade, and spectators. In the distance, surfers bobbed on boards behind others catching a wave back to shore.

I'd nearly lived under a beach tent one summer. The flat expanse of nylon fabric and retractable poles made it simple to adjust position as the sun changed direction, and I'd become a master before the Fourth of July. I spent my days people watching and reading romance novels, imagining what the tourists' lives were like when they went home, and dreaming of my future. There were often bonfires at night, and the ocean was right there for me all day if I got too hot or restless.

I slowed at the sight of Matt, seated on the hood of his truck, watching the surfers in the distance. He turned as I drew near, likely startled by the Beach Boys. I parked beside him and cut the engine.

He patted the space beside him, and I headed in his direction. "Are you following me?" he asked, a small, crooked smile on his tanned, handsome face. Mirrored glasses covered his eyes.

"Yes," I lied. "I'm thinking my new car will make it easy to tail people without their knowledge."

He laughed. "You might want to turn down the radio."

"I might," I agreed.

Matt extended a hand in my direction. "Come on up."

I accepted, noting the distinct lack of electricity in his touch. Nothing like when Grady was near. I took a seat at his side, sharing the beach blanket he'd spread over the hood.

"I hear you quit the play," I said.

He turned his attention back to the waves. "And I took the mandatory time off work. Boss's orders. I guess someone contacted him this morning with concerns about my ability to perform at capacity under all this pressure."

"Who?" I asked, appalled for him.

Matt shrugged. "I don't know, but I could've guessed it was coming."

And he *had* guessed, last night when we'd talked. My

heart broke anew. There was no kinder soul than Matt's, and someone was slowly taking his every joy. The play. His job. His reputation. Even surfing. I couldn't imagine what folks would say if he was spotted on the water right now, enjoying himself, doing the thing Kai no longer could.

"What about you?" he asked. "Any problems after you got to bed last night?"

I smiled. Matt had sent several texts as I'd slid into bed, apologizing for leaving the amphitheater abruptly and asking if I wanted him to come over to stay through the night like we'd discussed. I'd declined, but I was beginning to wonder if he wanted to stay for his own reasons as much as for my safety. Like, maybe he was sad and didn't want to be alone. He was too personable to be socially isolated and not be miserable. "Everything was fine," I assured him. "Grady came over for breakfast." I turned to watch his expression, hating the sadness in the set of his jaw. "Maybe you can come by tonight for a while," I said. "If you aren't busy."

He turned to me, lips curving slightly. "To make you feel safer? Or is this a pity friend-date for the sad sap accused of murder?" he asked. "Don't answer that. I'll probably take you up on it either way."

I laughed. "Good. I'll provide the tea."

My next stop was the Surf Daddy shop, just past the official *Welcome to Rodanthe* sign, and I pulled into the nearly empty parking lot on impulse. When I saw the woody station wagon, a thrill zipped along my spine. Maybe James could shed some light on the breakfast Kai had attended. Was he drunk and an embarrassment, or did the event go off without a hitch? I was also interested in how his tea with Tara had gone, but I wasn't sure how to bring it up.

I parked and hopped out as a group of young people in an SUV stared openly and laughed at Dharma and me. The base on their stereo blurred my eyes as they rolled out of the parking lot.

Surf Daddy was housed in a small clapboard home at the beach. The weathered wood was painted a bright yellow, and a large white vinyl sign, hanging from the porch railing, carried the company's bright blue and orange logo. The windows were covered by slatted blue shutters, which were pushed open, as were the front, back, and side orange doors.

A smaller version of the shop stood fifty yards away, at the water's edge, likely an old fishing shack turned welcome-point for students signing in for lessons.

My phone dinged with an incoming text, and I paused to check it out. Ryan's name appeared on the screen.

Ryan: Did you get my email?

I cringed. His email had been in my inbox while I'd looked into other things online, like Kai Larsen's life and the people in it, but I hadn't opened the message. I decided to be brief in my response, then read the email the moment I was home.

Me: Yep! Got it!

A series of bouncing dots appeared immediately. Then another text arrived.

Ryan: Have you spoken with the acrobats?

I snorted at the random and seemingly nonsensical question. Then I remembered he was serious. Right before the charging SUV had nearly killed me on Sea Spray, Ryan had asked me to help him surprise Amelia with a birthday party. *Cirque du Soleil meets enchanted library.*

I loved Amelia, but I couldn't get into this with him at the moment. There were more pressing issues afoot.

I typed another quick reply.

Me: Not yet.

The dots barely appeared before his response this time.

Ryan: When?

Me: Soon.

I watched as the dots bing-bonged again.

Ryan: Do you know any traveling sideshow members? Or librarians willing to play silent roles in the show? How about a magician?

I stared. Blinked. Then pocketed my phone. I definitely needed to deal with Ryan when I was home and could concentrate.

Two steps later, I watched in awe as a handsome, muscular young man I recognized from the Back to the Beach billboards and posters strode into Surf Daddy ahead of me. Locke Suarez. The same man I'd heard arguing with someone on the phone outside my home last night.

I hurried after him, admiring his perfectly fit physique and impossibly confident strides. As if the awful thing on my wrist could read my mind, the bossy bracelet buzzed and dinged.

BE MORE ACTIVE!

I slapped a hand over it, then ducked behind a rack of sunglasses and shook my arm to simulate steps. I grabbed a pair of sunglasses with my opposite hand, then jammed them on.

The Surf Daddy interior was bright and inviting. Lemon-colored walls had been outfitted with pegs and shelves to show swimsuits, surfboards, and beach chairs. Shelves and rounders of clothing, accessories, and novelties peppered the royal blue floor.

And it was completely devoid of shoppers.

Locke didn't stop moving.

I tracked him visually as he cut through the store. Then I began to inch along in his wake. I grabbed a ball cap from a table as I passed and put it on, pulling the brim low on my forehead.

"Hey," James Goodwin's voice boomed from somewhere out of sight. "Glad you could make it," he said. "Come on back."

I craned my neck from behind a bodyboard display, watching as James appeared and shook Locke's hand. The men turned down a short hallway marked Employees Only, and their voices grew muffled from distance.

I moved to the mouth of the hallway, straining to hear their conversation and pretending to look at string bikinis hung on pegs against the wall.

There was only one reason I could think of for Locke to meet privately with James like this. They were discussing the Surf Daddy sponsorship, a.k.a. money, notoriety, power, and influence. All solid reasons for murder.

What I couldn't understand was why Ted Osier, Locke's manager, wasn't present as well.

I also couldn't help wondering if the Surf Daddy sponsorship was the thing Locke had been arguing with someone on the phone about last night. His angry words warbled back through my mind. *"It was his…and it passes to me!"*

Then I recalled my latest threat. The arrows that had been delivered, only minutes after Locke had looked in my direction.

Was this the conversation he hadn't wanted me to hear?

I stared down the hall, no longer pretending to shop and considering how much closer I could get before I was caught.

An icy chill snaked down my spine before I could decide.

The fine hairs on my neck and arms stood at attention, and I knew without looking that I had a new problem. The sensation was familiar and intuitive, a sixth sense that had become steadily more profound. And came with a little puddle of heat in my core.

I turned to stare at the open front door.

A heartbeat later, Grady walked into view.

I dropped into a squat and looked for somewhere to hide, then waddled into a rounder of T-shirts.

I peered through a tangle of long shirt sleeves and considered my life choices.

Grady removed his sunglasses to scan the room. His brows furrowed, and I got the strangest feeling that he somehow sensed me too.

Belatedly, my brain began to scream. *Abort! Abort!*

I slipped free of the clothing rack and darted through the nearest exit, then around the building, realizing seconds too late that I'd unintentionally shoplifted sunglasses and a hat.

My stomach clenched while I considered my options. What was best for me? Or what was legal? I decided to come back in an hour and pay for my accidentally plundered goods. Meanwhile I'd find a place to lay low and hope Grady didn't recognize my car in the lot.

The newly formulated plan was foiled when Dharma came into view, along with the handsome lawman leaning against her door.

"Hey," I drawled, performing a little wave as I approached. "I didn't expect to see you here."

His jaw clenched and flexed, but he didn't respond.

"Do you like my new car?" I asked, patting the flower on her hood when I reached him. Then an interesting thought occurred. "How'd you know this one was mine?"

He extended an arm, pointing to the eight track tape in the dash.

"Okay," I hedged, "but how'd you know to look in there? What made you think I was here at all?"

Lines gathered on his tanned forehead. "I don't know."

"You don't know?" I tented my brows when he didn't answer. "Did you follow me here?"

"No. I came here to talk with James Goodwin. I walked inside, assuming you were somewhere mucking up my investigation, and hoping you weren't in mortal danger, then something told me to come back outside. I saw the car, then the tape, and knew you were here. I didn't see you inside. So, I decided to wait you out. We're too far away for you to walk home."

I lifted my chin and crossed my arms.

"What are you doing here?" he asked. "Tell me the truth this time. The whole truth," he added. "And don't change the subject."

"I wanted to ask James Goodwin about a publicity breakfast Kai Larsen attended the morning before his death," I said, then bit my tongue a few seconds too late. When that didn't work, I went on to explain why I wanted to know. I nearly slapped a hand over my mouth when I was done.

Grady rubbed one palm against a stubbled cheek. "Interesting. Maybe Nicole's obsession with Kai Larsen made it impossible for her to admit that he behaved so badly."

"So Osier was telling the truth?" I asked, relaxing with his willingness to discuss the situation. "That had to make him and James furious." I glanced back at the store, trying to imagine the local family man as a killer. "How did you confirm Kai's behavior? Was it on tape?" *Could I get a look at that footage?*

"I'm asking the questions," Grady said, tapping long fingers against the detective shield on his belt.

My eyes narrowed. I didn't like the implication with the shield tapping. "Are you questioning-questioning me?" I asked, daring him to say yes.

He ignored me and pressed on. "Did you speak with Mr. Goodwin?"

"No."

"Did you see or hear anything relevant to this case?" he asked.

I pressed my lips against the bubble of words expanding on my tongue. Then, it burst. "Locke is meeting with James right now. And I overheard him arguing on the phone outside my house last night, just before the threat arrived." I dished out the details without stopping for breath. Then I added my money-as-motive theory for Locke as Kai's killer.

Grady rocked back on his heels, whether in awe of my excellent info-gathering or my insightful working theory, I couldn't be sure. "I don't like how much thought you're giving this. Or that you're here, snooping, when I've been consistently asking you not to get involved in these things since the day we met."

"Yes," I countered, "but you've also asked me to work smarter and be careful if I must poke around. And I'm doing both excellently."

His big hands curved over his hips as he considered me. "I suppose I don't hate it when you actually answer my questions."

I smiled. "You like the money theory?" It made sense. "Locke was perpetually in second place with no hope of changing that until now. With Kai out of the way, Locke's the instant star. And let's not forget the manager, Osier," I added, still creeped out by his stalking ways and emotionless commentary on his dead client when we'd spoken outside the Charm Café. "He told me he was losing surfers due to poor behavior, following Kai's lead, which lead to sponsors pulling out of contracts."

A family with three giggling kids stopped in front of us and took pictures of Dharma, then smiled and waved as they walked away.

Grady rubbed a hand over his lips to suppress a laugh.

I pointed at him, and he went still. "I don't like you using that badge on me."

"I don't like it when I ask a question and you don't even try to answer it, which is almost every time I ask a question. You give me an intentional runaround," he countered.

"I give you a runaround because I hate when you scold me," I said. "I know you want me to leave this stuff alone, but I can't help myself."

"That's nonsense," he scolded. "Do you know how many other people live in your town? Know the victims and the accused? And never once decide to launch a personal investigation? A ton. In fact, I've never known anyone, anywhere who does what you do. You absolutely can help it," he said, emphasizing each of his final four words.

"I can't."

"You can," he said, raking his gaze over me, frustration turning to curiosity. "Why do you do this?"

"I like it." The words were out the moment I thought them.

The simple truth startled me, then hung on the ocean air between us, and Grady's lips twitched.

"Which part do you like?" he asked, shifting his weight and appraising me. "Nosing around? Stepping on my toes? Being threatened? Attacked? Abducted?"

"Not the last stuff," I said honestly. "But I like the intrigue. I like digging up information and putting the pieces together. I like asking questions and trying to beat you to the punch."

"Ah." He shook his head and averted his keen gaze as a smile slowly bloomed. "I thought that might be part of it. You know it's silly, right? You're not a detective. You run an iced tea shop. You bake and cook and make people feel like everything is going to be just fine, regardless of how awful their circumstances. That is what you do. This is not."

"Why can't I do both?" I asked, truly wondering. It wasn't often that anyone I knew was murdered, but when a case hit close to home, why couldn't I get involved? "I'm good at getting the information."

"And you're good at getting hurt." His expression froze into something like his blank cop face, then seemed to crumble. A rush of red rose up the column of his throat and colored his cheeks with pain "I don't like that," he said, voice low and gravelly. "I've already lost the first love of my life, Everly. I'm not sure I could survive losing the second."

My lips trembled, catching me off guard. Had he just called me the second love of his life? Compared me to his beloved wife? It was an honor I didn't deserve, and one I couldn't mentally manage. Before I was ready, another imperative question rose from my tongue. "Are you going to tell me you can't be with me if I don't change? Because, Grady..." I pulled in a long, steadying breath, then let out the thing that had been scaring me most. "I can't change, and I don't want to."

His handsome face crumbled, and for a moment, I assumed the answer was yes. Then, he pulled me into an embrace. He rested his cheek against my head and curled protective arms around my back. "If anyone ever asks you to change, they didn't deserve you to start with."

I set my cheek against his chest and hugged him back, but I didn't miss the fact that this time, it was him who didn't answer my question.

CHAPTER

∽

TWENTY

I pulled onto the street outside Surf Daddy feeling more confused and less enthusiastic than I had when I'd arrived. I hated being busted by Grady, but I was glad we'd talked. We hadn't had a chance to in far too long. He'd been in DC for a week helping his mother-in law, Senator Denver, move, and the night he'd returned, Kai Larsen was killed. Everything that had been stable and lovely between us before he'd gone to DC was suddenly disturbingly off-kilter, and I hated it.

At least he'd been gracious enough to return my stolen hat and sunglasses for me. He hadn't even commented on the hat's obnoxious logo, which I hadn't noticed until I'd removed it. The thick white embroidery had declared, *This is my resting beach face.*

The streets and sidewalks teemed with people as I rolled away. Shoppers and jaywalkers were out en masse, crisscrossing the main street between beach and retail establishments. I only made it a few feet before I was forced to stop for a horde of people in matching Roberts Family Reunion T-shirts.

Beyond the crowd, a white one-story building with black shingles and shutters appeared on my right. Pots of lavender plants filled the space on either side of a short walk to the door, and a black metal sign hung from white wooden posts out front. *The Write Stuff* was scripted on the sign and punctuated with the image of a fountain pen beneath.

I grinned, remembering my purpose, then carefully motored into the attached narrow lot.

A couple holding hands emerged as I reached for the front door to enter. They barely seemed to notice me, too caught up in one another's eyes. I slid around them, happy for their obvious joy and grumpy about my own current situation. Grady always assumed I was about to get myself into trouble, and it was offensive. It wasn't as if I was threatened every day. And I'd just been threatened with the arrows on my property, so I figured I had some time before he needed to worry again.

"Everly!" Nicole called, hurrying to meet me with a warm smile. "I'm so glad you came! Are you looking for invitations to a party? Something for a town event? Are you here on behalf of your great-aunt, Mayor Swan?" She motioned me inside, then opened her arms, as if to encourage me to look around. Her long dark hair was thick and pulled into a ponytail, much like my own. Though, her thin gold hoop earrings and delicate, matching necklace were far more elegant than my rubber fitness bully. My jewelry didn't even twinkle under the lights.

"I'm just looking today." I laughed. "But I might be back soon for invitations to a magical books and acrobats birthday party."

Nicole's smile thinned, but to her credit, she maintained professional composure. "Anything I can do," she said. "Count me in."

I made a trip around the store's perimeter, perusing the displays and paying special attention to the window facing the beach across the street. The Surf Daddy store was visible, as was the parking lot, but not the beach. Was that where the infamous PR breakfast had occurred?

"I specialize in invitations," Nicole said, popping up beside me, "but I carry a little bit of everything writing related. I fell in love with calligraphy in high school, and the obsession only grew. I teach classes now, if you're ever in the mood." She grinned. "And I sell all the supplies, from fountain pens and ink, to paper and wax seals."

"Wax seals?" I nodded, impressed. "Fancy."

"I try." Nicole had carried the black and white theme throughout the space, leaning heavily on the white. She'd mixed materials and fabrics in a way that gave the simplistic layout a chic and inviting feel. Very upscale modern. And expensive, based on the prices visible on the pages of open sample books.

I walked the plush cream area rugs, dragging my fingers over shaggy throw pillows in chairs and satin runners on display tables filled with candles, books, and crystal vases. "Your store is beautiful," I said, feeling a wave of fresh camaraderie as I took in the mix of romance and mystery titles on her bookshelf. "I think we're kindred spirits." I tapped a finger on the stack of novels. Each cover featured a shirtless surfer. "Mine all have cowboys, but you get it."

"I do." She laughed as she approached, a beautiful

chandelier casting rainbows across her and the whitewashed floors as she walked. "What can I say? I'm a sucker for love."

"Me too," I said wistfully.

I forced my thoughts back on track and raised my pointer finger toward the window overlooking the street and beach beyond. "You have a great view of Surf Daddy from here. I've been thinking about the PR breakfast with Kai. His manager said he showed up drunk and completely embarrassed himself and the sponsor." I turned quickly to gauge her reaction.

She blushed and glanced away. "I heard that too." She lifted one shoulder. "I didn't mean to lie. I just didn't see the point in speaking ill of the dead. Kai was already gone, and there was nothing that could be done to change or even improve the mess he made that day."

I offered an appreciative smile for her candor. "I can understand that," I said. "And you're right, what's done is done." I just couldn't help wondering if Kai's association with the family-centric Surf Daddy brand had been a detriment to overall sales.

A group of laughing women strode past the window, drawing my attention outside once more. It was funny how close Rodanthe was to Charm, and how different they managed to look and feel. "Busy day."

"Every day until fall," she said, moving into position at my side. "Tourists practically take over in the summer. Are you ever overrun in Charm?"

"No." But I'd nearly been run over recently. My gaze flicked to the bright yellow clapboard store once more. Was it possible the wholesome Goodwin family wasn't completely what they seemed? "The town council did its best to discourage tourists for decades. Aunt Fran is trying to undo a little of that now. We're run more by gossip than visitor traffic."

She laughed. "We deal with a little of that here too."

"Are there any significant Surf Daddy stories?" I asked. "The Goodwins seem like the nicest people, but I don't know them very well."

"No one knew them at all until the shop's brand took off a little while back," she said. "Well, maybe the local surfers knew James, but he rarely left the store, except to give lessons. So, the town as a whole didn't know him. His wife participated in some local events when she could, but with two small children, that wasn't often. Once the kids got a little older and James's surf lessons got really popular, everything changed all at once. Cindy dug her hands into the marketing and outreach, then suddenly, the store had lines around the building waiting for it to open. They expanded pretty quickly in response, putting out tables and umbrellas, erecting a shaved ice hut and bringing in local bands to play while folks shopped and ate. It was a lot of fun while it lasted."

I squinted through the glass at the Surf Daddy store and small matching shack.

Mr. Osier jogged across the lot toward the building, probably having tracked Locke there. Heaven forbid he miss out on a new business agreement.

I looked back to Nicole. "What happened?"

"I don't know. I hardly see anyone over there anymore, but we'll all wish the shaved ice had survived in another month or two."

I smiled, practically feeling the savage southern sun on

my skin at the thought of it. "Expanding too quickly is risky business, but that's the price of success, I guess."

Nicole leaned a hip against the nearby feather pen display. "I wouldn't know. I'm happy being this town's number one stop for stationery and writing supplies."

I felt exactly the same way. Except about tea.

"Have you made any headway on the murder case?" she asked, putting a little space between us, then circling around to the business side of her service counter.

"Not really," I admitted. "It's more complicated when everyone involved is from out of town." Except Matt. But I didn't need to learn anything more about him to know he wasn't a killer.

"Have you met Kai's wife?" Nicole asked.

I blew out a long breath. "Briefly. She's tough to nail down." And it bugged me that she hadn't seemed to care about her husband's death. For a woman who loved the spotlight, she was missing a perfect opportunity.

The other woman from Kai's life I'd talked to, however, had been an emotional mess. And she was only a teammate. Which brought me back to where I'd started. "Do you think it's possible Kai was cheating on Tara?" I asked.

Nicole pursed her lips, seeming to genuinely consider the possibility. "I don't know," she said finally. "Maybe. He seemed to love doing the wrong thing and being the bad boy. It'd become his main appeal to the fans, but I'd like to think he drew a line somewhere."

I nodded. "If Tara had time to decide on a divorce and plan a party, things probably haven't been great for them in a while."

"Sad," Nicole said.

I had to agree. "It makes sense that Tara would go to all his events if she thought he was unfaithful." Easier to keep an eye on him. Either to stop it from happening or to build her case for the split.

Nicole wrinkled her nose. "Tara never went to Kai's events. I was shocked to see her when she came to order invitations. It made more sense when I saw why she wanted them, but still. She typically stayed home and did something big to put the paparazzi's attention back on her. Not very supportive, but have you seen their Malibu estate?"

I had. The photos online were fabulous. "I wonder what made her come along this time?" Just to throw a public breakup bash? Or something more nefarious?

Nicole tapped a card against the countertop. "Maybe you can find out."

I moved in her direction. "How?"

"What would you think if I said the Goodbye to You party was still going on?" She slid the card across the counter to me. "She had me rewrite the invitations as memorial cards and mail them for her, overnight delivery."

I felt my face turn green. She'd turned the dump-him party into a memorial? "Gross."

"Yep."

I lifted the invitation and scanned for the day and time. "This is tomorrow night."

"She invited surfers, managers, sponsors, and media from all over the world," Nicole said. "If even half the invitees show, it's going to be the turnout of the century, and it's invitation only. Meaning you have to show your invite at the door to get in." She winked.

I smiled as I folded then tucked the invitation into my jeans pocket. "I see."

My mind worked overtime as I imagined showing up for the event. Crashing the memorial of someone I'd never met seemed incredibly rude, but what else could I do? Maybe just sit outside? Monitor the guests? Wait for an opportunity of some kind to strike?

I turned back to the window, my gaze drawn to the Surf Daddy shop and its nearly vacant parking lot. The missing tables, local bands, and shaved-ice hut. How much had Kai's bad boy ways hurt their sales? And how long could they stay afloat if things didn't turn around?

I thought of Mary Grace and her taunts about Eloise's tea shop. How I'd have to sell my business and my home. And I hoped the Goodwins weren't in trouble that deep.

I also hoped James's family-man image was more than the veneer of a desperate businessman-turned-killer.

"Do the Goodwins have another vehicle?" I asked, thinking of the SUV that had tried to kill me. "Besides the station wagon?"

"Mrs. Goodwin has an SUV," she said.

My muscles tensed as I formed my next question. "What kind?"

"I'm not sure. Something smallish but high end. One of those weird egg-shaped things women buy when they have to haul kids but don't want to drive a minivan." She snapped her fingers. "A Mercedes, I think. It's black."

I sighed in relief, then checked my watch. Mrs. Goodwin

hadn't tried to kill me, but my shopkeeper might if I didn't hustle. I'd been gone far longer than I'd intended, and Denise would have to leave Sun, Sand, and Tea soon.

I moved toward the door with a wave. "I've got to get back to Charm, but it was really nice talking you. Thanks again for the heads-up on that party." I patted my pocket, where I'd tucked the invitation.

"Anytime," she called as I strode into the sun.

Today had started out a little rocky, but it was definitely shaping up.

I rounded the corner to the small, attached lot where I'd left Dharma.

She had four flat tires. Each stabbed with an arrow.

"Dang it!"

CHAPTER
TWENTY-ONE

Grady drove me home more than an hour later. After the evidence had been processed. And Dharma towed.

I'd texted Denise while we waited, letting her know it was okay to close up shop at three, when she needed to leave and pick up Denver. Even if I'd somehow made it home in time to takeover at Sun, Sand, and Tea, I wasn't in any mental or emotional capacity to try. Better to call it a day four hours early and let the gossip fly. It was only a matter of time before everyone heard about what happened anyway.

Denise had been kind and comforting as usual. She was glad I was safe and with Grady, and she assured me that closing up early wouldn't be a problem. Business had been unusually slow. I could only hope it wasn't because my customers were lined up for teatimes with Eloise.

Unlike the chaos of policemen, reporters, and lookie-loos surrounding Dharma's unfortunate situation, the ride back to Charm was eerily calm. Grady hadn't even bothered to turn on his radio.

I alternated between squirming and embracing the

temporary quiet, which felt more like a brewing storm than peace.

"I'm sorry about your car," Grady said finally, after miles of charged silence.

"Thanks."

I was sorry too. This had been the first time I'd been able to leave town alone or on a whim. The independence of driving away from home had been better than any sugar high, and now the car that had made that possible was gone. At least temporarily.

I felt robbed.

Aunt Clara would say the tire stabbing was our family's curse at play. That's what I got for leaving Charm. I knew this because she also blamed the curse for the Beach Boys tape stuck in the dash. She'd told me over tea. Apparently Aunt Fran got around a little more than was acceptable in her day, and she was punished via the music situation. Fast forward several decades, and her bullheaded great-niece, a.k.a. me, didn't mind the blaring music, so I got four flat tires.

"It's fine," I assured him. "No one was hurt, and Dharma probably needed new tires anyway. Plus, you were right across the street, so that was actually good luck."

Grady slid his eyes at me, then back to the road.

The silence returned.

I locked my jaw and stared ahead. "If you're mad, then just say it."

"I'm mad," he said flatly and without hesitation.

I jerked around for a better look at him, causing the seat belt to tighten as if we'd been in an accident. "I was the victim here," I said, tugging uselessly against the crushing strap.

"Yeah, well, you're the victim more often than anyone I've ever known. At some point it becomes time to ask yourself about the common denominator."

I made my most offended face, wrinkling as many features simultaneously as possible. "Rude!"

"You're lucky none of the arrows being jammed into everything around you haven't been jammed into you. Yet." He tacked the final word on, as if what he'd described was inevitable.

"I'm figuring it out," I said. "And I'm not going to be shot with an arrow. Even Kai wasn't shot with an arrow. That was all for show. Smoke and mirrors to misdirect attention. The killer just doesn't know I know that yet, or he or she would've stopped using the arrows to try to scare me." I shot a superior look at Grady. "Where are the arrows coming from anyway?" I asked. Were they all made for the historic longbow? If so, was there somewhere people could buy them online? Could shoppers get free two-day shipping on four-hundred-year-old weaponry?

"I didn't say I was mad *at you*, by the way," Grady said, pulling my attention back to him. "I only said I was mad, and I am." He took the next exit toward Charm. "I'm infuriated that this is happening again. That every murder in a fifty-mile radius is somehow connected to you or someone you care about. That you are being threatened. On my watch. Again." He nearly growled the final word. "And there's nothing I can do about it."

I watched as the muscle along his jaw flexed and released.

I wanted to reach for him, to offer comfort in words or touch, but it wasn't like Grady to be so frank about his emotions, and I didn't want to ruin it. So I waited.

Grady stole a glance in my direction. "I'm mad that the person you're putting yourself in danger for this time is Matt Darning, the world's nicest guy, who you dated. And I'm mad at myself for being a little jealous about the lengths you will go to to protect him."

A little puff of breath escaped me, and Grady rolled his eyes.

"I realize that's ridiculous, which is why I'm mad about it," he said. "I'm a grown man. I carry a badge. I know what's reasonable and what's ridiculous, but it doesn't make it any easier. And that's all on me. Not you."

I scanned his troubled face as he pushed the painful, truthful words through tight lips. Grady Hays was jealous. And he'd admitted it. "It's almost like you're human," I said carefully, hoping he'd understand I was both teasing and encouraging him. "We all have thoughts and feelings we aren't proud of sometimes. The important thing is that you know you're being silly and aren't acting like a caveman about it."

He snorted. "A caveman?"

"Sure." I nodded. "You could be a total Neanderthal, but you're not, and I appreciate that. I think it's pretty appealing, actually."

He turned a pleased smile at me. "Yeah?"

"Yeah." I set my hand over his on the steering wheel, then lifted his fingers in mine and pressed them to my cheek. "I adore Matt," I said softly, and Grady grunted. "But I'm trying to figure out who killed Kai because I want to see justice served and my friend's name cleared." I did my best to emphasize the word friend. "Also because I've really missed doing this. No one's been accused or framed for murder in months."

Grady laughed, and his fingers relaxed against my jaw. "What am I going to do with you?"

"You could tell me more about this case," I suggested. "Maybe talking through the details will help you sort it out."

He dropped his hand, with mine, onto the seat between us. "Not having to worry about you being injured or abducted would do wonders for my concentration."

"Maybe we can revisit the self-defense lessons," I said, offering an olive branch.

"Self-defense won't protect you from arrows."

"But you will." I squeezed Grady's fingers as he pulled into my driveway and settled the engine.

He unbuckled and reached for me.

Movement near my home snapped us both to attention.

Matt jogged down the porch steps and gave an uncomfortable wave. His expression was apologetic. His stance, awkward.

Grady groaned, then climbed out.

I did the same. "Hey, Matt. What's up?"

"Sorry," he said. "I didn't mean to interrupt. I went home to shower and change, then heard a retro Volkswagen was attacked with arrows in Rodanthe and knew you were headed that way when I saw you." He shrugged. "I wanted to make sure you were okay."

"What were you doing in Rodanthe?" Grady asked.

"I was down at the S-Curves watching surfers." Matt slid his gaze to me. "You didn't tell him?"

I imagined smacking my forehead. *Or his.* "No. That didn't come up." Grady stared down at me, burning a hole in the side of my face. I refused to look up.

"I'm okay," I said, feeling strangely anxious. "Fortunately, Grady was there, so it was fine."

His eyes shifted to Grady at my side.

"So, you were in Rodanthe at the time of the crime," Grady said. "I don't suppose you have an alibi. Talk to anyone besides Everly?"

Matt shook his head. "No, and I headed home after I spoke with her."

I worked up the best smile I could manage. "At least no one was hurt. The car was probably overdue for a thorough once-over by a mechanic anyway. It's been mostly under a tarp for decades."

Grady shifted at my side. "What's the bag for?" he asked.

Matt and I turned our attention to the small duffel in his hand. "I grabbed my gym bag on the way over," Matt said slowly, his gaze sliding from Grady to me, then back. "Change of clothes, bathroom stuff."

"Matt is thinking of staying with me tonight," I said, daring a fast glance at Grady, who didn't look happy. "It's less likely anyone will bother me if he's around. And if anything else goes wrong, I'll be his alibi. It's a win-win, really."

Matt blew out a breath and raked his fingers through already messy hair. "I hate that you're wrapped up in this. I can't help feeling like that's my fault, and I want to apologize if I somehow encouraged you to get involved."

"It's not your fault," I said. "You know me. I'm always ready to dig into these things. And I usually end up with a warning or two along the way."

Both men hacked a throaty disbelieving sound.

"Okay," I said. "Sometimes I also get hurt, but that wasn't what happened today. So, don't worry about it. I'm good."

Matt nodded but didn't look convinced. "Any new ideas about who could've done this?" he asked Grady.

"Some." Grady crossed his arms and widened his stance. "I'd feel better if you could name one person who can vouch for your whereabouts at the time Everly's car was attacked."

I spun on him and frowned. "Be serious."

"I'm dead serious," Grady said, eyes fixed on Matt. "Any idea where all these arrows are coming from? I've collected nearly a dozen in the last two days."

I beamed. The arrows' origins had been my question.

Matt furrowed his sandy brows. "Actually, no. There was a limited supply at the amphitheater. A quiver full, but not more than twelve."

"The quiver we collected with your costume jacket at the crime scene was empty. Any idea where those arrows went?" Grady asked.

"No."

Grady waited.

"No," Matt repeated, his blue eyes flashing in the afternoon sun. "But I have a key to the *Lost Colony* wardrobe and supplies department. I haven't gotten around to turning them in yet. We can go and see if the arrows are there. Maybe someone put them away before heading home that night. Though I don't know why they would've left my jacket and the quiver." He dug into the pocket of his black board shorts and freed a small set of keys.

Grady dipped his chin. "I'll drive." He turned to me. "You good?"

I had whiplash from the speed the conversation had changed directions, but otherwise, I was great. Maybe even thrilled to see him work with Matt instead of against him. "Yep."

Grady kissed my cheek, then flicked a pointed gaze at Matt. "Bring your bag."

He headed back to his truck in long purposeful strides. Matt collected his duffel and followed.

Grady waited behind the wheel until I ducked into my foyer, then waved through the window to tell him I was safely locked inside.

I watched him drive away before going upstairs, then headed to my kitchen. I poured a tall glass of sweet tea, sliced a fat hunk of rum cake, then collapsed onto the couch. When the tea and cake were gone, and I was thinking clearly again, I pulled my laptop onto my legs and navigated to the *Town Charmer* for an update I could use. With a little luck, whoever was behind the blog hadn't reported on Dharma being towed, because I wanted to tell Aunt Fran the news myself.

An image of Subtle Teas appeared, and I fought the urge to stick out my tongue. A beloved local EMT was being framed for murder, and this was what the blogger had chosen to cover? It made no sense. The only thing newsworthy about the newest business in town was that the owner was a blatant gossipmonger. But I knew better than to think that was the story I'd find beneath the photo. For some reason, all the negative stories were usually about me. Or, at least, it felt that way.

Then, I saw the headline.

UNDERCOVER GOSSIP LOVER?

An image of Aunt Clara and me having tea ruined any hope I had that Eloise was being called out on her behavior. According to the text, I'd gone to Subtle Teas in disguise in an attempt to uncover information about the Kai Larsen murder by badgering the owner. "I knew Eloise recognized me!" I complained to the laptop, reading as quickly as I could. "Unbelievable!" She'd even reported that I'd asked about Tara Larsen's recent teatime!

I fought the urge to scream.

And worse, the comments were nearly sixty deep and all were appalled at my audacity.

"I was just checking out my competition!" I snapped. "Eloise is the gossip! Not me! And she was the one who'd provided all the fodder."

The article was completely unfair.

I considered creating a fake account to set all the other commenters straight, but every time I did that, they called me out.

I performed some creative swearing, then switched gears and opened my email.

Ryan's name was attached to the top four messages.

"Ugh." I hung my head and prayed for strength before jumping into that insanity.

Email one was a manifesto of sorts, outlining why Amelia was amazing and deserved to have a thirtieth birthday party she would never forget. Ryan was surprisingly enthusiastic and incredibly accurate on every count. He clearly knew her better than I thought. The two of them had been sort of long distance dating for a while, but I hadn't realized how close they'd become. Which made me wonder if I wasn't being a good enough friend to Amelia.

I slumped against my couch cushion, realizing the harsh truth. While I'd been absorbed in my new relationship with Grady for the last six months, I hadn't been properly holding up my end of the best friend deal with Amelia. And she'd been so busy being happy for me, she'd never complained.

I closed the first email, then opened the next, determined to do whatever I could to make Ryan's massive, somewhat nutso plans happen. Because he was right. Amelia deserved a birthday party she would never forget, and I was thrilled to be a part of it in any way I could.

My bracelet buzzed. BE MORE ACTIVE appeared on the tiny screen.

I shook my arm up and down as I skimmed the contents of each of Ryan's other emails.

My phone dinged, and I flipped it over on the coffee table with my free hand, balancing the laptop with my legs. Aunt Fran's number centered the screen. I swiped for a look at the message.

Fran: Clara says you'll teach a cooking class at Crooked Oaks

I shut my laptop and puffed out a breath before replying. I set the phone on my closed computer and pecked out a reply with my pointer finger, while pumping my other hand to shut up my badgering bracelet.

Me: RU sure they'd like that

Fran: Yes. Day after tomorrow? Noon?

Jeez. She already had it planned.

Eventually, I forced myself to tap the two letters she was waiting for.

Me: OK

I dropped the phone back on the table, then covered my eyes for a long beat, wallowing in the emotional overload of my day. Teatime was coming back to bite me in every possibly way. First with Eloise's ridiculous leak to the *Charmer*. Now with the cooking class Aunt Clara had suggested. I didn't mind doing the class, but I had my hands full this week already and no ideas what the folks at Crooked Oaks would want to make.

I opened my laptop and a new search window, deciding what to type first.

My phone buzzed again, this time with a text from Matt. I swiped the screen, then nearly rolled my eyes when I read the message.

Matt: Heading home for the night. Call if you need me.

Grady had officially scared him off. Hopefully that meant Grady was on his way over. I wanted to know what the pair had found in the supply closet.

I turned back to my laptop and navigated to Henrietta's button blog. Maybe a look at what the Corkers had been up to recently would spark an idea for recipes I could make, then serve as lunch. I couldn't afford to show up with some half-baked plan when at least one of these women had a YouTube channel. I had enough trouble already with the *Town Charmer*, and that was just a blog.

Henri's Happy Buttons appeared at the top of my search list, and I clicked immediately on her channel. She had dozens of videos, reaching back for more than two years. I scrolled through the topics. Jade buttons. Milk glass buttons. The history of buttons.

Henrietta was especially fond of historical buttons, and Matt, so I wasn't surprised when an episode taped at the amphitheater came up as one of her most viewed.

I started the video and watched as Henrietta interviewed members of the *Lost Colony* wardrobe crew. She asked intelligent and interesting questions about the historical accuracy of the buttons on costumes worn in the play, while including plenty of shots of Matt with his longbow, and ironically, no shirt. When the interviews concluded, the cameraperson scanned the scene, taking care to include images of the distant sea, the parking lots, trees, and seating beyond the stage.

I replayed the video when my intuition tingled and moved back to the item that had caught my eye.

A taupe-colored SUV was parked near the trees, and I was almost certain it was the same vehicle that had tried to kill me.

CHAPTER
TWENTY-TWO

I hung out with Denise the next day, splitting the café duties with her and planning for my cooking class at Crooked Oaks. We chatted between customers and did our best to catch up after missing our usual time together the day before.

She rang up the last of our lunch guests, then turned to me with a flummoxed expression. "You're sure the SUV in the video was the same one that tried to hit you?"

"Almost," I said. "I didn't get a look at the driver or plates that day, but the shape and color are the same." I hadn't even been certain of the color until I saw it on the video, then I'd been nearly positive. A little scratching sensation at the back of my mind assured me I was right. It was too bad my intuition wouldn't hold up in court. Then, Grady could figure out who owned the SUV, or had access to it the afternoon I'd been nearly run down, and make an arrest.

"You told Grady?" she asked.

"Yes, and I sent him the link to the video on YouTube. I even texted a screenshot of the vehicle in question so he wouldn't miss it. He responded with 'thanks, got it.'"

Denise frowned. "That's all he said? Weird." She lifted a rag to wipe the counter. "I wonder what he was in the middle of, because that's definitely not like him. Not in a situation like this and never where you're concerned."

I'd asked myself the same thing. Something as potentially case-breaking as footage of the killer's car was exactly the kind of news that would normally have landed him on my doorstep. He was onto something for sure, and I doubted he'd clue me in on what that was.

"Are you guys doing okay?" Denise asked, a look of concern replacing her frown.

"Better," I said. "We talked more yesterday than we have for a while. It felt nice." Until he left with Matt to explore the wardrobe and supplies at *The Lost Colony*. "He's barely responded to my texts since then."

"I'm sure he's just busy chasing a lead," she said. "But I'm glad you had the chance to talk."

I'd been glad too, at the time. I'd thought Grady and I were getting somewhere. Apparently I was wrong. Otherwise, he would've kept me in the loop.

I sighed. "Kai Larsen's murder really boggled things up for us," I said, cringing a moment later. "Not that I'm implying I have it worse than Kai Larsen." I wrinkled my nose. "You know what I mean." I waved my hands uselessly, then flopped onto a barstool at the counter.

Denise passed me a cold glass of Grandma's Old-Fashioned Sweet Tea. "I get it."

"Thanks." I took a long, deep drink of the century-old recipe and felt immediately refreshed. "My personal investigation has come up painfully short, so I'm trying to put my excess energy into planning a cooking class at Crooked Oaks Retirement Community tomorrow afternoon. Aunt Fran thought the residents would really like it, and I think she could really use the support of the group. I'm leaning toward crab cakes. If I print and laminate the recipe cards, they can keep them to use later, or give the set as a gift with some kind of cooking basket in the future."

"Nice." Denise dropped the rag, then dried her hands on a towel folded over my oven handle. "I wouldn't mind getting a gift like that."

I smiled. "I'll remember that."

My mind danced immediately away from the crab-cake concept, just as it had all morning, returning instead to the details surrounding Kai's case. I rubbed at the dull ache in my forehead. "If only I could get my stubbornly disobedient mind to cooperate."

"Anything I can help with?" she asked.

A smile spread my lips as a new, more entertaining thought arose. I still hadn't told Denise about Ryan's wild ideas for Amelia's thirtieth birthday. "Actually, yes." I bulldozed through the story, outlining all the best parts and highlighting the details from his myriad of emails.

Denise arched her back and hooted when I got to the magicians and fire eaters. She clapped silently as she straightened and cackled.

"I got three more emails this morning," I told her. "Every time something new comes to mind, he sends me a link or video about it. He's out of control."

"He loves her," she said softly, her bottom lip protruding. "The whole thing is really sweet in a big city way. She'll go crazy for all of it. She'll never see it coming. I want in. What can I do?"

"Dance in a cage?" I suggested.

She nearly collapsed from lack of oxygen with her next round of laughter.

The seashell wind chimes kicked into gear a few minutes later, and Denise wiped her eyes. "I've got this," she said. "You go online and hunt for fire-breathing acrobats."

I lifted my phone into view and opened a search engine, still giggling quietly. I navigated to the *Town Charmer* first, mostly from habit, and also because I didn't want to miss anything.

I regretted the decision immediately.

Pinning Down Our Local Sleuth Proves Trickier Than Ever

The article arranged images taken of the arrows outside my front door, alongside pictures of Dharma with arrows in her tires. I was lucky the little cartoon of my head rolling off wasn't as readily available as local police reports and cell phone photos. The horrible video would surely have accompanied the article if the *Charmer* knew it existed.

I scrolled through the post, counting my small blessing. The blogger had included details of my most recent threat in Rodanthe, allegations of Dharma violating Charm's noise ordinances, and images of me chatting up Nicole, Tara, and James. Though slightly sensationalized as usual, the article was based on facts. Unlike the bogus post I was sure Eloise had incited the night before.

My bracelet complained again, demanding I BE MORE ACTIVE, so I got off my stool to move around. I felt as if I never stopped moving, but my bossy fitness coach seemed to disagree. I swung my arms and worked my knees as I marched table to table, straightening chairs and fussing unnecessarily with a dining area Denise kept immaculate. My customers didn't pay any attention. My rocky relationship with the bracelet wasn't a secret. The *Town Charmer* could be thanked for that scoop too, after posting a photo collage of me glaring at it on a slow news day last winter. Thankfully, there had been an outpouring of camaraderie in the comments. At least I wasn't alone.

When the wind chimes sounded again, it was Tara Larsen who walked in. She wore white capri jeans with a mint green off the shoulder top and hot-pink, strappy wedge sandals. Her white leather clutch was tucked under one arm, and she'd worn her thick blond hair down, over her shoulders. She scanned the café as if she was looking for someone.

I hurried to greet her. "Welcome to Sun, Sand, and Tea." I waved and smiled, and hoped I didn't look as maniacal as I suddenly felt.

She looked me over, then selected a seat near the rear window overlooking the deck and ocean. "I hoped I'd find you here," she said quietly. Her tone was bored, but harsh, and I feared what might come next.

So, I changed the subject, hoping to cool her temper before she had a chance to yell at me. "I'm glad you came," I said, brightly.

Tara set her clutch on the table and stared. "I want to talk to you."

"Over tea?" I asked, interrupting again. "I serve twenty flavors of iced tea and a new menu almost every day. Are you hungry? Maybe we can share a meal or an appetizer and chat?" I pointed to the giant blackboard on the wall behind the counter. "Whatever you want. It's on me. Today's specials are spicy Carolina crab cakes with mango chutney, fresh avocado caprese salad, and coconut key lime pound cake."

Her gaze slid to the menu, and hope flickered in my chest. "I'll try the salad," she said. "And the strawberry mint tea."

"Excellent choices." I flagged Denise, then repeated the order for her to fill.

"I want to apologize," I told Tara, when Denise had gone. "I shouldn't have shown up unannounced the other day, or the time after that, and I'm sorry for running off the first time." I pressed my lips together and silently instructed myself to tighten up. "I'm a friend of Matt's," I said, suddenly exasperated. "I'm just trying to figure out what really happened to Kai, because there's no way Matt is responsible for his death."

"Of course he isn't," Tara shot back. "Matt's wonderful, and he's ten times the man Kai ever was. I know. I married them both." She pressed a palm to her chest, splaying white manicured nails over the pale mint material. "I loved them both, but only one of them ever loved me." Her bottom lip quivered.

I scanned the café for signs of an undercover blogger who'd report that I'd bullied a widow. "I'm so sorry. I didn't know."

I wanted to talk to Tara, but I didn't want her to cry, and I certainly didn't want to be the one who caused her tears if they fell. I yanked a napkin from the pocket of my apron and passed it to her. "That must've been awful."

She dotted her eyes and squared her shoulders, bristling at my words. "I know what you've been up to," she said, eyes narrowing. "That's why I came here. You say you're trying to help Matt, but you're really using your friendship with him to stick your nose into other people's problems because your own life is so boring. I read that blog. I know you were asking about me at the teahouse. Well, I wasn't there on some secret evil mission or whatever you're thinking. I was meeting someone on business. Not that it's any of yours. And no, I'm not some murderous gold digger who killed her rich husband so she could take all his stuff."

"I'm not trying to cause trouble," I said, wondering how things had gone so far south so quickly. "I'm trying to help Matt."

Tara leveled me with cold blue eyes, her beautiful face going feral. "You need to stop following me around. Stop slandering my name, and stop causing people to wonder if I'm homicidal."

"The article you read was sensationalized and intended to make me look bad, not you," I said. "As soon as I get the answers I need, I'll stop asking questions," I promised. "I'm glad to fill you in on what I know so far, if you'd like. Maybe you can help me fill in the holes. You knew Kai and Matt better than anyone."

She didn't walk away or tell me to go fly a kite, so I took that as permission to continue.

"I saw Kai's teammate, Ava, last night," I said. I watched Tara for a sign that Ava was the woman she suspected Kai of having an affair with, but Tara didn't bite. "She was sitting near the memorial by the amphitheater. And I heard

Locke arguing with someone on the phone about something he thought should be his," I said, testing another suspect's name. "I wasn't sure what he meant exactly, but I saw him at Surf Daddy meeting with James Goodwin yesterday." Now, I'd said all three names, and I waited to see which, if any, she responded to.

Tara's formerly placid expression turned livid. "Goodwin met with Locke?"

I nodded. "I didn't hear any of the conversation, but I watched them shake hands inside the Surf Daddy shop in Rodanthe, then retreat somewhere to speak privately."

Tara shoved onto her feet as Denise approached with her meal. She dug in her clutch and freed a set of bills, then tossed them onto the table, obviously furious. "Keep it and the change. I have to talk to my lawyers." She pulled a cell phone from her purse and tapped wildly at the screen.

"Is Locke angling for the Surf Daddy sponsorship?" I asked, unable to stop myself.

"Of course he is," she screeched. "It's a huge opportunity for exposure, and if they revise all the promo work to feature Locke, I won't see a penny of the cash owed Kai. I haven't even buried him yet, and the runner-up is already trying to take his place! What are managers for if they don't stay on top of sponsorships?" she ranted, raising the phone to her ear.

"Osier was there too," I said. "I saw him arrive a short while after Locke."

Tara jerked her eyes to mine. "Why are you still doing this?" she asked. "Why are you involved at all? None of this has anything to do with you. Just go away."

She spun on her sandals and marched off, head high and cell phone at her ear. A woman seated at the table near the doorway gaped, and Tara screeched. She grabbed the back of an empty chair and toppled it with one strong pull. "Stop staring!"

"Wait," I called, rushing after her, and picking up the chair as I passed. "Sorry!" I told the woman, then I kept running. "Tara, wait!" I came to an abrupt stop on the porch. "I didn't mean to upset you. I just want to talk."

She turned to face me, eyes hard and body rigid. "People are right about you! You're nosy! You need boundaries! And you're going to get yourself in some real trouble if you keep it up! So, go away!" She dropped behind the wheel of a small white convertible and drove away, while I stared after her.

Tara Larsen might've been planning to leave her husband, but after an outburst like that, I still wasn't convinced she hadn't killed him.

CHAPTER
❧
TWENTY-THREE

I didn't hear back from Grady all day, and I was in a snit by dinner. I had too much anxious energy and too many unanswered questions to manage a proper level of enthusiasm for customers, and more than one had ordered their meals to go.

I considered going for a long, brisk walk, or a swim, anything to help me settle down, but those things would only have fatigued my body. They wouldn't have quieted my mind.

Only one thing was going to do that.

I propped the invitation to Kai's memorial against my mirror while I dressed for the party. So far, none of my direct confrontations or face-to-face inquiries had turned up enough evidence to point me in any clear direction, so it was time to try something new. Tonight, I was going on a stakeout. I couldn't afford to ring the bell and crash the event after Tara had confronted me. But I could park outside her beach house and see what happened. Maybe witness or over-hear something useful. I decided to dress the part of a guest in case I was spotted. The last thing I needed was for Grady to show up because someone reported a lurker on the street.

The simple black A-line dress I'd selected was form fitting, hit just above my knee, and required my strongest Spanx. I'd broken a sweat wrestling the torture device onto my body and could've used another shower, but considering I'd probably have to cut myself out of the unforgiving material, I decided to lie on my bed and cool off instead.

The ceiling fan spun wildly above me as I struggled to catch my breath. I rolled onto my side, gingerly sipping in air. The industrial-strength fabric seemed to have smoothed my middle by relocating all my internal organs to somewhere beneath my rib cage, then pushed the contents of my bra beneath my chin like a beard.

I rolled off my bed, then moved breathlessly to the door. I rested a palm on the wall for support as I slipped my feet blindly into pumps I couldn't see over my amplified bust. Thankfully, I'd blown out my hair and added smooth, uniform barrel curls and makeup before getting dressed. Lifting my arms too high or repetitively now would likely cause a costume malfunction of Janet Jackson's Super Bowl halftime proportions.

I grabbed my keys and largest black purse, prepacked with snacks, bottles of water, and my e-reader, in case the party dragged on too long. I'd forbidden myself from making a casserole—because no decent southern woman would go to a memorial empty handed—and without it, I couldn't get any crazy ideas about going inside. My objective was to watch, not get involved. If anyone argued or behaved in a suspicious manner, I'd take notes, and their photo, then watch to see what they drove. I was also on the lookout for the SUV that had tried to flatten me, and the person who'd been behind the wheel.

A shiver ran down my spine at the thought, and I dashed to the carriage house before I could talk myself out of going. With Dharma in the shop, I was forced to take Blue, which wouldn't have much better luck outrunning a highway-worthy vehicle than I would. A golf cart also wasn't an ideal stakeout vehicle. She wasn't nearly as inconspicuous as a car, even in Charm. But to be fair, Dharma wasn't exactly inconspicuous in any situation. So, I had a six of one, half dozen of the other situation at best.

I set Blue into motion and made it as far as my mailbox before I reconsidered bringing a casserole.

Traffic was light and the wind was brisk as I motored along the boardwalk toward Sea Spray Drive. Silhouettes of couples holding hands as they walked the beach were visible in the distance, backlit by the periwinkle hues of a recently set sun. Laughter rang out from nearby homes, accented by the splashing of water in pools and heavenly aromas of seafood on grills.

I savored the sights, scents, and sounds, treasured the moments, though they belonged to others, because I knew how quickly, and often unexpectedly, everything could change. I'd lost Grandma while I'd been away. And I'd been unexpectedly hurt by bad people more often than I liked to think about. I'd learned to hang on to the good moments while they lasted and not to take them for granted whenever possible.

The muscles of my shoulders bunched and ached with

tension, and my teeth chattered, not from cold, but from adrenaline, fear, and anticipation. One too many run-ins with dangerous people had left me a little shell-shocked, and the plan to sit outside Tara's rental, at night, in a golf cart, had me severely on edge. Fortunately, the emotional attacks and flashbacks came only from time to time, and rarely lasted very long. I'd become an expert at pushing through them.

A dark sedan turned onto Sea Spray Drive ahead of me, and I slowed, hoping to avoid the driver's attention. The car parked outside the rental I planned to watch. I drove past, went to the end of the block, and turned around. I parked across the street, several houses away.

Mr. Osier climbed out of the car and buttoned his suit jacket before jogging up the steps to ring the bell.

Dozens of vehicles lined the street in both directions. I'd been fortunate to slide Blue between two late-model SUVs. The space was too small for a car, but just right for a golf cart, and the size of my current bookends would make Blue nearly invisible at this distance from the party. Thankfully, I'd packed my binoculars.

I settled in to watch guests flow in and out of the home, most wearing black, all dressed to the nines. It was easy to guess the surfers and their dates from the sponsors and managers. The latter two seemed to all be middle-aged and slightly out of shape, but with the confidence and swagger that often came with too much money. The ones I pinned as surfers and their dates looked as if they could qualify for *Sports Illustrated* cover models. Even from a distance, it was easy to see they were in the prime of their lives and knew it.

Bistro lights glowed and bobbed over the rear decks and

around the pool behind the home, partially visible from my position. Music drifted softly from outdoor speakers. Overall, Kai's memorial seemed to be a respectful, understated event. Not a ploy for attention from Tara, as I'd originally suspected. Though it was impossible to know what was going on inside.

Movement caught my eye at the end of the block, and I used my binoculars to take a closer look. Locke strode up the sidewalk toward the home, fastening the button on his iridescent navy blue suit jacket. He took the steps two at a time, then ran a hand over his hair when he rang the bell. A moment later, the door opened, and Locked stepped inside.

I examined the other vehicles before putting my binoculars down. Most were high end, and many had bumper stickers from rental companies. No sign of the SUV I feared most, but James Goodwin's station wagon was parked three vehicles away.

"Seems like the gang's all here," I whispered, cracking open a bottle of water, then liberating my bag of Her Majesty's Munch Mix. "Now, I wait and see."

I alternated between noshing handfuls of the caramel corn, pretzel, and potato chip snack and peeking through the binoculars. When my fingers brushed the bottom of the bag, I frowned. An incoming call from Grady interrupted my confusion. Surely there was a hole in the bottom of my bag. I turned my phone around to answer as I confirmed the shocking truth. I'd somehow eaten all Her Majesty's Munch Mix, and I hadn't been on my stakeout for a full thirty minutes. At this rate, I'd run through all my snacks inside an hour.

The phone rang again, and I refocused on a new conundrum. Why on earth was Grady calling? He never called. He was always in a hurry, and preferred saving conversation for moments when we were together. I wet my lips and steadied myself for whatever might've happened to cause the call.

"Hello?" I crumbled the empty munch mix bag, then stuffed it to the bottom of my purse and pulled the other snacks onto the top.

"How's it going?" he asked.

"Okay," I said, suddenly hyperaware he wouldn't approve of my mission. "Having a little snack."

"Oh, yeah? Anything going on tonight?" he asked. "I was thinking of coming over."

"No." I stilled, then peered across the street at the house with every one of my suspects inside. "Tonight's not a great night for me," I said. "How about breakfast?"

"I hope nothing's wrong," he said, a strange edge to his tone. "Maybe there's something I can do to help."

I shook my head, a thread of panic rising in me. I was fibbing again, exactly the way he'd asked me not to. "I'm just...tired," I said. That was true enough, though I didn't think it counted as being truthful.

A new set of headlights swung into view, and I ducked as they drew near. The lights blinked off directly across the street from me, and Matt exited his truck. I slumped in my seat, hoping he wouldn't notice me. "Hold on," I whispered to Grady, tipping over in Blue's front seat.

I listened as the sounds of Matt's dress shoes against asphalt moved swiftly away.

"I guess you are tired," Grady said, his voice coming in stereo, both through the speaker and directly above my head.

I started and jerked upright.

He glared down from Blue's passenger side, wiggling the cell phone in his hand.

"Oh," I uttered, at a complete loss for words.

"Yeah. Oh," he said, moving my purse out of his way and taking a seat beside me in the golf cart. He was dressed in black from his long-sleeved compression shirt to his military boots. The usual serious look on his stubborn face. "You're awfully dressed up for a stakeout."

"I considered going inside," I said, not bothering to make up excuses as I peered over my medieval bustline. "But I didn't bring a casserole."

He nodded in faux understanding as he dragged his gaze carefully over me. "What'd you do to your hair?"

I touched my unusually tame locks. "I curled it."

"Isn't it usually curly?"

"This is different. These curls are intentional," I said.

"I like it," he said, releasing a long sigh. "It's pretty. But I don't like the fact you lied to me about being here."

"I didn't say I wasn't here," I hedged, feeling heat rise in my lying cheeks. "Did you find the owner of the SUV from the video?"

"I'm working on it," he said, "and I was rightfully worrying about you, it seems."

"I'm okay." I smiled and opened my bag to search for a snack to offer.

Grady raised a hand, declining the cookies I produced.

"I thought we'd agreed you would stop lying to me, and I'd accept you as the meddler you are."

I opened my mouth, but a witty retort didn't arrive. Instead, I asked a more personal question. "Why haven't you been responding to my texts?"

"I've been swamped," he said. "I'm sorry about that. I mean to respond right away, but I'm in a meeting or an interview and I have to wait. Then I don't remember until the next text comes."

I nodded, brows furrowed. I didn't like it, but I supposed this was what it was like to be involved with a lawman. He wasn't as available as someone in another profession, *like an accountant,* I thought, then felt my frown deepen. How dull would that be?

A better question was how much I wanted a boyfriend who responded to me. Reliably.

His gaze moved to my lap. "Are those your birding binoculars?"

I rested my open hands over the device in question. "All my suspects are in there," I said, gaze flicking to the rental home. "Osier, Locke, Goodwin, and Tara. Plus half the surfing community, and Matt just arrived," I reported. "Not that he's a suspect. He could be a great inside source though."

Grady rubbed his eyebrows. "I'm aware."

I gave him a long once over, taking a minute to ask myself why my personal cowboy was dressed as a ninja. "What are you doing here? Where's your truck?"

Our eyes locked in a silent stare.

"You're on a stakeout too!" I said, pointing a finger at his chest.

"No," he said. "I am on a stakeout. You are stalking. If anyone calls in a complaint, I'm going to have to ask you to leave."

I frowned. "Offense."

His phone buzzed, and he looked at it briefly before climbing out.

"Where are you going?"

"Back to work," he said, already moving into the shadows.

"Why? What did your phone say?"

He didn't answer.

"Aren't you going to tell me to go home?" I called after him.

He shot a disappointed look over his shoulder. "Would it matter? And could I believe you if you said you would?"

"You're being dramatic," I called. "And coy." Neither were looks I liked on him.

"I'm making a point," he growled, then vanished into the night.

CHAPTER
TWENTY-FOUR

I waffled between wanting to go home and wanting to ring the bell at Tara's place. I had my invitation, so as long as she wasn't the one who answered the door, I could slip right in. If Tara answered, on the other hand, I would have some explaining to do. And no casserole to smooth things over.

My heart rate increased as I tried to decide. I certainly wasn't accomplishing anything sitting out here, and I was walking a fine line with Grady. Something had to give, but entering a home with all my suspected attackers drew sweat across my brow. I hung my head for a long beat and forced myself to decide. Then I sat tall and powered up Blue's engine.

Grady had the event covered. I would go home and wait.

My phone rang before I had a chance to pull away from the curb, and Amelia's face graced my screen. I answered immediately.

"Hello?"

"Tell me the truth," she said, in lieu of a greeting, "Do you know what Ryan is up to? Because he's definitely up to something, and you said he's been in touch with you."

I bit my lip, unsure what to say. I didn't want to ruin her birthday surprise, but after being chastised by Grady for fibbing, I felt a little icky telling more half-truths and lies.

"You're too quiet," she said. "You know something. I'm coming over."

"I'm not home," I said, releasing the steering wheel. Maybe my luck had improved.

"Where are you?"

I froze, cursing the urge to make something up. "I'm outside the Kai Larsen memorial on Sea Spray. Hoping to see or hear something that will make sense of the bits and pieces I've found so far, but it's just a normal event. No drama. No one with a neon sign announcing themselves as the killer."

"Where on Sea Spray?" she asked, the sound of a car door and engine joining her voice through the line.

"Tara's beach house rental. 1128. I'm sitting across the street at the end of the block in Blue," I said.

"Fine, I'll come to you."

I cringed. "Or we can talk after I get home," I suggested. "I wasn't planning to stay much longer."

"I can't wait," she said. "I've been pacing the store all day waiting for closing time. I think Ryan might be planning to break up with me. Is that why he wanted to talk with you? So you can help him cushion the blow?"

Tara's front door opened, and Ava darted out, clearly distraught. Her black dress flounced against her thighs as she ran down the steps in heels I wouldn't have been able to walk a straight line in. She wiped frantically at her face as she rounded the corner of the home, then stopped abruptly and collapsed onto the grass in a total breakdown.

Osier appeared on the porch a moment later, scanned the scene for her, then headed in her direction.

My intuition spiked. "Hang on," I whispered, lifting my binoculars to my eyes for a clearer look at the situation. He'd shown up the last time I'd seen Ava upset too. Did it mean anything? If so, what?

I watched intently as Osier crouched before her and offered her a handkerchief. He cast repeated looks over each shoulder as they spoke, and for one long, nerve-wracking beat, I was sure he locked his gaze with mine. I reminded myself that I was tucked between two larger vehicles and probably invisible, dressed in black, covered by shadows. I ducked anyway.

"Something's going on with Kai's manager and one of his teammates," I told Amelia.

He helped her onto her feet, and she swayed before leaning heavily against him.

"She's crying really hard, and he's trying to help her walk."

Amelia made a soft, compassionate sound. "I hope she's okay."

"Me too," I said, a frown tugging at my brow. Ava and Osier were at the same event tonight, but how had he found her on the beach the other night? Did he track her, the way he'd tracked Kai?

"Do you think there was something going on between her and Kai?" Amelia asked.

"I'm not sure," I said. "Tara thought he was cheating, but Ava's young, and called him her mentor. It could be nothing, but it would also be easy to fall in love with an idol, especially one she spent so much time with."

"It could've even been a one-way affection," Amelia said. "I bet the manager would know. That's kind of his business, right? To babysit them, keep them in line and all that?"

I wasn't sure what Osier's role was in the surfers' lives. I'd never had a manager. "Is that how it works with your agent?" I asked. Amelia had recently published her first children's book and had a literary agent in New York.

She snickered. "Hardly. I only talk to my agent a few times a year. Surf managers travel with their athletes. They spend a lot of time together during the season. I guess it makes sense for him to keep a close watch on her. Is she the next in line to be the star in Kai's absence?"

"I'm not sure. There's also another surfer named Locke," I said, setting my binoculars down as the pair disappeared back inside. "He's technically the next best surfer, and Tara thinks he's moving in on the Surf Daddy sponsorship, but the fans love Ava." I sighed. I needed to mark someone off my suspect list before it got any longer. "I should've brought a casserole."

Amelia laughed. "No, you shouldn't have. I bet that's the only thing that's kept you outside."

"That and the fear Tara Larsen will bowl me back down the steps to the sidewalk if she sees me trying to crash."

An odd sound pricked my ears, then stopped abruptly, ending in a gentle thump at my side.

"I'm here," Amelia said, as a set of headlights flashed into view. "Passing the house now. Good grief. Is the whole world at this party?"

I stared, momentarily frozen, at an arrow lodged in the headrest beside mine.

I screamed and jumped out, bumbling backward into the path of the headlights, turning my head wildly in search of a killer with a longbow.

"Everly!" Amelia's voice rang through the night and my phone. "What happened?" she stared up at me, terrified, from the driver's seat of her convertible. "Are you okay?"

I pointed to Blue, and Amelia turned to look. She sucked in a breath. "Get in," she said. "Get in, get in, get in!" I scrambled into the passenger side of her car, and she peeled away.

My phone rang as we raced down the street and around the corner.

I stared at Grady's face on the screen while I struggled to buckle my seat belt.

Amelia took the device from my hand as she sped through the night. "Grady?" she called, having apparently initiated the speaker function. "This is Amelia. I have Everly. She's okay."

"What happened?" he asked, the steady sound of footfalls pounding across the line. "Why'd she run into the street? Why didn't she answer her phone?" He cursed before she could respond.

"Arrow," she said.

"Got it," he growled. "Take her home and stay with her?"

"Yes."

"I'll send a cruiser to sit outside." Grady disconnected.

Hot tears slid silently over my cheeks, and my teeth began to chatter once more. Whoever had shot the arrow into Blue's headrest could've easily hit my head if they'd wanted. Just like in the little video sent to me earlier this week.

"Are you okay?" Amelia asked, slowing at the light on Middletown Road as we headed back toward my home.

"No," I said, wiping my cheeks and trying to shore up my nerve. "I'd been hoping to shorten my suspect list," I said with a humorless laugh. "But they were all at the memorial. Any one of them could've shot that arrow."

I tried to imagine James, Locke, Osier, Ava, or even Tara sneaking away from the group of alibis to collect a hidden weapon and creep into position without me knowing. "Whoever shot the arrow had to be Kai's killer," I muttered. "It's the only reason to use that weapon." Grady hadn't told me if there were any more arrows left at *The Lost Colony* when he went with Matt, and I needed to know more than ever. I considered texting him, but knew he had his hands full.

"I'm only partially following what you're saying," Amelia said. She pressed the gas again as the light turned green, then reached across the console to pat my hand. "We're going to need lots of cake and tea to sort this out. You can catch me up while we wait for Grady."

I nodded, batting back another round of tears. "Okay." A friend to bounce my thoughts off of was exactly what I needed. And cake never hurt.

We left Amelia's car in my driveway, then raced inside. We went all the way to my living space, pausing only to dead bolt doors behind us as we ran.

She helped me out of my dress, then went to cut the cake. I was on my own to escape the Spanx.

Twenty minutes later, we'd curled on deck chairs outside, wrapped in blankets and enjoying our second slices of rum cake. I'd slipped into yoga pants and a long-sleeved T-shirt

with the words *I'm a bit cooky* in messy script across the bust.
A gift from Amelia's dad who thought I was extremely kooky
and loved me anyway.

I explained everything I knew about Kai Larsen's life and
murder to Amelia while Lou stood guard. He'd arrived only
a minute or two after we'd come outside to talk and looked
appropriately shocked and horrified at my many recent
unfortunate encounters.

Amelia listened carefully, filing away the details as she
ate. When her plate was empty, for the second time, she
sighed and offered a deeply apologetic look in my direction.
"You've had an awful week, and I haven't even been around
to encourage you."

"You were here tonight," I said. "You rescued me."

"I was only there because I was worked up about my own
stuff," she said. "I should've known all of this sooner. I'm so
sorry I didn't,"

"It's okay." I shrugged. "Life, right?"

"Yeah," she agreed. "Life."

I watched as she scanned the darkened sea, pale brows
pulling low before her bright blue eyes flashed back to mine.
"I'm sorry I've been placing lunch orders at Subtle Teas. I
know you don't expect me to only order from you, but I also
know you think that place is your competition, which it's
not, and I hate that I was a traitor."

"You're hardly a traitor." I laughed. "I can't fault you for
needing a hazelnut fix. Hazelnut is amazing."

"It is," Amelia whispered, and I giggled. She set her plate
on the broad wooden railing, allowing Lou to eyeball the
crumbs. "Do you like rum cake?"

"Squawk!" he answered, moving immediately in the plate's direction.

She jumped, then looked to me, eyes wide.

"He's a scavenger," I said. "And I normally feed him, so he expects it."

"He really does seem to understand everything we're saying," she said, hugging her middle against the night breeze. "I've never noticed that in a gull before."

I looked at Lou, my personal protector and friend. "He's special."

"Okay." Amelia cleared her throat, then shifted on her chair, tucking both feet beneath her blanket. "What do you think Ryan's up to?" she asked, catching me off guard once again.

"I'm not sure," I said, lifting my nearly empty tea glass to my lips.

"You said he was trying to reach you," she reminded me. "What did he say? Exactly. I need to know every word so I can try to figure this out. Something's wrong. I can tell. Look." She poked an arm free of the blanket. "Goose bumps."

I smiled. "I'm sure nothing's wrong. That man adores you."

She shifted again, pulling her knees to her chest and resting her chin on top. "Do you think he wants to break up with me?"

"Absolutely not. Why would he want to do that?"

"Because men are dumb?" she guessed.

I couldn't disagree. Some men were dumb. As were some women, and I felt as if my habitual twisting of truths, especially to Grady, landed me firmly in that category. But this wasn't about me, and denial was my superpower. So, I refocused on the worried woman at my side. "Ryan makes me nuts on occasion, but he's not dumb. He's a good guy, and he's crazy about you," I repeated the last part, hoping to drive the notion home.

She smiled. "You're right. I'm probably being paranoid. But he's definitely acting squirrely."

"I think that's just his personality."

Amelia laughed. "Grady's a good guy too, you know. He really cares about you. It's evident in everything he does, and the whole town's talking about it."

I dared a long look at my best friend. "He's mad at me for all the times I'm not straight with him, but I only do that to avoid arguing."

Amelia smiled. "The irony."

I snorted a small, indelicate laugh. "Right? I don't want to be deceitful. I want to keep the peace, and I always come clean later," I said.

She rested her head against the seat and turned her body to face me. "You're the best person I know. You're independent and smart. Brave and fun. You don't have a malicious bone in your body, and Grady knows that. But if you're falling in love, you're both going to have to make some adjustments, because your world will stop being only about you. That means he'll have to forgive you for your half-truths, while you work on being more direct. That's what being in a relationship is. It's treating the other person the way you want to be treated. Always. And being treated the way you want in return."

I released a heavy breath. "He and I are going to do a lot of fighting while I figure this out."

"Good thing the makeups are so nice."

I barked a laugh, then reached out to push her shoulder. "Thanks for being here tonight. I needed this. And the getaway ride."

"What are friends for?" she asked.

And I took a long moment to count my many blessings.

CHAPTER

TWENTY-FIVE

It was late when Grady stopped by, and he didn't stay long, but he'd wanted to make sure I was okay. He hadn't had any luck finding the person who'd sent an arrow into Blue, but he'd confirmed the shooter hadn't used a longbow. The arrow I'd seen had actually been a bolt, used by a crossbow. I tried hard not to let that sink in.

I also learned that Grady and Matt hadn't found any arrows with the amphitheater's supplies. They'd made a trip to the police station from there, and Matt identified the arrows collected outside my house and from Dharma's tires as ones he used regularly in practice. His fingerprints had been all over every arrow except the murder weapon. Only a few of his partial prints had been found there. Grady believed the killer tried to remove his or her own prints after killing Kai, but hadn't done a thorough job, possibly due to panic. That person had likely begun using gloves afterward.

Grady had tucked me in and locked up on his way out, but I'd found him outside at dawn when I woke. I suspected he'd spent the night in his truck, keeping watch, but he refused to admit it. We had breakfast with Lou, and talked again about what we wanted, needed, and expected from one another. He, like the living saint of a human he was, reiterated his understanding of why I did the things I did, including fib about what I was up to on occasion, and even vowed to never fault me for telling the truth. Then, just like Amelia said he would, he promised to be patient while I learned to trust him enough to do it. And I warmed impossibly further to the idea of having him on my team forever.

After seeing him out, I'd run through a few recipes with Denise, searching for the perfect one to present at Crooked Oaks this afternoon. Anything I chose had to be simple enough for a novice, with standard ingredients students could find in their pantries or at the local market without overspending.

We decided on a tried and true café favorite, my great-grandma's honey garlic chicken. It was my go-to option whenever I had trouble deciding what to add on the daily menu, and it sold out every time. As a bonus, chicken was readily available all year, and most folks were comfortable cooking it.

The seasoning was simple. Salt, pepper, and garlic, which were staples in most pantries, and the sauce was made in the pan as the chicken cooked, keeping production and cleanup to a minimum. The recipe worked with breasts or thighs, dealer's choice. A little something for everyone. Honey, water, vinegar, and soy sauce were all it took to finish things up. My favorite thing about the simple recipe, beside the fact it was delicious, was that the results were versatile. Honey garlic chicken worked as easily in a wrap or salad for lunch as it did beside a bed of rice and veggies for dinner.

The Crooked Oaks crew was going to love it.

I stripped off my apron and hung it on a hook behind the counter, then gathered my bags.

Denise offered me a high five on my way out the door.

I'd packed everything I needed into a pair of extra-large insulated totes and was eager to get going.

Blue waited in the driveway. She'd appeared out front while I'd been getting ready for work after breakfast. Grady was clearly behind her return. The hole in my headrest, where an arrow had been lodged before, now had a tidy star-shaped patch over it. Like the one Grady had made for my other headrest after Blue was attacked last year. The first star had meant everything to me because I'd known what it meant to Grady, having been a U.S. marshal before moving to Charm. This star meant just as much; it was one more way he reminded me that he had my back.

I thanked him by text, and he responded by asking me to stay home. I rolled my eyes. He'd made it clear, over quiche and coffee, that he was onto something with the Kai Larsen case, and that I should reschedule the cooking class. When he'd refused to tell me what he was on to exactly, I'd decided there wasn't a good reason to stay home. For all I knew, Grady was headed in the complete opposite direction. He would neither confirm nor deny. So, I saw no reason to change my plans. The ladies were counting on me.

My upcoming class at Crooked Oaks had made the *Town Charmer* headline. Apparently Henrietta and Pearl had submitted the article. Henrietta had mostly used the space to direct folks to her button channel, and Pearl had focused on the fact Crooked Oaks was the best place to retire on the islands. In truth, the article had said very little about me. Regardless, I'd been right to suspect I needed to impress those two. They were motivated to get the word out on things, and I didn't need an article outlining my failure as a chef later today.

I stopped short of Blue when Matt came into view, looking sweaty and forlorn in a T-shirt and board shorts, as if he'd spent the morning moping on the beach. "Hey," I said. "You okay?"

He bobbed his head, suggesting he was fine while his face told the real story. He was miserable.

"What's going on?" I asked. "Did something happen?" My hackles rose as I spoke. He'd already been dragged through the emotional and social ringer. Everyone needed to leave Matt alone, or better yet, start supporting him. There wasn't anything he wouldn't do for someone else, and Charmers knew it.

"I got a call from my boss," he said. "Apparently my position in this murder case has caused a number of people to bring my oath into question." He wiggled his phone, clutched in one hand.

"Your oath?" I asked, moving closer, in case he needed a hug.

"When EMTs are sworn in, we promise, among other things, to honor physical and judicial laws. Being accused of murder suggests I might be guilty of both. And my status as an emergency medical technician is being brought up for review," he said.

I opened my arms, and he curled his big frame around mine.

"What is happening?" he whispered, sounding desperate and dumbfounded. "One minute I was enjoying my life. The next minute I had a black eye and was being accused of murder. Now I could be stripped of my job?" He straightened, then scrubbed both hands over his face. "I feel like I'm living in a nightmare."

"We'll figure it out," I told him, gripping his strong biceps. "It's going to be okay. Grady says he's onto something solid right now, and it's not you." I hoped. In truth Grady hadn't been specific.

Matt blew out a long breath, then dragged the fingers of one hand through sweaty hair. "I shouldn't be complaining to you again. At least no one is trying to hurt me."

"I'm fine," I said. "I promise. And I'm here for you, anytime you need to complain about anything. I have to run over to Crooked Oaks and teach a class now, but you should go inside and get something cold to drink. Visit with Denise. She's an excellent listener, and trustworthy."

He looked toward my front door. "I can do that."

"Good." I offered a warm smile. "Why don't you stay with me tonight?" I asked. "We can sit on the deck and talk through all the crazy things that have happened this week. Maybe we'll figure out who's behind it all. Even if we don't, at least neither one of us will be alone."

He nodded, expression warming at the proposal. "I'd really like that. But what about Grady? Your guy was crystal clear on his feelings about me staying with you before."

I frowned, recalling the way Grady had instructed Matt

to take his duffel bag when they'd left together the other day. "Did he say something to you about it?"

Matt grinned. "Yeah. He said, 'You are not staying at Everly's place.' There really wasn't any room for misinterpretation."

I smiled sweetly as my eyes narrowed. "Well, it sounds as if I need to speak with him about that." Because clearly "my guy" needed to be reminded that I was the one who decided what I did and who I did it with.

"Good luck." Matt chuckled.

I waved, then climbed behind Blue's wheel and headed down Bay View toward Subtle Teas. The water was peaceful and blue, polka-dotted with sailboats and kayakers. I smiled and waved at passersby. Then I saw Mary Grace and Eloise outside the teahouse, laughing and hugging like old friends, and my mood soured. What were the odds of my oldest nemesis and newest competition being so chummy? I'd have to look into that later, but I didn't believe in coincidences. I suddenly wondered if Mary Grace had used her new real estate license to draw Eloise and her teahouse straight to Charm. And if she'd done it just to spite me.

Someone honked, and I jerked my face forward, eyes back on the road.

The driver behind me waved to a family on bikes.

I smiled at my unfounded paranoia, then pressed the pedal underfoot a little harder. The mechanic caring for Dharma had promised it would only be another day or two on repairs, and I didn't mind the wait. I was glad to know she was getting the attention she deserved. Someone her age had earned a few days at the spa.

I took the winding road toward Crooked Oaks, enjoying the colorful flora and gorgeous spring landscaping. It was easy to see why so many people chose to retire here. And according to the community's website, the clubhouse had all the trimmings of a cruise ship, without the hassle of being at sea. Everything from food to entertainment was available on site twenty-four-seven, and anything that wasn't, was only a short drive away.

I paused when a familiar car caught my eye on the horizon, and I altered my course out of curiosity. James Goodwin's station wagon was angled in a spot at the small public parking area near the beach, and two figures stood together at the hood.

Blue eased to a stop along the perfectly manicured street, and I dug into my bag for the binoculars. I identified the men in the space of a heartbeat.

James and Locke stood shoulder to shoulder, gazing out at the sea. James moved one arm in a sweeping arc, as if describing something to his companion. Locke nodded, then turned to shake James's hand.

A flash of light from the sun off my binoculars glinted across Locke's cheek, causing him to squint before angling away.

James's gaze, however, moved in my direction, quickly tracking the light.

I ducked, dropping my binoculars back into my bag and slumping in my seat until I could barely see above the wheel. I jammed my toe against the pedal until it touched the floor and cruised away before I proved Grady right and got myself into trouble again.

A valet was waiting with Pearl at the Crooked Oaks clubhouse doors. I hopped out to greet her with a warm handshake and a smile, then I grabbed my bags and handed my cart key to the young man standing politely aside. His crimson vest had a small, crooked tree embroidered on the left breast above a golden pin with the name Chris engraved on it.

"Thanks, Chris," I called as he swung Blue into a parking spot just beyond a massive fountain in the paved turnaround.

"This place is gorgeous," I told Pearl, gazing around. She'd walked me through a set of wooden doors at least twenty-feet tall. An expansive marble tile foyer stretched ahead of us, with a grand oak welcome desk on one side.

"It is," she agreed. "Tell all your friends. We could use some new blood in here. Liven the place up."

I laughed. "Will do."

Pearl took my bags, then handed them to the woman at the desk. "We'll be back," she told her. Turning to me, she asked, "How about the two-cent tour?"

"I'd love it!"

Pearl locked her arm with mine, then led me around the first floor. Meeting rooms, ball rooms, parlors, dining areas from casual to elegant, a rec space, indoor pool, gym, and library. I wasn't sure I could've found my way back to the lobby without her help.

When we returned, Locke was at the front desk.

His gaze landed on me, and my stomach clenched.

Had he caught me spying earlier? Was he here to confront me on the subject?

He dipped his chin in a casual, albeit disinterested,

greeting, then turned back to the woman at the desk. He'd dressed all in white, showcasing his perfectly tanned skin. His crisp linen suit and shoes gleamed in the fluorescent light. His T-shirt bore the Surf Daddy logo.

Pearl released me at the sight of him. "You came!" she exclaimed.

He swung his attention back in a double take. His dark-brown eyes turned friendly as Pearl clutched onto his massive biceps.

"Of course," he said, patting her hand. "It was nice of you to invite me."

"Locke is here to meet the residents, and he's going to give us some bodyboarding lessons later," Pearl informed me. I smiled. "Fun."

"Is this the sign-up sheet?" he asked, his bright smile slipping as he looked over a paper on the massive desk. "No one wanted the lesson?"

Pearl batted her eyes. "We all want the lesson," she assured. "But we're getting older. You understand. We'll watch from our private beach while you show us how it's done."

I'll bet, I thought, struggling to suppress a full-out laugh.

His gaze returned to me, seeing me for the first time, it seemed. "Everly Sams, right? The local sleuth?"

My jaw dropped, and my brain struggled to process the statement. I chose my next words carefully. "Swan," I corrected, "But I'm no sleuth. I run an iced tea shop on the beach." I pointed to the logo printed on my shirt as evidence. "Sun, Sand, and Tea, see?" A nervous little chuckle wiggled from my lips, and I smashed my mouth shut tight.

His brow furrowed. "Sorry. I must've mistaken you—"

"Tsk." Pearl cut him off. "Everly is a marvelous investigator. She's just being humble. This woman has single-handedly beaten the police to the killer on a bunch of local murder cases over the last two years. In fact, she's looking into another murder now." She stage winked.

I imagined running away.

He nodded. "I thought that was you. Pearl turned me onto using the town's blog for tide schedules, and it was hard not to get sucked into the posts about you. Especially after..." He trailed off.

It wasn't hard to fill in the blank. *Especially after Kai died.*

"It's not something I talk about," I said, trying to cover my previous denial. "I wish I had answers for you, about what happened to your friend, but I've come up short at every turn. I'm sorry." I offered an apologetic smile with the hard truth. Hopefully it was enough to keep me safe, if Locke was the killer who'd been threatening me.

He narrowed his eyes in curiosity. "There's no need to be sorry. You aren't a detective, right? Just a lady who likes answers? My mother is like that. Not with murders, but she's into the TV shows and books. She's all about guessing who-dunit before it's revealed. You like those too?"

"I read a lot of romance," I said, shaking off the comparison to his mother, a woman surely twice my age.

He laughed. "Romance? Now, that's the real mystery to me."

I joined him and Pearl in a giggle, then changed the subject. "You must be getting excited about the upcoming competition," I said. "Hopefully things will be sorted by the time you return for Back to the Beach and the Spring Surf Classic."

"I hope," he said, kneading his hands and fighting a small grin. "My mother's flying in from Hawaii for it. She hasn't seen me surf professionally on the mainland yet. It's a pretty big deal."

I smiled, hoping to show him it was okay to find happiness, even in times of loss. Then, another question came to mind, and my big mouth opened. "I think I saw you with James Goodwin on the beach earlier. I noticed his station wagon when I was headed this way."

"You know Mr. Goodwin?" he asked.

"A little. He seems like such a great guy. Nice family too, and he's local, so I love that. He must be a lot of fun to work with."

Locke paused, his gaze moving from my face to Pearl's then back. "He's great. And Surf Daddy is a great. Great products. Really great."

I fought a frown. *That was a whole lot of greats*. "Will you be the new brand ambassador?" I asked, lifting a finger toward his T-shirt. "It's important to love the things you represent. Sounds like you will."

Locke shifted his weight. "You're really into the details for someone who isn't investigating." He raised a smile to Pearl, then looked back to me.

"I'm just…such a fan," I said, bobbing my head to punctuate the lie. "And honored to see a major player like you here in Charm. Usually the big guys don't come to our little beaches." I put on a bright smile.

"You're a surf fan?" he asked.

"Mm hmm." I nodded. "Absolutely! A total diehard."

Pearl looked confused.

He didn't look convinced either. Actually, he looked a little uncomfortable.

I bit my lip against a deep internal groan. I was lying again! And poorly.

Panic spiked in my core, and I lunged for the desk, grabbing a permanent marker from a mug beside the sign-in sheet. "Can I have your autograph? I can't stand being this close and not asking. Do you mind?"

Locke rocked back on his heels. "Sure, but I don't have any headshots or promo with me. Do you have something you want signed?"

I looked down at myself. "Sign my shirt," I said, trying to sound more like a fangirl than the bad actress I was.

Locke reluctantly took the marker, and I pointed to a spot near my belly button. He doodled his name across the fabric of my Sun, Sand, and Tea shirt.

"Thank you," I said, already wondering if the ink would come out with some extra-strength stain stick. Those logoed café shirts weren't cheap!

The massive lobby doors opened behind him, and a tall, broad silhouette appeared, backlit by the sun. I sighed in relief as Osier came into view. His focus latched onto me for a long moment, eyes narrowing, before he dragged it over to Locke, who'd already turned away to greet him.

Osier seemed to flip a switch, laughing and grinning as he overplayed his friendly manager role. "Ava will be here in just a few minutes," he said, glancing at his phone. Probably tracking her every step through town.

Pearl shook Osier's hand, thanking him for coming and promising she'd be out for the bodyboard event as soon as she got me set up for my cooking class. She collected my bags from the desk, then darted back to my side and grabbed my elbow. "Come on. I don't want to miss it when he takes off his shirt."

"You're completely inappropriate," I told her, as she dragged me away.

She didn't bother denying it.

"Is Ava coming to help with the bodyboarding lesson?" I asked, unsure why she was coming to the show.

"She agreed to a beach volleyball demonstration with the staff," Pearl said. "Our male residents bought tickets for that. We collected enough money to take a bus trip this fall."

I shook my head, not bothering to point out all the things that were wrong with that statement.

"Here you are," Pearl announced, leading me into a large room with round tables, plus a row of long rectangular tables arranged at the front. A rolling cart stood against the wall behind the podium. A hot plate and camp stove were set up nearby.

Pearl squatted before the podium and reached for the white cloth covering the nearest rectangular table. "I put all your cooking items under here," she said. "I thought I'd let you arrange things the way you want them." She lifted the cloth to reveal a set of boxes with mixing bowls, measuring utensils, pans, cutting boards, and a trash receptacle. "If you think of anything else you need, just buzz me, and I'll get the message over to our kitchen staff. Someone will run whatever you need out to you."

She stood, and I followed her to the cart with the hot plate and camp stove. "This is a mini fridge," she said, opening one panel on the cart. "You can store your cold things here."

"Wow." I raised my brows, then whistled. "You really thought of everything."

"I try," she said. "The way I see it, anyone willing to volunteer their time here should know they're appreciated. And I hope the overall experience will be good enough that all of our presenters will want to come back."

I smiled. "That's nice."

"Thank you. Now, I'd better go check on Locke," she said with a wink. "He was nice enough to come on such little notice. I need to get him set up too."

I waved goodbye, already pulling cold ingredients from my insulated bag to store in the fridge.

Pearl spun away on silent orthopedic sneakers and burned a path back to the lobby.

CHAPTER
TWENTY-SIX

There was nearly an hour before my session began, giving me plenty of time to get my workspace and thoughts in order. Today was supposed to be a day when I kept my nose out of Grady's investigation, before the next arrow landed between my eyes. But fate seemed to be intervening. First, Matt had fallen into my lap as I was leaving home, weary and carrying heavy news. Then, I'd driven past Locke and Goodwin on the way to Crooked Oaks. And to top it off, Locke and Osier had shown up in the lobby, with Ava on her way! I wasn't trying to be superstitious, but it seemed as if the universe was telling me something. Like, maybe, it wasn't time to let Kai's death go just yet.

I fought the urge to go hunting for the surfers and their manager, just to ask all the questions still rolling around in my head. At least there would be plenty of witnesses wherever the young, beautiful people had gone. And I had a feeling the Crooked Oaks residents would protect me if one of the others turned out to be homicidal.

Except, I wasn't meddling today. Today, I was cooking.

Just cooking.

I fixed my feet to the floor and focused on prepping and arranging my seasonings and equipment.

Concentration was maddeningly difficult, knowing the possibility of real answers was somewhere on Crooked Oaks property, but I doubled down on my resolve. Maybe I would never know who killed Kai Larsen or why. Maybe I'd never know if Tara was right about him seeing someone else or who that person was. Maybe I'd never know who'd been stalking and threatening me.

And I hated it.

I lined my spatulas by size, then color, repeatedly talking myself into staying where I was. Until the warm tickle of anticipation I'd come to accept as my intuitive sense that Grady was nearby kicked in.

The muffled but familiar tenor of his voice was barely a heartbeat behind. I followed the sound to the window. Grady stood just outside with Henrietta. She peered up at him and smiled like her life depended on it. Her narrow fingers stroked his biceps, and I shook my head.

These ladies clearly had a signature move, and I could hardly blame them. Grady's muscles were quite nice.

She swept an arm in my direction, then started when she saw me watching. I waved.

Grady adjusted the brim of his signature cowboy hat against the sun and peered inside.

When the two turned for the front doors, I checked my reflection in the glass. My ponytail hadn't drooped, and my mascara was still in place. Not bad for a windy golf cart ride across town. Then I saw the scribbled signature across my middle and winced. Nothing would make me look as if I'd been meddling faster than a suspect's signature on my belly.

I scuttled behind my table and crouched low, hidden by the table cover. I whipped the shirt off, turning it inside out, before tugging it back over my head. The ink was significantly harder to make out, but the seams along my sides were now exposed. "Dang it."

The door to my room opened, and I sprang to my feet. "Hello!" I called. "Grady! Hi, how are ya?"

His brows pinched, whether in amusement or suspicion, I couldn't say and probably didn't want to know.

My heart pounded as he moved closer.

"What are you doing here?" I asked, rambling nervously through the half second of silence. "I didn't know you were headed this way." He certainly hadn't mentioned it over breakfast.

"I told you I had some things to follow up on." He scrutinized me, and I moved against the table, hoping to hide any visible hint of Locke's signature. "I thought you had a cooking class."

"I do." I opened my arms to draw his attention to the display between us. "Here."

He shifted. "How long will you be here?"

"A couple of hours." I looked to Henrietta who'd turned her attention to her phone. "I want to stick around and answer questions afterward. Why?"

Grady grunted. "Let me know when you're ready to go. I'll follow you home."

That sounded fine, but it reminded me of something else

I wanted to say before he took off. "Matt's staying at my place tonight, by the way."

He stilled and his jaw locked.

"I ran into him on my way here, and it turns out that thanks to him being a murder suspect and all, he's about to lose his job. He didn't do anything wrong, but he's losing everything," I said. "It's not right."

Grady's eyes flashed with challenge, but I didn't need to remind him whose fault it was that Matt was being treated like a pariah.

"So, to be clear," I said softly, trying to be less than obvious in front of Henrietta. "I invited him, and he is staying."

Grady dipped his chin.

I relaxed by a fraction, relieved he was smart enough not to argue. Then, something else blazed to mind. He'd told me earlier that he was onto something, and he'd asked me not to teach my class. Now, he was here and planning to follow me home. "Is something wrong?" I asked, my stomach plummeting. "Did you come here to talk to someone specific?"

Was he here to speak with Locke? With Osier? Ava? Or maybe James Goodwin, who wasn't far away. I turned the puzzle pieces over in my mind. What was I missing?

Grady pursed his lips. "Just stay here. I'll come back before your class ends."

I nodded, sensing the imperativeness in his tone. "Okay."

"Is your shirt on inside out?"

I shook my head. "Nope."

He rolled his eyes, then turned for the door.

Henrietta perked at the sight of him leaving my table. "Good luck, Everly!" she called, then grabbed hold of his arm once more. "I love your hat," she cooed. "Cowboys are a long-honored tradition on the islands, you know. I have a beach house in Corolla I rent out for added income. You're welcome to it anytime. Plenty of wild horses. Your son would love it. The house is right out on the beach."

I pursed my lips as they vanished in the distance, wondering what had brought Grady to Crooked Oaks. Or, more specifically, who.

And Henrietta's talk of a beach house in Corolla reminded me of the Goodwins. Hadn't Cindy Goodwin said the family was staying there for a few days? Until the hoopla surrounding Kai's death settled down?

Images of the beautiful and often rustic area rushed to mind. The sand dunes were tall, the homes often on stilts. And many properties were virtually unreachable without a four-wheel-drive vehicle.

Like the SUV that had gunned for me.

My breaths hastened as memories and facts began to arrange themselves in my mind.

Nicole had said Cindy was the driving force behind the extensive Surf Daddy expansion, which had ultimately failed. What if she blamed Kai and his behavior for their financial complications? Or for embarrassing her and then creating a scandal that could have derailed all her hard work?

What if the Goodwins owned a third vehicle?

The woody. The Mercedes. And the SUV that had tried to kill me.

If they didn't own the SUV, they could've rented it to manage the terrain on their trip to Corolla.

A handful of Crooked Oaks residents trickled into the

room as I tried my new theory on for size. Could Mr., or even Mrs., Goodwin have been so irate at Kai's behavior, and the possible black mark on their family brand, that they'd confronted him about it?

Could one of them have asked Kai to do better and the conversation escalated? It seemed reasonable that he would let down his guard and literally turn his back to walk away from either. One being a family man, older and kinder, the other being a petite woman. How could either possibly hurt the great Kai Larsen?

I rounded the presenter's table and drifted toward the door, heart racing as I mentally plugged the Goodwins into my theory. First James. Then his wife.

I nodded and smiled tightly at the residents as they found their seats, more than fifteen minutes early, then I began to run.

The lobby was empty when I arrived, save for the woman behind the desk, who I hadn't been introduced to earlier.

"Hello," I waved. "Did you happen to see which way Henrietta took Detective Hays?" I asked.

"Of course." She pointed down the hall where I'd walked through a maze of rooms with Pearl earlier. "Head east toward the kitchen, then follow signs for the pool and locker rooms. The double glass doors to the private beach and shuffleboard courts are down that hall."

"Thank you!" I rushed over the wide marble tiles, reading signs and peeking into each open door I passed, in case Henrietta and Grady had stopped somewhere along the way.

The building was enormous and infuriating. I just needed to find Grady. He needed to know I'd seen Goodwin near the beach earlier, and that his family was staying in Corolla. If he was here to talk to Osier or Locke about the local sponsor, he didn't need to. He needed to go straight to James. Or his wife.

I stopped at an intersection of hallways with too many signs stuck to the wall. I ran a hasty gaze down the list, in search of the pool, locker room, or shuffleboard icons, then burst back into motion when I found them. "How big is this building?" I complained.

Locke appeared outside the locker rooms several yards later, a distant set of glass doors at the end of the hall behind him. "Hey," he said, brows furrowed. "In a hurry to watch the show?" He'd changed into black board shorts and a rash guard with water shoes. His curious gaze traveled over me. "Are you all right?"

"No." I stopped to catch my breath. "Have you seen Detective Hays?" I panted, pressing a palm against the budding stitch in my side.

"Who?"

"Detective," I repeated, lifting my arms over my head. "This tall. Cowboy hat, jeans. Grouchy looking. He's with Henrietta. Do you know her?"

Locke nodded. "That guy's a detective?" he asked, swinging his gaze away from me. "I saw them when I was on my way to change. They were headed outside."

"Perfect! Did they go through those doors?" I asked, pointing in the direction Locke's gaze had gone.

He turned back to me, a stunned expression replacing the confusion. "Yeah, come on." He started down the hall, and I followed. "Can you call him?" he asked. "In case he's moved on? This place is ridiculous. It took me five minutes to find the locker room."

"Good idea." I pulled the phone from my pocket and tried to keep up.

Locke glanced over my shoulder, then turned in one swift move, knocking the phone from my hands. He stomped one massive foot against it before I could utter a complaint or response.

I raised my gaze to his, confused and quickly understanding I'd made a huge mistake. "Oh no."

Locke grabbed me in the space of a heartbeat, then spun me into a headlock, one hand over my mouth, as he backed me into a darkened room.

He kicked the door shut behind us and applied pressure to my neck until my head swam. I screamed against his fingers, trying to bite as I also tried, uselessly, to escape.

Then slowly, my eyelids fell shut.

❧

I woke to a blinding headache and a multitude of confusing sounds. It took a minute to recognize the scanning radio. The steady hum of tires and whoosh of rushing wind. The unforgiving floor of a vehicle stretched hard and flat beneath me. The world was dark. My body was curled, cramped and stiff. My knees had been bent and angled up to my chest in the most indelicate of ways, parted to accommodate my round middle.

I tried and failed to straighten. The arm I'd been laying on ached and stung, having fallen partially asleep. Full realization of my situation hit like a sledge to my heart.

I'd been wrong about Kai's killer, and I was about to pay the price.

My breaths sped, heating my face. I pressed my hands against the fabric surrounding me, slowly peeling back the heavy blanket.

I gulped the fresh air as it rushed in.

A phone rang and I stilled, terrified it was mine and the sound would draw Locke's attention. Then I remembered. My phone was gone. Crushed. Along with my chances of calling for help.

The volume on the radio lowered, as I watched the scenery whip past the windows, identifying signs for Corolla.

"I'll be right there," Locke said. "Just stretching before I head into the water. Go ahead and get set up on the beach."

I sucked in a deep breath, then screamed. "Help!"

The vehicle swerved, and Locke spluttered. "I didn't hear anything. I'll see you in a few minutes."

"Help! Help! Help!" I shrieked at the top of my burning lungs as he spoke.

"Shut up!" he yelled a moment later, presumably having ended his call. "Shut up, or you're going into the ocean wearing zip ties on your wrists and ankles!"

I paused to consider the possibility. Getting out of this vehicle was the goal, and I was a strong swimmer, but I wasn't convinced I could survive without the use of at least two limbs.

"Let me go," I croaked, deciding the ocean wasn't a good option. I stretched upward, unfurling myself from the bag. "Pull over and let me out."

"I can't," he said, catching my eye in the rearview mirror

as I rose. "Be quiet so I can think." The agitation in his gaze made him appear borderline unhinged, nothing like the laid-back surfer I'd spoken to earlier this afternoon. "This wasn't supposed to happen," he growled. "None of this was supposed to happen." He pounded his hand against the steering wheel, causing the vehicle to swerve once more.

"Maybe I can help?" I suggested, trying to sound reasonable as I dragged my attention over everything in sight and through the windows.

We were in a big SUV, presumably the one that had tried to kill me, and racing away from Charm. "Why are we headed for Corolla?"

"That's where I'm staying," he said. "I wanted to be on my own for this trip. Away from Osier, always looking over my shoulder. Away from Ava, fawning over Kai, and as far as I could get from Kai, always ready to remind me I was second best."

I tucked all that into my frazzled mind to come back to. The most important question perched on my tongue. "You're the one who tried to run me over?" I asked, voice pitching and cracking with fresh fear.

"I just wanted you to go away!" He smashed his fist into the dash and cracked the screen on his GPS. The SUV swerved, hitting loose gravel along the roadside as he shook out the pain in his now bleeding hand. "Shut up! I can't think!"

I wet my dry, cracked lips and released a long, shuddered breath. I had to get away from Locke when he stopped the car, but he was stronger and faster. I needed a plan.

I gripped and kneaded my stinging arm while I thought,

inching up for a better view outside. Despite being choked out and abducted, I wasn't injured. The fresh air rushing through the windows had cleared my head. Adrenaline had pushed away the pain.

"You don't want to do this," I said, catching sight of a silver stake wedged between the back seat and hatch where I lay. If he'd wanted to kill me, he could've done that already. He didn't have to bring me along on this ride. "You can let me go," I suggested. "Then make your escape. It'll be easier for one person to run than two. You can be back on the mainland before anyone knows what's happened."

"And then what?" he asked, half livid, half pitiful. "Then my career is over. Before it ever had a fair chance to begin. And all of this is for nothing. I hurt you. Killed Kai. Just to run away and live my life in a hole somewhere? Hoping I won't be found? I can't do that! My mother's flying in to see me surf next month."

I turned my eyes to the open road, trying to catch the attention of a driver or passenger in another car. No one seemed to notice me, a grown woman riding in the very back of an SUV.

"Kai had everything," Locke said, utterly miserable in the front seat. "He was the absolute worst person, and he had everything. Fame. Glory. Skills. Money. A gorgeous wife. The respect of every hopeful surfer. And Ava," he whispered the final two words, pulling my attention to him once more.

"Kai and Ava were involved?" I asked. Images of the wholly distraught Ava flashed back to mind. She had been more to him than a teammate.

He lowered his chin by a fraction, confirming.

"Tara suspected Kai was cheating," I said. And she'd been right. "Never ignore your intuition," I muttered.

"It wasn't right," Locke spat. Blood flowed faster from his fresh knuckle wounds. "Kai didn't deserve any of the things he had, and he was so cocky. So proud. So mean." Locke released a feral roar. "I hated him!"

"So, you killed him."

"That was an accident," Locke said, looking back into the rearview, his expression almost pleading. "I wanted to talk to him, so I followed him to the amphitheater, then he got into a blowout with that EMT before I had a chance. I waited for an opportunity to start a conversation, but he was fuming. I followed him to a bar a couple miles away and tried to buy him a drink, but he lashed out, still mad the other guy had walked away, I guess. He kept saying they weren't finished, then I remembered seeing the other guy storm off and leave his phone on the stage. I took a chance and went back."

"You knew he'd be willing to meet with Matt again," I said, filling in the missing pieces I'd been waiting for.

Locke's gaze flickered to the rearview mirror, then back to the road. The SUV began to pick up speed. "He came back, then got mad when he realized I'd tricked him. He sent me away like I was some kook instead of his biggest competition. He told me I was stupid for caring for Ava because women didn't settle for second best. Then he called her a name I couldn't let stand. At first, I was just going to defend her name, tell him he couldn't talk about her like that, then something came over me. I lost control."

"You stabbed him with a stake from your tent," I said, curling my fingers around the sharp metal anchor at my feet.

The slender piece of equipment had the strength to hold small nylon tents in the sand, so surfers and swimmers could get a break from the sun on a long day at the beach. It was also the right size to be mistaken for an arrow. "Why'd you bring the stake with you, if you only wanted to talk to him?"

Locke didn't answer.

The SUV picked up speed again, and I knew the truth.

Locke was lying. He'd gone there to confront Kai and assert himself. To put a stop to the bullying and bragging, and it had all gone terribly wrong.

"You framed Matt with the arrow to cover your crime, because once you'd done it, you knew you'd ruined everything and you needed to cover it up."

Locke's gaze jumped back to the rearview mirror, and he swerved once more. His skin paled, and the vehicle lurched forward, moving impossibly faster and raising my heart rate in the process.

I turned to look behind me, wondering what he saw.

A massive black truck with a familiar silver star decal on the windshield was making good time toward our bumper, despite Locke's efforts to get away.

I knew that decal. Knew that truck. And that driver. I extended an arm in his direction, thinking his name with all my soul.

Grady.

Grady had come for me. My heart soared, and tears welled. I felt as if I might burst with hope, relief, and love. The idea startled me, but I let it settle in. I loved him. I'd gotten myself into a little trouble, as he'd predicted, but I hadn't gotten hurt, not really, and Grady had come to save me. My life wasn't cursed. It was blessed, and all I wanted in the world was to tell Grady he was right. I wasn't cursed in love, because I loved him, and we were both going to be okay.

I didn't pay any attention to the SUV's next swerve, one more of so many already, until we began to spin.

And suddenly I was rolling.

CHAPTER
TWENTY-SEVEN

The SUV rocked to a stop, landing back on its wheels, while my head spun and wobbled.

I was covered in beads of shattered glass. The SUV's rear window had burst. The hatch had bent and come ajar. My eyes struggled to focus. The vehicle was angled at the edge of the road, and Grady's big black truck parked behind.

Whoever once said scary things happened in slow motion was a dirty liar, because one minute I was happy, and the next minute I was being thrown against the SUV's window, then the ceiling, before crashing back to where I'd begun. The experience was over in what felt like nanoseconds, and my brain was still struggling to catch up.

I pushed my way through the hatch on numb, wooden legs, moving on autopilot more than thought.

"Hands up!" Grady's voice boomed and I started, swinging my gaze away from his truck. "Charm, PD! Put your hands where I can see them."

He approached the driver's door, where I presumed Locke was half loopy from the accident too.

"Hands up," Grady repeated, inching forward, hand at his holster while he approached.

I stumbled awkwardly over the sandy berm in his direction, silently taking inventory of my body. All parts were present and accounted for. Bruises, to be sure. A few little cuts from the beads of shattered glass. Nothing terrifying or significant. I squinted against the brilliant southern sun and marveled at my lack of life-threatening injuries, despite the dilapidated shape of the SUV.

And the good luck kept piling on.

Warm ocean breezes rushed over me, throwing my hair against my sun-kissed skin and making me feel more alive than I ever recalled.

Everything was going to be okay. And it was a miracle.

An oncoming car stopped to gawk, apparently unsure how to proceed around the situation. One wrecked car and one intimidating pickup with flashers racing through the grill.

Grady stopped before the driver's side door, and sirens began in the distance.

When Locke didn't respond to his voice, Grady extended a hand through the open window, pressing steady fingers to the young man's neck.

My ears rang as I hurried ahead, pulled by the invisible band that had somehow formed between us long ago. "Grady?"

He turned his face to mine, and the parade of emotions was unmistakable. Relief and regret. Joy and pain. "Everly."

I ran at him without thinking. I wrapped my arms around his strong, protective frame and cried. "I'm so sorry."

Grady kissed my head and hugged me back. "You've got nothing to be sorry for. I should've been faster," he said. "I should've protected you. I've been doing everything I can to build a case against Locke, but it's been tough. When you identified his SUV in that YouTube footage, I thought I had him, but the plate was obscured. I started second-guessing myself."

"Well, you did better than me," I said, laughing despite the tears rolling over my cheeks. "I thought it was one of the Goodwins."

I peeked at Locke, out cold behind the wheel, his head lulled and his limbs limp. The seat belt held him in place.

Grady turned me back to him and cupped my face in his hands. "My little detective." He rested his forehead on mine. "Are you okay?"

"Yeah."

The sirens grew loud as they closed in, but I didn't care about any of it. My world was right, and I felt wildly free.

Beside us, the sound of shuffling reached my ears.

Grady and I turned in unison to see Locke had awakened. He'd released his seat belt and slipped onto the passenger seat.

"Freeze," Grady commanded, with all the authority of the seasoned lawman he was.

Locke opened the passenger door, then climbed out, turning to face us from the opposite side of the vehicle.

And he raised a crossbow.

I gasped, confused and terrified by the look in his desperate eyes.

"I'm walking away," he said, forcing the words through

ragged breaths. "I didn't mean for any of this to happen, and I can't take it back, so I'm leaving. And you're going to let me." He swung the weapon in my direction, and Grady shoved me aside, then behind him.

I complied, careful not to startle Locke and letting Grady work his magic.

Locke's nervous gaze made the circuit from Grady, to me, to the stalled traffic and approaching first responders. Then, to the beach and ocean at his back.

"Put your weapon down," Grady repeated in the most fatherly voice I'd ever heard. And I knew he saw the fear and panic in Locke's eyes too.

I turned to survey the new arrivals over my shoulder, hoping to find armed backup, but finding only ambulances instead. Matt climbed down from one driver's seat. His stance was tense and his expression hard as he evaluated the unraveling scene.

A soft, unthinkable sound rang out. One I remembered clearly from Kai's memorial.

I spun back, my heart in my throat as I looked at Locke. The shock and pain in his young, desperate face made my stomach clench in sudden fear.

His crossbow was no longer loaded.

I followed his gaze to my cowboy, an arrow protruding from his core. Blood bloomed around the wound in his torso as I stepped forward, taking in the horror.

His knees buckled, and I fell with him, my arms outstretched to catch him the way he always caught me.

"Grady," I whispered, cradling him as his body fully collapsed.

The sound of heavy footfalls and Matt's voice boomed behind me.

Locke ran over the dunes, toward the beach, and I no longer cared what happened to him. If he was caught. If he was punished. Everything I cared about was already in my hands.

New sirens raged through the air as Grady's backup arrived too late.

Images of Denver's small face raced across my mind. I imagined telling him what had happened to his father, and the anguish that would come. The pain and horror of a little boy who'd already lost his mother, and survived the exodus of his grandparents.

I ignored the fact that this was all my fault. That I was stupid and stubborn and... A sign welcoming us to Corolla caught my eye and stalled my thoughts.

I was cursed.

Grady groaned, and I turned back to him, my tears dropping onto his forehead.

His eyes were shut, and I realized what I'd done.

I'd tempted fate.

I was no longer in Charm, and I was deeply in love with Grady.

Matt moved into view, lowering at my side. "Are you hurt?"

I shook my head and sniffled, biting into my lip to stop the building sobs. I wasn't physically injured, but I was a liar. I'd never been in as much pain in my life.

"You're going to have to give me room," he said gently, nudging me away.

Grady's fingers tightened on mine when I tried to release him.

"I need to assess the damage, clean the wound, and get an IV going," Matt said, sweeping his gaze from Grady to me. "She needs to give me room."

I obeyed, moving to Grady's head and taking his hand with me.

Uniformed officers appeared near the vehicle. Some dashed by in the direction Locke had gone. Others made a slow exploration of the ruined vehicle, their sullen countenances and worried gazes returning regularly to Grady.

"He's losing a lot of blood," Matt said, his face turned up to an approaching EMT. "The bolt's lodged deep. Call ahead to the ER. Let them know we're coming. They should meet us and probably prep for surgery."

My breath caught and time began to slow, just like other people had claimed. It hadn't happened during the car accident, but it was happening now.

Maybe it only happened when someone became more afraid than they'd ever been. When they were sure they wouldn't survive the situation at hand.

The second EMT placed an orange backboard at his side. She and Matt arranged their grips on Grady, moving him expertly while I watched.

"I love you," I whispered, unable to hold it in any longer.

His hand squeezed mine as the EMTs moved him again, this time onto a waiting gurney.

I pushed to my feet, letting the truth settle over us, and batting tears as Matt looked my way.

"Everly," he said, softly. "We need to get him to the hospital."

I nodded, then stepped aside.

Grady's eyes opened, and the usual, ethereal gray of still waters I found there was gone. Replaced by a turbulent brewing storm.

Grady was fighting.

I cried as they whisked him away and pressed my palms to my temples, my life coming apart at the seams.

"Come on," Matt returned to me, taking my hand carefully in his. "You need to go with him." He guided me to the ambulance, then helped me into the bay where Grady lay, unnaturally still.

An oxygen mask covered his handsome face, and machines monitored his vitals.

"I'm so sorry," I repeated, the words clanging and echoing in my ears. "This should never have happened."

And if he lived, I'd make sure Grady was never hurt again because of me.

CHAPTER
TWENTY-EIGHT

I slept in the hospital waiting room that night, surrounded by my loved ones.

Matt had cleaned my plentiful scrapes and cuts with care after they'd taken Grady into surgery, and I'd done my best to wash up in the sink of the public restroom. My aunts had brought my favorite sweatpants and T-shirt, along with a quilt from their home. I hadn't had to tell them it would be a long night.

The vast and steady outpouring of care and support from Charmers made me prouder than I'd ever been. It was nearly enough, at times, to offset my fear and heartbreak. I supposed that if I was truly cursed, there was no better community to be stuck in than mine.

My aunts tipped against each other for support in the hard, uncomfortable chairs across from mine. Wyatt sat on the floor at my feet, his head on my knee as he softly snored. He'd given his chair to one of the many Corkers who'd come immediately after hearing what had happened, then refused to leave until they knew Grady was okay.

Flowers, balloons, and well wishes poured in consistently

through the night, along with food donations and guests, arriving as their various work shifts ended. A fruit basket the size of one of my aunts had a note of goodwill from Henrietta and the Corkers.

Denise was home with Denver, where she had to put on a brave face and tell the little guy that his daddy was working late. A call with Denver's counselor had agreed it was best to see what the outcome would be before dragging him into emotional quicksand.

I shifted, unable to get comfortable, my thoughts consumed with sad, ugly things.

Amelia rubbed my hand, lying on our shared armrest. Her dad had brought her to me as soon as I called. She'd been too upset to drive, and they'd simply closed the store right then and there.

Matt had checked in repeatedly throughout his shift before collapsing in a corner seat, head in hands around two a.m. He looked a lot like I felt, except, he seemed to be sleeping. At least he had that.

Grady didn't have any family in Charm, aside from Denver, so the doctors were incredibly tight-lipped about his progress. The surgery to remove the arrow and repair internal damage had taken hours. I only knew that because Wyatt had unleashed the full power of his charm on an unsuspecting young nurse, who'd agreed to give him a heads-up when Grady was moved to recovery.

The air in our overcrowded waiting room smelled of bleach and bandages, underscored by the faint aroma of stale coffee and a weird floral scent I assumed was the product of hidden air fresheners.

I looked at each tired, worried face and said little prayers for them. Prayers of hope and of thanks. And of all the things I couldn't tell them aloud without bursting into tears.

A row of uniformed officers sat along the wall, hats in hand. Waiting. They'd come in after their shifts. Traded time and meals with their families for a hard hospital floor and cold casseroles from an accruing collection.

One of the cops had assured me early on that Locke had been caught. That Grady had amassed a hefty file of evidence loosely linking Locke with multiple island crimes. There was enough now, coupled with my abduction, Locke's confession, and his attempt on Grady's life, to put him in jail for a very long time.

But I didn't care about any of that. I just wanted Grady to open his eyes.

Someone touched my hand just after sunrise, pulling me out of a shallow, fitful sleep.

Ryan stood before me, a comforting expression on his brow. "Hey, champ," he said warmly. "I came as soon as I could."

I rose on wobbly legs, shifting Wyatt gently away from me as Ryan drew me into a tight embrace. "He's going to be okay, you know," he said. "It takes a tough cookie to put up with the likes of you the way he does. This is nothing." He kissed my head, then pulled back to look into my red, puffy eyes.

I laughed, and Wyatt stretched to his feet, then shook Ryan's hand.

"Hey, man," he said. "Glad you're here."

"I wouldn't be anywhere else," Ryan said. He turned

and motioned someone into the room with us. A parade of people in uniform shirts from the local coffee shop streamed inside, each with a tray of disposable cups and at least one white pastry bag. "I bought three dozen coffees," he said. "Scones and a few turnovers as well. I suspected I'd find half your town here, circling the wagons, with one of its own in need."

I sobbed. Without choice and without warning. Because Grady was one of us now. Not the new guy. Not the stranger. He was part of my world, my community, and a part of me.

I sat back down, and Ryan let me be.

He turned to shake Mr. Butters's hand, then lifted Amelia in a tight hug, while everyone else in the waiting room moved in a slow wave toward the coffees and scones.

Only Aunt Clara and Aunt Fran remained seated, eyes fixed on me. Heartbreak evident on their pale features. And I suspected for the thousandth time in my life that they could somehow read my mind.

Matt stopped on his way toward the refreshments and lowered himself into the seat beside me. "No coffee?"

"No." I leaned into him. "Maybe when the line dies down."

He set a hand on mine, curling strong fingers around my palm and squeezing gently. A punch of remorse swept over me, as if I'd tapped into his mood. And I realized I wasn't the only one hurting deeply.

"This isn't your fault," I said, understanding instinctually that he somehow blamed himself.

He squinted and rubbed his forehead. "Funny. I was about to say the same thing to you."

We stared at one another in miserable camaraderie. We'd both played a role in the events leading to Grady's injury, and while neither of us had actually caused any of it, we were both carrying the heavy burden.

Amelia and Ryan returned. They each carried two cups of coffee and each offered us one.

"Thanks," we accepted in near unison, cracked open the lids, then sipped.

My attention flickered to the waiting room door, where two more familiar figures walked stoically inside. Grady's former mother-in-law, U.S. Senator Denver, and her husband nodded as they headed my way.

Amelia, Ryan, and Matt gave the incoming couple plenty of space as they approached.

The older couple's normally shellacked confidence was visibly puckered and flaking. Her makeup was smudged. His tie slightly askew. They'd spent more than their share of time in a similar waiting room, no doubt, following their daughter's surgeries as she'd lost her battle with cancer. I couldn't imagine the kinds of pain this trip brought back for them.

"He'll be okay," I told them, in lieu of hello, determination fortifying the words. They looked as if they might need to hear it as much as I did.

"How did the surgery go?" the senator asked. "Were there any complications? How long is the anticipated recovery?"

I shook my head, hating that I didn't have anything to offer her. "I don't know." A wedge swelled in my throat, making it painful to finish. "I'm not family."

Her eyes flashed with indignation, and her chin lifted.

She reached for my arm as her husband indelicately proclaimed, "The hell you aren't family."

And they dragged me away, out of the room and down the hall to a massive nurse's station where the senator threw her weight around, HIPAA be darned, and attempted to set the record straight about who I was to Grady Hays.

My heart splintered, irrevocable as she took her pain out on the poor, patient woman behind the desk. I could never be his family. Just being his girlfriend might've contributed to the fact he was here now.

A doctor appeared, stopping the verbal push and pull in progress. "Senator?" he said, cradling a small laptop. "You're asking for an update on Detective Hays?"

"Yes," she said, grabbing me again and towing me along with her. "Proceed."

The older man's gaze flickered briefly to me, then back to the woman practically holding me up. Her husband rounded my back, bookending me between them. Their arms crisscrossed at my back, and I wondered if I might be holding them up a little too.

"Surgery went well," the doctor said proudly. "The internal damage was miraculously minimal, and there weren't any complications. Grady's recovering nicely, as expected. Like the strong young man he is. We weaned him from the anesthesia, then let him rest through the night. He's awake now and has received the same information I'm giving you. Though the painkillers in his system may make it necessary for you to repeat some of this to him later. He can go home tomorrow. A full recovery can be expected in about ten days. He'll need a temporary caregiver while he rests for the next week or so."

"He has an au pair," she said. "Denise can help, and I'll stay as well."

"We'll stay," her husband said, reminding her she wasn't alone.

"I can send meals," I said. "So none of you have to worry about cooking. I know what Grady and Denver like. Denise too." I chewed my lip, wondering how else I could help. "Actually," I said, untangling myself from the Denvers. "Denise has been with Denver all night, and I know she wants to be here. I'll head over there now. I can take him to school, so she can come in and see Grady. She's probably worried sick."

I didn't wait for their response. I nodded at the doctor, then hurried away as a sudden and inexplicable panic welled and burst in me. All the waiting to be sure he was fine had rooted me in place, but knowing he'd lived, that he had a second chance, was enough to eject me through the roof. I couldn't get away from him fast enough. And all I wanted in that moment was to be free of the sense of building suffocation and to breath in the balmy seaside air.

My great-aunts stood in the waiting room doorway, apparently waiting for me. "Where do you think you're going?" Aunt Fran asked.

"To relieve Denise, so she can visit Grady. He's awake. Doing well. But I have to go. I won't be long."

She exchanged a look with Aunt Clara. "I guess this is good timing then. You can take Dharma." She presented me with the fuzzy hot pink pompom and key. "You just missed the mechanic. He heard about what happened and decided to bring the car to you. Hoping to add a little bright spot to your day."

I took the key, closing my fingers over the fuzzy ball. "That was thoughtful. I'll make sure he knows I appreciate it. Did he leave a bill?" Maybe figuring out how to pay for whatever had needed done to a car that wasn't driven for the better part of fifty years would be a great way to distract myself from the pain spreading through my body and soul.

Then again, seeing the total might actually kill me.

Aunt Fran lifted her brows. "You didn't know? Grady took care of the bill."

"What?" I swept my gaze down the hallway behind me. "How?"

"Days ago," Aunt Clara said, smiling warmly. The only way she knew how. "Frank said the detective gave clear instructions when she was hauled in. You weren't to get the car back until it had been deemed safe in every way. And he had the invoice directed to him."

Aunt Fran stepped forward and kissed my cheek. "Aren't you going to stay and see him? I'm certain he'll be asking for you."

"No. I need a little time first. His in-laws are with him now." I crossed trembling arms over my chest and forced a tight smile. "I'll be back soon."

"Or," Aunt Clara said, raising a hand, as if she might try to physically hold me in place. "You can stay here. I'm sure Denise already plans to come as soon as she drops Denver off."

The urge to run, to scream, to collapse became more than I could manage, and I leaned closer to kiss her cheek. "I won't be long," I repeated.

They traded cautious looks again but let me go.

I burst from the hospital with a crashing sob, then scanned the lot for Dharma.

She was easy enough to spot. Her bright yellow paint and flowers had been washed and buffed to a shine. I climbed behind the wheel and stared at the place where a Beach Boys tape had once been stuck in the half-century-old dash. A modern stereo stared back. A tiny gift tag dangling from the volume button identified the gift as being from my aunts.

Before me, tied to a string around my rearview mirror, beside the aged bouquet hung by Aunt Fran's mother, was a tiny cowboy hat with a silver star on its brim.

I touched the hat with one gentle fingertip, then looked back at the hospital, now bathed in bright morning light.

A familiar silhouette strode out, and for a moment, my heart seized. Then I recognized the set of his shoulders, his gait and stride.

Wyatt lifted a hand as he approached. "He's asking for you, E." His eyes searched mine, seeing too much and understanding too deeply. "Don't go."

I glanced from him to the building. Torn. Afraid. Guilty. Thrilled.

"Come on," Wyatt said, opening my door. "Your aunts told me you were on your way to Denise, but she's already en route. It's after eight. Denver's in school. She'll be here in a few minutes."

I wet my lips, then released a long slow breath. "I can't."

"This wasn't your fault," he said, tipping his head over one shoulder in the same cocky way he always did when he thought he was right. "You aren't cursed. And you aren't responsible for this."

"How can you say that?" I asked. "You, more than anyone else, should know." I batted stinging eyes, willing him to see what I saw. "You think this is a coincidence too?"

When Wyatt and I had been together, he'd nearly died a number of times. He'd been thrown from bulls. Trampled. Gored. I'd spent countless nights in ERs all over the Midwest, hoping he would survive. And once we'd broken up, and I'd come home, his body had healed. His riding had improved, and he'd been okay.

"I've told you," Wyatt said. "I was hurt all those times because I was young and careless. I was more focused on the buckles and the glory, than anything else. Including you. Which was why I lost you and failed on so many of my rides. I took unnecessary chances, and I did stupid things." He leaned in close and locked serious blue eyes on me. "I was a complete idiot. I would think you, of all people, would know that."

I fought a grin as he threw my words back at me. "You were," I agreed.

He'd broken my heart, and I'd been sure I would never recover.

"Come on," he repeated, reaching across me to unfasten a seat belt I didn't remember buckling. "That man of yours has been through a lot. He wants to see you, and you're here, so there's no reason to keep him waiting."

"Fine."

"Fine," he echoed, a smug smile on his lips.

We returned to the hospital and rode silently in the elevator. Then Wyatt walked me to Grady's room, where he handed me off like the father of a bride. "Here she is."

Senator Denver and her husband smiled as they excused themselves, following Wyatt and leaving Grady and I alone.

"Hey," he said, using the buttons on his bed to sit up taller and wincing as he moved.

"How are you feeling?"

He scanned himself, then me. Small purple crescents underscored his eyes. The bandages from his surgery were hidden beneath a hospital gown and blanket. "Not bad considering," he said. "I'd be better if I knew you were okay."

"I'm okay," I said. "Possibly cursed." I offered a self-deprecating smile. "You know how that is."

"You aren't cursed. I'm the one in the bed," he said.

I nodded. "This is worse."

Grady's expression flattened. All pretenses of casualness were set aside. The storm returned to his eyes.

"Don't say this isn't my fault," I said, cutting him off. "If it wasn't my family curse that got you, then it was the fact I never listen, and I continued my personal crusade to clear Matt's name when you had it under control."

"I was going to ask if you meant what you said before, when the EMTs were prepping me for transport."

My cheeks flushed at the memory of my lips on his head. Not knowing if he'd be okay. Not knowing if I'd missed my chance to tell him how I felt. So, I'd blurted the truth.

"You said you love me," he reminded me. "Is it true, or were you just scared?"

I bit my lip, unable to say it again, not when he was hurt because of me.

"Everly," he whispered, taking my hand in his, the IV line

stretching with his movement. "Is it true?" he asked, speaking each word with great intensity and reverence.

I nodded, my heart breaking as I realized what I had to do. "I do," I said.

Which was why I had to let him go.

CHAPTER
TWENTY-NINE

Three weeks later

I 've had the best day," Amelia said, turning onto Ocean Drive as she drove me home.

We'd taken a road trip, shopping, eating, and sightseeing our way through the islands, stopping at all the touristy things we typically paid no attention to and pretending to be newcomers in our own land. We'd climbed hundreds of stairs at historic light houses, admired art in local galleries, sipped iced coffee on piers, and emptied our bank accounts while shopping at the outlet mall. For one long carefree day, we'd allowed ourselves to simply be.

To be young.

To be hopeful.

To be happy.

At the moment, I was hopeful to pull off the surprise happening next, and that Amelia would be utterly happy as a result.

She peeked at me as we motored along. "I thought thirty would feel worse. Heavy or disappointing somehow," she said. "So far, I feel pretty great. It's been too long since we spent a day together like this."

"True," I said, my tummy flipping with anticipation while my face struggled to remain cool.

As Ryan had suggested, Amelia's dad and I had thrown our typical beachside buffets and gatherings two days ago, on the weekend before her birthday, in our traditional, predictable style. Then, Mr. Butters had insisted she spend her actual birthday with her fabulous best friend, while he watched Charming Reads and Aunt Fran took the afternoon shift at Sun, Sand, and Tea.

In truth, the entire town had put out their Closed signs before dinner, so they could get ready for Amelia's surprise party. An event designed and orchestrated by her adoring boyfriend.

Amelia squinted at the empty sidewalks and darkened shops as we rolled through town. "Is something going on?" she asked. "Why'd everything close already?"

I thought of a dozen wild tales I could spin, but decided on, "Wow. That is weird."

She nodded, then gave me an examining look. "What's wrong?"

I avoided eye contact. I'd been trying not to tell so many fibs these days, but my face was another story and couldn't be controlled.

"Is it Grady?" she asked. "You never talk about what happened the last time you spoke."

I felt the proverbial arrow lodge in my chest at the

mention of his name. The last time I'd seen Grady, I'd told him I was sorry, but we needed to take a break from one another.

Since then, he'd recovered fully from his injuries, according to Denise, but I'd steered clear. At least, as clear as possible while living in the same little town.

"I was just thinking about Locke again," I admitted, his name popping into mind immediately after Grady's.

"Have you heard anything about the upcoming trial?"

I nodded. "Yeah, it sounds like Locke confessed on the record and cooperated fully," I said. According to Denise, my new source of information, since I'd stopped taking Grady's calls. "He gave a play-by-play, from seeing the argument between Matt and Kai at the amphitheater, to using Matt's phone to lure Kai back there. He saw Matt use his password to unlock his phone at the beach, when he'd shown up to help Kai. He said he left the body so Osier could clean up Kai's mess one last time."

Amelia wrinkled her nose. "Awful."

"Pretty much."

"You won't have to testify or anything like that?" she asked.

"No."

I'd also learned the fight between Matt and Kai had started when Tara invited Matt for drinks, then confessed she'd made a huge mistake by leaving him. Ava had overheard and told Kai, in the hopes that he'd leave Tara for her. Instead, he'd hunted Matt down to express his humiliation in the form of anger.

Then, I'd shown up at the crime scene with Matt. Locke

had overheard an officer mention my involvement in previous crimes, from wherever he'd been lurking, then he looked
me up and discovered the *Town Charmer*. Things had only
gotten worse for me from there.

He'd tried to frighten me with the cartoon and the
arrows. He'd tried to run me down in a fit of anger after
seeing me speak with Tara. He was sure I'd put it all together
from there. When none of that worked, he took a shot at me
outside Kai's memorial, and he hadn't meant to miss.

She shifted into park in my driveway and offered a comforting smile. "Do you feel like company or just want to be
alone?"

"Come in," I said. "I'm trying something new in the café
and I'd love your input."

"Excellent." She hopped out with a grin. "I hope it's
hazelnut."

I laughed. There were definitely strawberry and hazelnut
treats for her to sample, because there was no way I'd let
Eloise be the one making my best friend's favorite sweets
any longer.

I worked my key around the dead bolt on my front door
like a drunkard, rattling the knob and doing my best to be
sure everyone inside knew we were there.

"Do you need help?" she asked, moving into my personal
space.

"I've got it," I said, slowly pushing the door wide.

A cascade of lights in diamond shapes moved in over the
dark walls in an arch, projected from a desk in the middle
of the room. Stacks of books surrounded the projector and
tipped against the desk's legs on the floor. Black lights had

replaced every bulb throughout the first floor, and an abundance of novels had been suspended from the ceiling by invisible wire, covers spread, as if the books were in flight. Their pages glowed in the strange purple light.

"What on earth?" she said, moving inside and marveling at the odd scene.

I smiled, then extended an arm, indicating she should continue into the café.

The soft cadence of calliope music drifted throughout the room. Cotton candy in white cones hung from looping strings between windows, while an old-fashioned popcorn machine filled its glass belly with newly burst kernels.

The floor was covered in loosely rolling balloons of every size.

"What is happening?" she asked, arms out slightly at her sides. "This is like a delicious book circus."

My tables had been covered in white clothes. The centerpieces flickered with faux candles stacked on books. A trio of acrobats dressed in ruff collars and silver bodysuits contorted near the rear windows.

"It's a magical bookstore with acrobats," I said, smiling as a man moved into view from the shadows.

Ryan smiled as he approached. Dressed in a sharp black suit with a bolero hat, he offered her an enormous white rose bouquet. "Happy birthday."

Amelia squeaked, then covered her mouth with both hands before leaping at him.

I took the flowers as he pressed them to her back, easily supporting her weight.

Slowly, the guests began to unpack from my ballroom,

where they'd been hiding. They lined up to wish Amelia happy birthday for the second time in a week.

Aunt Clara and Aunt Fran joined Denise behind my counter and began to raise prepared trays of foods and sweets onto the counter. Cookies shaped like books. Brightly colored paper cones filled with roasted nuts and popcorn. And a cake the Mad Hatter would've been proud of, wacky tilted tiers and all.

A blast of fire drew our attention to the wraparound deck outside. A man dressed as a vintage detective swallowed, then breathed fire. Beside him, a woman in a flowing white gown danced in dramatic, sweeping arcs and turns.

I set the flowers on a nearby table, then slipped silently away, attempting to manage my overwhelming juxtaposition of emotions on Amelia's special night.

The ocean breeze fluttered over me as I climbed into my gazebo, and for the first time in half a year, I looked up at my widow's walk. I thought of my ancestor, Magnolia Bane, and the price she'd paid for love. Of my grandma and aunts, my mother, and me. What had someone done to deserve a punishment that would never end?

And why hadn't I believed before it was too late?

The wind picked up around me, rocking the branches of bushes and producing Maggie from the shadows, her luminous eyes flashing.

Lou landed on the gazebo's handrail across from me.

"It's not fair," I whispered weakly, knowing quite well that life rarely was. "I want him back."

As if I'd conjured him with my words, the hairs rose on the back of my neck and along my arms. And Grady appeared outside my gazebo.

"Everly?"

I sucked in a wretched breath at the sound of his voice and my name on his tongue.

"Am I interrupting?"

I shook my head and wiped an errant tear, unsure why he was there. He'd been invited, of course, but until now he'd avoided me as carefully as I'd avoided him.

He wore black suit pants and shiny shoes. His tie was loose and the button beneath it unfastened. His sleeves had been rolled up to his elbows. "I think it's time we talked," he said, stepping forward when I began to nod.

There was something in his hands as he reached for me, and my world began to blur through heavy unshed tears. I looped my arms around his strong, steady frame and felt immediately lighter as his heart beat against my cheek.

He brushed the hair away from my face and pressed a gentle kiss beside my ear. "I've got something I need to ask you," he whispered.

And I held my breath as I looked into his hopeful gray eyes.

RECIPES FROM SUN, SAND, AND TEA

Her Majesty's Munch Mix

A perfect sweet and salty snack combo to enjoy any-time. Pairs especially well with *The Lost Colony* and other island dramas.

Serves: 8–12 | Total Time: 25 minutes

6 cups popcorn
2 cups broken ruffled potato chips
1½ cups Chex cereal
1½ cups broken pretzels
*optional 1 cup peanuts
Caramel:
1/2 cup butter
1 cup packed light brown sugar
1/3 cup corn syrup
1/4 teaspoon salt
1 teaspoon vanilla
1/4 teaspoon baking soda

Preheat the oven to 350°F. Line a baking sheet with parchment paper.

In a large bowl, mix together the popcorn, potato chips, Chex cereal, pretzels, and nuts. Set aside.

Melt the butter in a medium saucepan.

Mix in the brown sugar and corn syrup, stirring often, until it comes to a boil.

Reduce and simmer for 2 minutes without stirring.

Remove the saucepan from the heat.

Stir in the salt and vanilla.

Add the baking soda and stir until the mixture is lighter and creamy brown in color.

Pour the caramel mixture over the party mix. Stir well.

Spread onto the baking sheet.

Bake for 4 minutes, stirring after 2 minutes.

Remove from the oven and let cool. Then, break it up and place in a serving dish.

Swan's Southern Tea Cakes

Indulge your sweet tooth and impress your friends with a taste of island history. This Swan family recipe has been enjoyed for generations. Make it your family's newest tradition!

Serves: 12–14 | Total Time: 15 minutes

4 cups flour
2 cups sugar
2 eggs
1½ sticks butter, melted
1/2 cup milk
1 teaspoon pure almond extract

Preheat the oven to 400°F. Line two baking sheets with parchment paper.

Pour the flour into a large bowl. Set aside.

In a medium bowl, whisk together the remaining ingredients until smooth.

Pour the wet ingredients into the bowl of flour and stir carefully to combine.

Work the dough into balls, and drop onto the baking sheet.

Bake for 7 to 9 minutes or until lightly browned. Serve.

Bubbling Basil Raspberry Tea

This gently bubbling tea is sure to impress and refresh! Adjust sweetness to taste and enjoy all summer long.

Serves: 6–8 | Total Time: 30 minutes + chill time

5 cups fresh raspberries, mashed
3 cups sugar
1½ cups packed fresh basil leaves, coarsely chopped
1/3 cup lime juice
3 black tea bags
1 (1-liter) bottle carbonated water
*optional additional berries and basil for garnish

In a large saucepan, combine the raspberries, sugar, basil, and lime juice. Cook over medium heat for 5 to 7 minutes.
Remove from the heat and add the tea bags. Cover and steep for 20 minutes.
Strain, discarding the tea bags and raspberry seeds.
Pour the tea into a two-quart pitcher. Cover and refrigerate until chilled.
Before serving, add the carbonated water.
Serve over ice and garnish with fresh berries and basil.

CHAPTER
❧
ONE

"Congratulations, Mrs. Miller," I said, embracing my childhood friend, Judy, who was still glowing from her recent exchange of wedding vows. "You look beautiful. Has anyone told you that today?"

"One or two people," she said, beaming back at me. "I can't thank you enough for doing all this, Everly. When you agreed to cater the wedding reception and be the local liaison, I never dreamed you'd manage all of this." She motioned at the crowded beach behind us, where half the town and a handful of her new husband's guests mingled and danced in bare feet on the sand.

I'd worked diligently for weeks with a local rental company to create the elaborate beach wedding of Judy's dreams, and I'd even petitioned the town council to close the portion of beach outside my home for the entire day to accommodate the big event. Everything had come together seamlessly. A blank check from Judy's new husband had definitely helped.

Judy had grown up in Charm with me. Her family lived on the more rural end of the island, near the maritime forest, and they'd struggled financially more than most. I hadn't been especially close to Judy as a child, but I remembered hearing her say in high school that she'd leave the island—and North Carolina—as soon as she graduated, and never worry about money again. Marrying Craig Miller, one of *Entrepreneur* magazine's Wealthiest Thirty Under Thirty, basically guaranteed she would accomplish that goal.

Judy smiled and bopped her head to a Beach Boys song rising from the DJ booth positioned outside my home and newly opened iced tea shop, Sun, Sand, and Tea. A salty summer breeze tousled the light-brown hair at the base of her neck. Her elegant chignon had loosened significantly during an enthusiastic round of the chicken dance. "I never thought a single day could be perfect, but this one really is. I've even eaten whatever I wanted since I got here Wednesday, and my dress still fits." She patted her perfectly flat stomach, which was currently wrapped in a designer white lace gown. Barefoot in the sand, under waning sunlight, she looked like an angel who might break into a graceful pirouette at any moment.

My fitted coral sundress, on the other hand, hugged all my many curves. I'd briefly considered a more flattering A-line, but Judy had insisted I looked like a shorter Jessica Rabbit in this dress, and I didn't hate that idea.

Judy's bright blue eyes sparkled as she watched her new husband limbo beneath a striped pole several yards away from my iced tea tent. "Can you believe he's brilliant *and* silly? How did I get lucky enough to find both in one man?"

"Well," I said, handing her a Mason jar filled with crushed ice and my newest sweet tea creation, "he married you, so you don't have to convince me about the brilliant part."

She turned the full force of her smile on me and accepted the tea. I popped a coral-colored straw into the jar and folded my hands while I waited for the verdict.

"This is delicious." She took a long pull. The ice rattled as the tea line neared the jar's bottom. "Oh my goodness, what it this?"

"Hibiscus tea, cinnamon sticks, a dash of sugar to taste, lemon for garnish. I call it the Blushing Bride. It's a signature creation for your special day." I bobbed a goofy curtsy, then stood with a casual shrug. "Or the J. C. Miller, for Judy and Craig, if Blushing Bride seems like too much. What do you think?"

"I think this is the reason I heard about your shop all the way up in Massachusetts when you've only been open a few months."

My cheeks warmed with pride. "Thanks."

I'd left Charm several years ago to follow my dream of becoming a culinary mastermind—and also to chase a cowboy through the Midwest on a rodeo circuit. The cowboy had eventually broken my heart, and I'd high-tailed it home to the island without finishing culinary school, but I was working to turn that unfortunate series of events into something good. For starters, I'd opened Sun, Sand, and Tea, a seaside café and iced tea shop, where I served recipes from my family's old cookbooks with my own unique flair. I might not have finished all my culinary classes, but I was happy, healthy, and home. What more could a lady ask for?

My superstitious great-aunts would say I was happy *because* I was home. According to them, my adventures couldn't have ended any other way. Aunt Clara and Aunt

Fran harbored several outlandish beliefs about women in the Swan family. For starters, they believed we weren't supposed to leave the island. Our female Swan ancestors had helped found Charm, and we were therefore irrevocably tied to it, as was our happiness, health, and livelihoods. If that wasn't stifling enough, we were also, allegedly, cursed in love.

Personally, I'd never believed in my aunts' myths, so I did what I wanted, and I was certain that my heart was neither the first nor the last to have been broken by a cowboy, curse notwithstanding.

Despite the lost love, I was thankful the tide had turned and brought me back to Charm. My dream home had gone on the market almost immediately, at the exact asking price I could afford. Even better, the property was zoned for commercial use and ready for a business to be tucked into the first floor below the living quarters. These days, I was in love with a massive hundred-and-seventy-year-old estate on a cliff near the sea.

Judy set her empty glass down beside the pitcher. "Hit me again, bartender. It's hot as aces out here."

I refilled her jar with the hibiscus and cinnamon concoction and enjoyed the pretty red glow it cast over her hands as she lifted it to her lips.

Craig made his way through the sand in pale gray suit pants, a white dress shirt unbuttoned halfway down his chest. The tie and jacket had been abandoned pre-limbo. He kissed his bride and enveloped her in his arms. "I love you."

"Tea?" I offered, passing him a jar of Blushing Bride.

"Thank you." He accepted the drink without releasing Judy. "For everything," he said, smiling. "I doubt any amount of money could have accomplished all this without you at the helm. This party is unbelievable. I don't think an army could have pulled this off, and you did it all by yourself."

Judy laughed. "If we'd asked my mom to be our local liaison, we'd be eating fish off paper plates next to Daddy's backyard grill right now and fighting mosquitos."

I gave the twenty-foot buffet of finger foods a long, prideful look. The dishes were displayed under little mesh screens on long tables covered in white linens and manned by the rental company's staff. Each recipe had come from one of my family's ancient, crumbling cookbooks. "Have you had a chance to eat anything?" I asked Craig.

He nodded. "I've eaten everything. I'd eat at your café every day if I could. Have you thought of opening a satellite location in Martha's Vineyard?"

"No." I shook my head. Possible curses aside, I liked Charm, and since I'd come home I couldn't imagine ever wanting to leave again. Plus, the shop had only been open a few months, and I was still working to establish a predictable income—preferably one that would pay the bills and rebuild the savings account I'd drained to make my iced tea dreams come true, not to mention the endless maintenance and improvements needed for a house as old as mine. The small amount of money I'd accepted for my work on the Millers' wedding was already set aside for aesthetic improvements to the café and a membership at one of those big-box stores where I could buy supplies in bulk. "I love that you decided on a Friday wedding," I said. "I hope your out-of-town guests will stay and enjoy Charm through the weekend."

Craig set his empty tea jar aside. "We chose today because it's the six-month anniversary of our first date."

"Wow." I dragged the word into several syllables. "I knew it was a short engagement, but I had no idea you'd just started dating that recently."

Judy curled her fingers under the collar of Craig's shirt to tug him closer. "I was so distraught when I lost my teaching job in Boston that I drove to Martha's Vineyard, rented a cottage, and just sat by the sea contemplating what to do with my life. I thought it was over. I thought I'd have to move, start over. Look at school districts in need of educators, maybe even come back to Charm and bait hooks for Dad and my brothers' fishing crew. Then I ran into Craig while we were waiting in line for shrimp tacos, and here we are."

Craig kissed her nose.

"Did you find a teaching job in Martha's Vineyard?" I asked.

"Nope." Judy didn't take her eyes off her husband. "Craig asked me to move in with him a few days after we met, and I've just been hanging out with him ever since."

I tried to imagine a man who could make me want to stop working and move into his house less than a week after meeting him, but my imagination wasn't that good.

"Wait until you see our room," Judy told Craig. "It's amazing. I almost felt guilty staying in it without you last night."

Craig looked at me with gratitude. "You aced that too, I guess."

"I did my best," I said. I might've gone a little crazy giving my largest guest room a wedding-themed makeover: white eyelet lace duvet, pillow shams, and bedding, fluffy white rug, white pillar candles. Heirloom crystal vases and silver candlesticks. Roses on the nightstand, vanity, and every flat surface I could fit them on. Judy had spent her last night as a single woman in there, and she would spend her first night as Mrs. Miller in there as well. I wanted the space to be worthy of creating the highest caliber of memories.

She turned her cheek against his chest, catching my eye. "I still can't believe you bought this old place."

"My house?" I glanced at the historic beauty with satisfaction.

"I've heard so many stories about it over the years," she said. "My brothers used to tell me it was haunted. I always ran past it whenever I came to this part of the beach or boardwalk, even as a teen."

"Haunted?" I asked. "I love this place." Though if she'd asked my great-aunts, they would've heartily agreed with Judy's brothers.

The wedding coordinator cut through the crowd at the buffet and made a beeline for my tea tent. "Time to cut the cake," he called.

A woman holding a big camera followed along behind him, sliding and sinking in the soft white sand with every step. "I'd love to get a photo of Craig and Judy cutting the first slice together," she said. "The sun's setting fast, so we have to hurry if we want the good light. Then I'd like to relocate to the bay for a few shots at twilight."

The planner opened his arms to herd the happy couple along. "We're arranging transportation to the bay as soon as the cake is cut," he said, "but we've got to keep moving."

The bay was just across the island from my home, not ten minutes by car. Charm was part of North Carolina's barrier islands, the long narrow strips of land separated from the mainland by channels, also known as the Outer Banks. The sun rose over the Atlantic outside my back door and set over the bay. The lighthouse-like tower that rose from the top of my old Victorian made views of both possible—and perfect.

I followed the foursome through the soft, warm sand to the cake table and waited while the photographer clicked away. Judy gripped the cake knife, then Craig slid his hands gently over hers. They smiled. They cut. It was adorable.

The photographer checked the screen of her camera and frowned. "Can we try that again? This time, tug your sleeve over the bracelet."

She mimed the act, and Craig obeyed, dipping his chin and blushing slightly as he stuffed the edges of a braided hemp band beneath the cuff of his dress shirt. "Sorry."

Judy's face paled. She stared at Craig's wrist for a long beat, then dragged her attention back to the photographer without making eye contact with her husband. Her smile was suddenly hollow and staged.

I jumped in to help the waitstaff finish cutting the cake. Nearly three hundred slices later, all fifty of Craig's guests and more than two hundred of Judy's were enjoying a light almond torte covered in edible beach-themed bling.

Craig's brow pinched as he pulled his phone from his pocket. "It's Pete," he said softly, then turned and paced away.

"Pete is the business partner?" I asked Judy. I was doing my best to remember names, but I'd heard a hundred new ones since breakfast.

"Yeah," she said with a frown. "I was sure I saw him here."

She turned in a small circle, peering at the crowd. "What did he do? Leave after the ceremony?"

"Would he do that?"

"Maybe," she said. "Who knows with Pete. He and Craig have been buddies since college, but Craig's the only one who grew up. Pete is as irresponsible now as he was ten years ago, which makes him a millionaire mess. Bad investments, tons of debt. He drives Craig batty, but Craig's too nice to ever say so." She stopped and wrinkled her nose. "I'm sorry. That was such a downer. What's important is that Craig is wonderful, and I'm happy."

My best friend, Amelia, emerged from a group of nearby guests and headed our way. Her sleek blond bob danced in the wind and over her shoulders. "Congratulations!" She wrapped Judy in a big hug and rocked her back and forth before stepping away to admire her. "You look absolutely stunning."

"Thank you," Judy said. "So do you."

Amelia always looked amazing in her vintage pinup ensembles. Today's aquamarine sequined sheath, which enhanced the color of her already bright blue eyes, was no exception.

"I can't believe you're really here," Amelia told Judy. "It's just like old times, except now you're married!"

Judy's smile widened. "I know you had a huge hand in this amazing party too, so thank you. Words aren't enough, but seriously, thank you so much. I can't stop smiling."

"*That* is enough," Amelia assured. "Besides, friends do things for each other. Sometimes Everly helps me stock my Little Libraries with books, and sometimes I help her make two thousand hors d'oeuvres and fifty gallons of iced tea."

I laughed. Amelia wasn't a chef, but she was loads of fun, a great listener, and an incredible friend. She'd been by my side through every quiche and kabob that made this dinner possible. I owed her about a month of trekking around the island with wagonloads of books to fill the Little Libraries she maintained, where townspeople could pick up free books to read or leave some behind for others to enjoy.

"You picked the perfect weekend for a party," Amelia told Judy. "Summer Splash starts Sunday, so some folks are literally painting the town."

Summer Splash was Charm's annual arts festival. Local vendors and artists came out in droves to display and sell their wares.

"We picked today for the wedding because it's the anniversary of our first date," Judy said, her smile slipping slightly as she scanned the area where Craig had disappeared. "I'll be right back. Too much nerves and tea, I think."

"Do you think we might be the ones in a fancy white dress one day?" Amelia asked as Judy walked away.

I tried to imagine myself in Judy's narrow, custom-designed gown but couldn't. Not just because I'd left for college in a size six and returned in a twelve, but mostly because the idea I might really be cursed in love sometimes got the better of me.

"Are you setting up a booth at the festival for Charming Reads?" I asked, changing the subject.

"Right outside my shop," she said. "Are you going to be there?"

"I hope so. I plan to see Craig and Judy off tomorrow morning with a massive breakfast before their flight to Maui. After that, I'll be helping my aunts brainstorm ideas for a video they want to shoot. Apparently a honeybee advocacy group called Bee Loved is accepting video applications from beekeepers across the country for a chance to appear in their upcoming documentary on the plight of the American honeybee."

Amelia raised her brows. "That's going to be interesting."

"Tell me about it."

Amelia laughed. "Your aunts are the bee's knees. They have this in the bag. Maybe next you can reach out to some ghost hunters about filming in your house."

"My house isn't haunted," I said. "Unless you count Lou." Lou was the seagull who seemed to have come with the place. He often appeared on my deck out of nowhere and made me scream.

"I don't know how you grew up in your family without believing in curses and ghosts and legends."

"Oh my," I said with a smile. "And I'm not sure how you grew up in a normal family and believe everything my aunts tell you."

"It's safer this way," she said.

I rolled my eyes.

ABOUT THE AUTHOR

 Bree Baker is a mystery-loving daydreamer who got into the storytelling business at a very young age, much to the dismay of her parents and teachers. Today, she is an award-winning and bestselling author. When she's not writing the stories that keep her up at night, Bree stays busy in Kent, Ohio, with her patient husband and three amazing kids. Today, she hopes to make someone smile. One day, she plans to change the world. You can learn more about Bree and her books at breebaker.com.